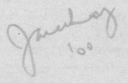

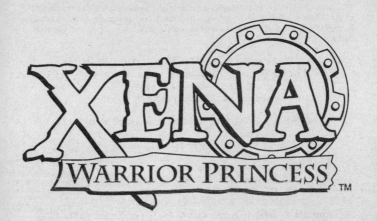

XENA
WARRIOR PRINCESS ™

QUESTWARD HO!

A NOVEL BY RU EMERSON
BASED ON THE UNIVERSAL TELEVISION SERIES
CREATED BY
JOHN SCHULIAN AND ROB TAPERT

ACE BOOKS, NEW YORK

XENA: WARRIOR PRINCESS: QUESTWARD HO!
A novel by Ru Emerson. Based on the Universal television series
XENA: WARRIOR PRINCESS,
created by John Schulian and Rob Tapert.

An Ace Book / published by arrangement with
Universal Studios Publishing Rights,
a division of Universal Studios Licensing, Inc.

PRINTING HISTORY
Ace edition / February 2000

The Penguin Putnam Inc. World Wide Web site address is
http://www.penguinputnam.com

ISBN: 0-441-00659-0

ACE®
Ace Books are published
by The Berkley Publishing Group,
a division of Penguin Putnam Inc.,
375 Hudson Street, New York, New York 10014.
ACE and the "A" design are trademarks
belonging to Penguin Putnam Inc.

PRINTED IN THE UNITED STATES OF AMERICA

10 9 8 7 6 5 4 3 2 1

To Doug

To Roberta

and with apologies to the vegetable beds
and the mountain bike.

Next year, guys. . . .

Acknowledgment

This book could not have happened without help above and beyond from several sources, whether inspirational, research, or other.

Ginjer: Thanks. Really. And Lea, we all know how much you hate trolling for books at Powell's in Portland; you deserve a medal for this one. Kathi, for the e-mails, silly cards, calls and other help, including the killer vitamins.

Many thanks to the Xena fans for support, kind notes, and information when I needed it. Special thanks to Chris (she knows why).

And if any of you reading this would like to get signed, personalized bookplates, or your copy of this book signed, I can be reached on-line at:

XenaBard@aol.com

Prologue

It had been too long, Xena thought. Too many days apart, too much distance. *And all that, for what? Here she is on a ship once again. Poor Gabrielle.*

And as much as she'd like to, she really couldn't blame Joxer, even though the two women would still be up in northern Thessalonika if not for him. *Ya gotta blame someone, blame his mother, and his brother Jett, for making him the way he is. Blame King Menelaus for coming up with this lousy quest idea and roping Joxer in on it.* Gods, blame herself and Gabrielle for snarling at him all the time and giving him reason to want to prove himself to them. Or her *or* Gabrielle for not simply saying "good riddance" and letting him go.

Not that he didn't bring it down on himself, with that whiny voice, his attitudes, the incredibly annoying and often stupid things he said and did. Still—*Yeah. I couldn't let him just walk blindly into danger, any more than she could.*

Too late to change all that anyway; she shrugged it aside. Joxer'd been ripe for picking when the Spartan king's men found him in that northern village and convinced him that Menelaus was seeking heroes—make that, A Hero—to retrieve some gods-blessed artifact. *Yeah, well, sure he'd fall for that. He's not the only one.* Everyone from wide-eyed village lads to the battle-hardened and normally wary Draco had converged on Sparta for a chance at the king's quest.

Supposed quest. Even before she'd reached Sparta and eavesdropped on the king, she'd been almost positive that any search Menelaus had set up would have Helen as its goal.

Xena's lips twitched. The look on Draco's face when he'd found her in his apartments back in Sparta! Better yet, the look he'd given her earlier this evening as she sent him flying over the rail of that pirate ship and into the water so she could use that ship to catch up to this one—and Gabrielle. *Wonder if Habbish went back to pick him up?* Unfortunately, the old Gael probably had: like most of his kind, he kept a certain code of honor, particularly where coin was involved—as he'd said just before Xena left his ship to vault onto this tubby merchant vessel, "He paid." *Which means he'll be behind us.* With luck—something she wasn't going to count on anytime soon—he'd stay *well* behind.

Her arms tightened briefly around her companion; Gabrielle sighed quietly and leaned into her. *Poor Gabrielle; she's had a bad time of it.* First Joxer getting hissy and storming away from camp, back north. But when Gabrielle'd tried to follow, she'd gone into the lake—a particularly green-slimed part of it—and emerged only to find three of Sparta's finest blocking her way. The warrior smiled grimly. *Yeah, she does just fine, these days.* She only needed to watch and wait while Gabrielle flattened all three. And though two had gotten away, there'd still been one left behind to tell them what little he knew about what Menelaus might be up to.

Of course, he hadn't known anything. Poor old fool of a stableboy, Botricas. But thanks to Botricas—and the nasty little device that had been slipped into his pike hood—she'd figured out right away that Menelaus' pet priest, Avicus, was involved. Only a priest of Apollo could utilize a listening thing like the *rhodforch*. Only a devious priest of Apollo *would* use such a thing.

Which meant that whatever the king was up to, it wasn't good. *That figured anyway,* she told herself. Menelaus was an arrogant old tyrant; she'd been certain all along he hadn't given up hope of getting Helen back— no matter what Helen wanted. But with Avicus involved. . . .

She didn't like the Apollo priest; never had, any more than she'd trusted him. He was as devious as either of the masters he served—king or god. *He was when I first ran across him—when he was working the machinery for the plays in Athens.* She'd find out what he was up to, what he thought he'd be getting out of all this. Eventually.

Her eyes narrowed; she gazed across bright hair, across the deck of the *Euterpe* and out to sea without properly seeing any of it. Another time and place, a slender, fair woman, Helen. *And Menelaus, watching her, eyeing his allies and his men to be certain none of them paid close attention to her. Possessive, smothering. No wonder she ran off with Paris of Troy. Not that he was much better.* Paris hadn't seen beyond her incredible beauty, like Menelaus. Unlike the king, however, he hadn't wanted to keep her all to himself. *Yeah? So it's better that he wanted to display her like a prize instead?*

She put it aside. At the moment, it was enough she'd finally caught up to Gabrielle, who'd been pursuing Joxer. *And* Joxer. *My mistake. We shoulda gone after Joxer right then and hauled him back to camp.*

Well, but she'd had messages—important ones for Hercules and Iolaus, and another for her old friend Mannius. *I still shouldn't have sent Gabrielle after him alone.* She smiled down at the young woman who leaned against her, arms clasped fiercely around her waist, and brushed dampish golden hair off Gabrielle's forehead.

Gabrielle glanced up and smiled wanly, then leaned against her shoulder once more. "You *said* you'd catch up with me," she mumbled.

"Meant it, didn't I?" the warrior demanded quietly.

Gabrielle sighed faintly and let her eyes close; she nodded.

"I didn't mean for it to take so long, or to work out like this, Gabrielle. You know that."

Gabrielle nodded.

"Hey. You feeling ok?"

A shake of the head this time.

"Sorry about the boat, Gabrielle. I've got some plain bread—"

"*Joxer* has bread," Gabrielle muttered sourly. "A little green, but, hey! What's a little *mold* among friends, right? And this—this sausage or something that's—"

"Don't think about it." Xena gave her a mild shake. "Just remember, you get to mangle him this time. So—where's the boat going?"

Gabrielle swallowed, licked her lips. "Um—out to sea? I don't know, I just climbed on board to grab Joxer and next thing I knew, we were moving, and our 'gallant' captain refused to go back and put me ashore."

"I'll talk to him," Xena said grimly. She sighed then, and tucked a windblown strand of pale hair behind Gabrielle's ear. "But I was afraid all along we'd wind up at sea."

"Great," Gabrielle muttered. "I thought you turned King Nestor down so we wouldn't *have* to go to sea this time of year! Storms, you said, and no—" she swallowed hard "—no squid. I remember, see?"

"Gabrielle—hey. C'mere. Come on." Xena moved to sit with her back against the ship's rail, where the planks blocked the wind and the younger woman's gear was shoved out of the way. She shook out the blanket one-handed and draped it over Gabrielle's shoulders, then settled down next to her. Gabrielle managed another wan smile and leaned back. "We can't let Menelaus send all these guys out after Helen. . . ."

"All?" Gabrielle frowned. "What other guys? Wait—you're not gonna tell me that *Draco*—?"

"Draco, Joxer, some village boy named Briax—"

"Not that innkeeper's son from up north?" Xena nodded; Gabrielle closed her eyes and shook her head. "I *told* him there wasn't a quest. I was afraid he wouldn't believe me. But I didn't think he'd—"

"Yeah, well, he did. And Menelaus and his pet priest gave him something to go look for—something that Helen supposedly took when she left Sparta."

Gabrielle stared at her. "For a—a what?"

The warrior shook her head. "I'm not gonna second-guess that pair. All I know is, Joxer thinks he's searching for one thing, Draco another, this Briax something else—I don't know why, either. Except, Draco. . . ." Her voice trailed off.

"Draco *what*?" Gabrielle asked warily.

5

"Hmmm? Oh, yeah. Draco's looking for Helen, the king asked him to find her and give her a message—and if she falls for it, he's supposed to escort her back to Sparta."

"Falls for it?" Gabrielle considered this briefly. "Wait— no. Let me guess. 'I really love you, I've changed, let's start over?' Except *you* said it's not like that with him, and she knows it. So, how dumb does he think she is?"

"I don't think that's the point, Gabrielle," Xena said evenly. "Because each of the men who got in to see the king, and were picked, each of them got a badge from Avicus. Some kind of thing that lets him see where they are."

Gabrielle sighed heavily. "Great. So Joxer's got one, right?"

Xena nodded.

"Which means the king knows where he is—and probably me, and you, too."

"Yeah, well. I spent a lot of time on that ledge in the king's reception chamber, listening to him and Avicus. Avicus knew Joxer goes around with us; he also knew you were behind him. He figured I was somewhere close by, and he'd have to figure I wouldn't just let the two of you go off alone."

"Thanks," Gabrielle said dryly. "I think." She considered this. "But, then. . . ." Another, longer silence. She finally shook her head. "I can't work it out; I don't think I slept the last two nights, my feet hurt from trying to keep up with stupid Joxer all the way down to the coast, and I feel sick. Does the badge come off, or does this mean we can toss Joxer overboard?"

Xena smiled and tossled her friend's bangs. "Sounds good to me—but no, I can get the badge off. Thing is . . ." She glanced around to be sure Joxer was nowhere close by, then turned her back on him and prudently lowered her voice. "I've been thinking about this—a lot, since I started south after you. I think we—you and I—need to find Helen and warn her. Avicus didn't get close to either of us, so we aren't marked. He shouldn't have any way to figure out where we are, and what we're up to."

"Once you get that badge off Joxer," Gabrielle amended. "Because unless we dive off the ship, or clonk him one and sneak off, he'll be right with us, all the way." Her eyes narrowed as she gazed down the deck.

"Save that thought, we may need it, Gabrielle. But right now, as far as we know, Helen may think she's safe, wherever she is. Oh," the warrior added as Gabrielle gave her a disbelieving look. "Sure, she knows him; she wouldn't think he'd ever give up trying to find her. But even if she's got some king's protection, that may not be enough."

"Yeah." Gabrielle sighed heavily. "Her luck and ours, so far, *Joxer* would be the one to find her, and lead Menclaus to her."

Xena nodded. "Exactly. You and I know what we're up against, we know to be careful. And I have an idea or two where she might go. We find her, we can at least warn her. If she'll let us, we can protect her ourselves then. Or she can get protection from whoever's sheltering her. Or we can see that she gets to someplace safe."

Gabrielle frowned, and tugged the blanket closer around her shoulders. "That's all fine. But how do we find her?"

"I don't know yet, Gabrielle. Settle down and get some sleep, if you can. If you get hungry, remember, I've got plain, fresh bread."

"Later," Gabrielle mumbled as she eased herself down flat. Xena watched her get settled, tugged the blanket down over Gabrielle's ankles, and got to her feet.

She looked up as someone came clomping across the deck. By rights, the captain should have come around long since to bellow at her for intercepting his ship and coming aboard despite his orders. *Yeah, it's hard to blame him; he's probably down in his cabin trying to figure out how to appease Poseidon.* Unfortunately, all too many ships' companies knew Poseidon had sworn vengeance against Xena. They figured just her presence—even as a paying passenger—was enough to provoke the god's anger, and send the ship, its cargo, and crew, all to the bottom.

The warrior's mouth twitched. It wasn't the captain, it was worse. Joxer came toward her in a wobbly, side-to-side lunging stride, arms flailing for balance as the ship rode the waves. *Gods. It's as calm as it ever gets out here. What in Tartarus would he do in a storm?* There was nothing wrong with his spirits, it seemed. He was grinning hugely, obviously pleased to see her and no doubt proud of himself.

"Gee, Gabrielle, and now you! This is—"

Xena leveled a finger at his nose, and he fell abruptly silent, the smile gone, his eyes suddenly wary. "One more word outa you, Joxer, except when I *ask* you something— One!—and I will tell Gabrielle *everything* you said to Menelaus and Avicus about her!"

"Huh?" He stared, slack-jawed.

"I was there," she said flatly.

He shook his head. "No! Where? I mean, if you'd been there, *I* woulda seen you, all right? And even if the king hadn't, on account he's so upset and everything, Avicus

8

woulda, because he's got all these really neat things he got from Apollo. You know he can—?"

"Jox*er*!" Silence. His mouth went sulky, but he was quiet. "Better." She closed the distance between them, glanced at Gabrielle, and lowered her voice. "You can't keep her off you, remember?"

"Ahhhh—I can explain," he began nervously. Xena snatched at the throat of his shirt; he swallowed hard.

"Don't—explain—anything," the warrior growled. Her fingers shifted, moving until they found the priest's badge, and closed around it. It was harder to free than Draco's had been. Maybe because he'd worn this one longer than Draco had had his. *Don't try to figure it out, okay?* she warned herself as she ripped it loose. It was the work of a moment to drop the thing overboard. "Just listen to me. No—wait. C'mere." She glanced down at Gabrielle, who seemed to be asleep, and dragged him up-deck, toward the stern, where he'd tossed his bedding and pack in a corner, well out of the way. She shoved him down onto the pile, then knelt, blocking his way. "Listen to me," she said flatly and quietly. "There is no quest."

Joxer sighed heavily. "You know, I cannot believe you came all this way to tell me *that*? Xena, for your information, I *ate* with King Menelaus and his priest. They were very nice to me, and. . . ."

"And that didn't get your suspicions up? Joxer, when was the last time someone like the king of Sparta was nice to you—unless they wanted something?"

"Yeah, they do," he replied huffily. "I find Helen and there's this thingie, looks like a necklace or something? And—"

"—And you get it back so Avicus can lay some member of the king's family to rest, and if she gets angry,

9

it burns her." Joxer stared. Xena smiled, a movement of lips that didn't reach dark, hard eyes. "Told you I was there. I heard what you told them, what they told you—and I also heard what they said to each other after you left. About all this and what Menelaus really wants." He gazed down at his hands, lips twitching. The warrior waited. He sighed finally.

"Yeah, all right, okay, so maybe it didn't seem likely. Even when I really wanted to believe it, I didn't. I mean—I . . . Yeah. Okay, you're right. Anyone wants something from *me,* it's the opposite of what they say, on account of I'll screw it up. Like breaking up that marriage for Aphrodite, and—"

Xena slewed around and sat next to him. "Hey, Joxer, I didn't mean it like that. There's a lot of good in you, and sometimes you do the right thing. And I know. you *mean* to do the right thing, even when it doesn't work out that way. And I don't know why they picked you. Maybe the men in that village decided you fit the king's description. Maybe Avicus—or Apollo—saw something in you."

"Yeah, right," the would-be hero said bitterly.

"All right, then. Maybe I'm right; maybe they *did* pick you because they know who you travel with these days." He looked at her blankly. "Menelaus knows I was in Troy at the end. He's probably guessed, or learned from someone that I helped her get away. He may think I know where she is now—or that Gabrielle does." He still looked blank. "Joxer, I'm not saying this is it—it's just possible. Maybe they planned to keep you hostage, wait for Gabrielle to come looking for you, and then, maybe with both of you locked up, I'd have to tell the king where she'd gone."

He considered this, eyes wide, and a self-satisfied smirk

turned the corners of his wide mouth. "Gee, you think so? You know, I just *knew* there was a good reason for me to get outa Sparta early!"

"You did that fine, Joxer," she assured him. "Woulda been better if you'd waited with Gabrielle. But getting out was good."

"But—*now* what do we do? I mean—"

Xena sighed. "Joxer, I don't know yet. Menelaus is bad enough; with Avicus involved, I'm not even gonna try. All I know is that Menelaus wants Helen back. Whether she wants to return to him or not." He was shaking his head stubbornly. "Joxer, will you remember I was *there*? Not just when you were, but for a long time before and after. I heard what those two said."

"Yeah, But—that's crazy!" he protested.

"Joxer." She smiled. He tittered nervously and settled back on his blanket. "You gonna tell me I'm *lying*?" He spluttered wordlessly, then fell abruptly silent as she chopped a hand. "And it's not just you—it's a lotta guys. All kinds."

The fight went out of him, all at once; his shoulders sagged. "Yeah. I think I saw some of 'em, back there in the palace." He hauled the helmet off and dropped it, ran both hands through his thatch of brown hair. "So, now what?"

"Now what?" She shrugged. Best thing just now would be to tell him as little as possible—*business as usual,* she thought tiredly. "I don't know. Maybe we'll just all go back north and forget about it."

The inept warrior struggled to his feet and clutched the rail. "Yeah, but . . . suppose one of those other guys get lucky? I mean. . . ."

"I'm thinking about it," she replied evenly. "Get some

sleep, Joxer." She turned and strode down the deck. She could feel his puzzled gaze following her.

A few sailors were down in the depths of the tubby merchant ship—shifting cargo, from the sound of things. One man was aloft, and another manning the wheel on the high stern. It was quiet at the moment, and nearly full dark. She could just make out a dim light behind thick curtains—captain's cabin, likely. He didn't seem interested in seeking her out. *Fine with me,* she thought, and settled down next to Gabrielle. She tugged a free end of the younger woman's blanket across her shoulders, and resolutely closed her eyes.

Some distance away, another ship rode south and east, trailing the *Euterpe* from a prudent distance but keeping close enough not to lose her. Draco, still dripping sea-water, stood next to Captain Habbish on the upper deck, a thick drying cloth draped over his bare shoulders. His eyes, like the captain's, were fixed on the pale spot between dark water and dark sky: a small blob that was the merchant vessel's sail. Habbish cleared his throat, took a long pull from his wine sack, and passed it to his companion, who swallowed briefly. Draco wiped his mouth on the back of his hand and returned the sack, but Habbish pushed it away. "Keep it, man," the Gael said. "Warm y'self inside, at least."

The warlord nodded absently; his eyes remained fixed on the distant sail.

"It is good coin ye've offered and I'll take it gladly— but I'm no so sure why ye want to follow Xena."

"It's not her," Draco replied slowly. A smile touched his lips. "It's what she's after. I want it, too." Habbish eyed him doubtfully, then fell silent.

• • •

The vast reception chamber of the Spartan king was dark, and so was the priest's private room behind it. At this late hour, the halls were largely deserted. Menelaus allowed very few guards near his private apartments, most of the servants were asleep or at tasks in the distant kitchens. And by now, all the "heroes" had gone—some heading north or west, one going south toward Pylos and beyond. Most had taken the broad east road to the sea. King Menelaus reclined on the couch in his apartments, moodily picking at a late supper, listening as Avicus detailed things for him. He seemed moody and preoccupied, and finally sat up, raising a hand for silence.

"I don't care about the details, priest. Not unless one of them finds Helen. What about that Joxer?"

"He took ship late today, sire," the priest said. "From Phalamys, heading east toward Rhodes.

"And?"

"And?" Avicus raised an eyebrow; the king snorted.

"That girl—did she catch up with him? And what about Xena?"

"The girl left on board the ship with him. But just now, I saw both of them, sire. In my mirror." *Just before a strong sword-hand came down on the seeing device, tore it free, and tossed it into the sea,* he thought gloomily. No point in telling Menelaus that just now. Any more than he'd willingly admit Draco's badge was gone—torn free by the same hand.

But in Joxer's case, it didn't matter—there was another. *And a good thing you chose to have Stroez go through the fool's room and find a safe place to put a second badge,* he told himself. He smiled faintly and inclined his head as the king dismissed him—he hadn't actually

13

caught the last thing Menelaus had said, but it probably wasn't important. Probably nothing he hadn't heard at least ten times, the past few months. He bowed again at the door and let himself out. Once within his own sumptuous rooms, he stretched out on his couch and stared up at the ceiling. *Helen. Where are you, my own fair lady-to-be? I wonder . . . ?*

Well . . . he'd know soon enough.

1

Xena woke to a predawn that was already too warm; the air was heavy and a hot wind billowed the sails one moment, then died away to nothing. The eastern sky was a dull red. *Storm weather,* she thought. No point in letting Gabrielle know that. At the moment, fortunately, the ship moved smoothly; the waves were less than they'd been the previous night.

She sat up cautiously, making sure not to pull the blanket from Gabrielle, yawned and stretched, then got to her feet so she could look out over the rail.

Not that she could see very far in the early gloom. There were islands ahead—the outlines of one or two low peaks off the port side, and another, higher and nearer, off the starboard. At the moment, she couldn't tell which—if any—of them might be their goal.

Overhead, the watch in the crow's nest called out; she couldn't make out what he'd shouted, but it sounded routine. Either nothing to warn about, or nothing he could see. More likely a regular call—possibly so the deck watch, or the tillerman, would know he hadn't gone to sleep up there. The tillerman called back—they must be using some merchanter slang, Xena thought, because it wasn't Greek or any other language *she* knew.

At her feet, Gabrielle moaned softly and shifted to her side, her face close to the railboards, but when the warrior looked down, she'd gone still again. Still asleep. *She might not think so, but she's better on one of these than she used to be.*

Joxer. The warrior could just make out the motionless lump farther up the deck, surrounded by helm, assorted bits of armor and other things he'd strewn out the night before. She wasn't too concerned about him at the moment. In the middle of the sea, he wasn't gonna sneak off. There wasn't a whole lot of trouble he could get into, either.

Still no sign of the captain. *Fine with me,* she thought, remembering his infuriated bellows of the night before when she'd launched herself onto his deck. She took one last look around, then settled down cross-legged with her back to the rail, close to Gabrielle but not so close she'd accidentally bump the other woman if the ship lurched. Her stomach growled loudly, and she cast up her eyes. *Time for some of that bread; you didn't eat much yesterday, and nothing at all after you got on this wobbly excuse for a ship.*

She fished out one of the cloth-wrapped bundles and tore off a generous hunk, ate quickly, and washed down the last of her share with a good swallow from her water bottle. She sat then, gazing around her, as the sail turned from a muddy gray to rosy as day broke. Suddenly, there were ship's men all over the deck, and as sunlight broke over the topmast, the captain came yawning from his cabin.

It sounded like a little too much excitement just for morning, Xena thought, suddenly wary. Several men clustered along the stern rail near the wheel, gazing out behind them, and someone was talking to the captain now, waving his arms and pointing the same way. The warrior eased onto one knee and gazed back west.

The mainland was a dark, distant blur. Habbish's ship *Wode* was considerably closer—near enough that there was no mistaking the vessel.

The warrior swore under her breath. *Of course the old pirate went back and got Draco, just like you figured. Like he said he would. And then Draco—instead of going off on his own search—paid him to keep this ship in sight. 'Cause he figures if anyone knows where Helen is, I do.*

Maybe not just that, of course. Where Xena went, there went Gabrielle. And Draco was still under the spell of Cupid's love arrow. *And whose fault is that?* the warrior asked herself angrily. *You coulda got Cupid to put him back, take off the spell that made him nutty for Gabrielle. But no, you had to tell the smirky little winged god that being in love with Gabrielle suited the warlord!* Well, all right, it did. She'd never been able to convince him to do good herself—his love for Gabrielle had. He was *trying* to do the right things, anyway.

All the same, he was going to be damned inconvenient just now. For one thing, he never had believed—still didn't—that he'd been god-touched, oh no! Love at first sight with Gabrielle, and nothing she'd ever said had convinced him otherwise. *Stubborn, difficult, arbitrary . . .* But it wasn't just that. A Draco who was trying to perform heroic deeds and great quests to win over Gabrielle wasn't going to relinquish the chance to reunite Menelaus and

Helen if he thought that would do the trick. As he apparently did.

I'd feel better about it if I thought for a minute that he'd thought about what I'd told him about Helen.

The warrior had tried. And he'd *said* he was willing to give her the benefit of a doubt. At least *ask* Helen what she wanted, which was more than most of the men in her life had ever done. Xena scowled at the deck, then beyond the peacefully sleeping Gabrielle. *Hah. Draco would say anything—you know better than to trust him!*

That worked both ways, of course. For some reason—she bit back a sly grin—he always seemed to think she was trying to manipulate him. *Just because you usually are—like you always have. And he still falls for it every single time.*

All the same, she didn't doubt he was gonna be underfoot a lot in the next few days; in the way, and where he was least wanted. *Figure out how to get rid of him,* she ordered herself. At sea, that wouldn't be easy. Once they reached some island port, though, she could surely find a way to distract him, lose him away from the coast, maybe, then be gone and well out to sea before he got back to the wharf.

Bottom line was, she simply didn't dare let him be anywhere close by, from any direction, if she did happen to locate Helen. *If he wanted to take her back to Sparta, willing or no, I'd have to hurt him. These days—yeah, I'd rather not.* Not because she cared—not like that. Just—if he was trying to do good, the way she'd tried to get him to do for so long, then he deserved whatever chances he could get.

Another glance along the rail, where she could just make out the lump of blanket that was Joxer. *He* complicated things all by himself—but now you had to factor in that Draco considered Joxer a rival for Gabrielle. . . .

Cupid, the warrior told herself flatly, *still* has a lot to answer for from *that* little mess. Gabrielle "in love" with Joxer; herself madly adoring Draco, she and Gabrielle fighting over him, Gabrielle furious when her close companion said anything rude (*true*) about Joxer. And Draco still saw Joxer as a rival, unfortunately. *Remember what he said in Sparta; he thought she'd gone off with Joxer. Yeah. That's all I'd need, having to protect Joxer from Draco!* "Give it a rest," she growled through her teeth, and began shoving blades into their various sheaths. But as she stood to clip the chakram at her waist, the captain came storming down the deck, his face an unhealthy red in the new-risen sun.

She gazed down at him, her face blandly curious, one eyebrow raised. He really was a little man: shorter than her old friend Mannius—the neatly built Mannius had barely come even with her shoulder—and much, much rounder. Fat little hands were clenched into hard fists— red-backed, white knuckled, and the air hissed in and out of him, rather like Gabrielle's water kettle. She bit back amusement. He looked funny, but he was clearly very angry and about to work himself into a fit. "Captain?" she asked politely.

"None o' that!" he snapped, and leveled a shaking finger along their back-path. "What's yon ship? 'Tis the one ye left last even, I wager, and them aboard it pirates! *Your* pirates, mayhap?" He glared at her; she merely looked at him, and finally waved him to go on. Seething, he did. "Aye, I'd heard Xena had give over her hard ways along t'sea, but *I* never believed it! Cousin of mine and his pa went down under attack from your ship, time was! *And*

19

villagers I once knew—well, thanks to *you*, I'll see none of 'em again until Captain Plice fetches up in the lands o' the dead!"

"And since I'm still an evil warlord or a pirate, or maybe both," she drawled softly, "you're trying to get me angry enough that I'll send you down to join them right now?" The color left Plice's chubby face rather suddenly, and he staggered back a pace, but when she would have steadied him, he swore and threw her arm off. "Take it easy," she said. "I'm no raider, no warlord. I needed that ship just long enough to reach yours and join my friend." A wave of her hand took in the still sound asleep Gabrielle. "Whatever that captain's doing, it's his choice, not my order." The captain glanced her way and snorted indignantly.

"Aye. *That* 'un! Him—the warrior with t'odd armor, *he* owes me for his girlfriend, there, but I was willin' t'let it go until we reached port."

"She's my *friend*," Xena corrected him flatly. "And he's a companion of mine—sometimes." She drew out several coins and let them clink together. "Her passage and mine both—as far as Rhodes."

Plice eyed the coins briefly, then stepped back and clasped his hands behind his back. "Not touchin' a coin from *you*, Xena! And t'other one? He gets *his* back this very morning! Poseidon sees me take coin from you or yours, and where's the *Euterpe*? Bottom of t'sea, that's where, and all her crew with her. That includes my sister's two sons, she'd curse me to Tartarus and back, they drown for any cause. I give passage to Poseidon's sworn enemy, she'd curse me anyway."

"Poseidon's quarrel is with me, not you," Xena said flatly. She shifted the coins between her fingers, letting

20

them clink. The captain watched them hungrily, but kept his hands securely clasped together behind his back. "The sea-god has his faults—"

Captain Plice waved both hands frantically. "Shhh! Woman, are y'daft, ill-speaking Poseidon in the midst of his own sea?" The warrior cast her eyes up, and waited for silence.

"Faults," she repeated firmly. "But he doesn't sacrifice people like you because of people like *me*." He eyed her in patent disbelief. She sighed heavily, and turned away, shoving the coins back in the small, belt pocket. "Think what you want, then," she snarled. At her feet, Gabrielle groaned and shifted, then snorted sharply, rolled face first into the rail, back again, and sat partway up to blink at them.

"Do you people *mind*?" she asked muzzily. "Some people are trying to *sleep* around here!" She glared through slitted eyes, then curled into a ball and resolutely tugged the blanket over her head.

Xena gazed levelly at the captain, who glared back at her. "We can talk about this up there," she gestured toward the raised aft deck and the wheel with her chin, "or we can talk later. The coin's yours, if you decide to be sensible about it." Plice looked as though he wanted badly to say—or shout—something back, but after a moment, he merely turned his back on her and strode toward the aft deck, scrambled up the five steep stairs, and vanished into his cabin; the door slammed ringingly behind him, briefly silencing the crew.

Not for long, of course; *now* they had something new to gossip about. She was grimly amused to notice that few of the crew members actually looked *at* her. Except for one.

At first she thought there was something familiar about the hulking brute who came stalking along the deck, but on closer inspection, she decided he was just one of a given type: bad clothes, big muscles, massive neck, shaven head. Instead of a tattoo, this fellow's skull was marred by thick scarring; his eyes were deep set and beady, chips of pale blue under a single, thick, black brow. He stopped mid-deck; Xena flexed her shoulders and moved away from Gabrielle as the brute gestured at two other seamen, who came up behind him.

"Xena," he spat. "Heard last night, when we was shifting the load below, that you'd come on board." He smiled, revealing broken, blackened teeth. "Didn't believe my luck. It usually isn't this good."

"What makes you think you're so lucky?" she asked, her voice low and menacing.

He ignored the tone and grinned briefly at his two comrades—as if he'd scored some point by getting a reply from her. "Luckier'n my brothers," he snarled, and the grin was gone. "They were ships' men, good ones."

"There are a lot of good ships' men out there, it's a big ocean," she countered, and leaned casually against the mast. "Why should I care about you—*or* your brothers?"

He took a step forward, but stopped cold as one of his companions caught hold of his elbow and the other muttered something to him. He nodded briefly. "They never served you, any more'n I did. They were on a ship following a man named Cecrops. While back. Maybe you remember now?"

She yawned neatly. "I remember. So what? Cecrops captained his own ship; whoever was in charge of the other ship—he wasn't under *my* command, either."

"So thanks to *you*, Cecrops didn't fall into the whirlpool—but the other ship did! Maybe I wouldn't'a known at all, where they went, 'cept I heard a couple of Cecrops's men in a tavern, just south of Athens. Bragging about how they'd escaped Poseidon's curse, and how the other ship had gone down."

Xena shrugged. "Anyone serving on that ship knew what he was doing, who he was serving, and what the risks were. I didn't put them there—and I didn't send them to their doom."

"Yeah," he sneered. "So you say."

"Niros, the captain's already warned you off for fighting—" The other man caught at his arm; Niros shook him off and drew a long dagger from his belt.

"Captain'll probably promote me for getting rid of her, and I owe my brothers." Beady little eyes fixed on hers. "I'm gonna enjoy this, Xena," he said, and threw himself at her.

But she was no longer there; Xena evaded the man easily, letting him crash headlong into the mast as she caught his companions each by the shirt and knocked their heads together. They sagged slowly to the deck as she spun back.

Niros moved quickly for a man of his bulk; he'd already righted himself and turned back, one hand briefly braced on the mast, the other holding the long knife at the ready. She gave him a broad flash of teeth and went into a crouch, arms spread wide, her hands empty.

Behind her, she could hear Gabrielle's sleep-fogged voice demanding, "Does anyone *mind*? Some of us around here would like a little *sleep*!" A loud thump followed as the younger woman resettled and dragged the blanket back over her head. Niros glanced that way; Xena shifted sideways two quick paces, putting herself between the brute and Gabrielle. He gave her an unpleasant grin.

"Friend of yours, isn't she? Maybe once I've tossed what's left of you overboard, I'll—"

"You talk too much," Xena snarled; she ran up his chest, snapped a foot up under his chin in passing and flipped back off his shoulders. He staggered back and shook his head as she landed on the deck, shifted his dagger from hand to hand, and began stalking to the left. *Trying to get around me to get at Gabrielle, or maybe to distract me so his friends can,* she thought, as the two slowly rose, wobbling against each other. Didn't matter either way. The other two didn't look like they wanted to fight her, and Niros was too clumsy to do any real damage.

She flipped the chakram into her hand as he shifted his grip on the dagger once more, then suddenly threw it; the deadly metal circle deflected it neatly, and Niros's friends threw themselves flat as the dagger flew between them to lodge in the far rail. Niros himself stared blankly for a long moment, then fumbled at his belt for another blade.

Xena cast up her eyes and shook her head; she was smiling in genuine amusement now. "You're no challenge," she said softly, and launched herself in a tight flip, came down on his shoulders, and slammed the flat of the chakram against his head. He staggered, and as he went down, she launched again, this time landing on the deck behind his companions. The two men stared at the unconscious Niros, turned to eye her sidelong, then gazed at each other.

The entire ship was quiet, she suddenly realized. What crew was on deck was staring at what was left of a very one-sided battle. "You two are smart, you'll drag him off

24

and talk some sense into him when he wakes up," she said.

The two men looked at her, eyed each other again, then bent to grab hold of his arms. Niros groaned faintly.

But before they could drag the bulky sailor aside, a cold voice from overhead broke the silence. "Salini. Holin. You both swore last night you'd back Niros. I knew you were cowards."

"That's not fair," one of the two complained in a high, reedy voice; one hand shaded his eyes as he looked high into the rigging. "Moldawic, if we hadn't, Niros woulda beat us flat! Holin *tried* to tell him it wasn't *our* quarrel, and that if *he* couldn't take her, *we* sure's Hades couldn't!"

"Cowards," Moldawic spat, silencing him. Xena took a step back from the mast to gaze up. Halfway down from the crow's nest she could see him—at least his outline against the rising sun. He must be sure of his footing, she thought. Most men wouldn't try to climb down a main-mast aboard a moving ship with a drawn sword in one hand. He did move quickly and easily; at just above her height, he pushed off and dropped to the deck with a loud thump.

She blinked in suprise—for just a moment, his coloring, the shape of his head. . . . *It could almost have been Marcus,* she thought. But Marcus was taller than this Moldawic, better muscled, and this fellow wore a beard. *Besides,* she reminded herself flatly, *Marcus is dead.* She stood where she was, chakram hanging loosely in her right fingers, watching him. His grip tightened on the sword hilt, but he made no other move.

"You really think you need that?" she asked finally, a gesture taking in the long, broad blade as she dropped the chakram back onto its clip. He laughed mirthlessly.

"Against *you*, Xena? I'm good in a fight—good enough to know a smart man doesn't go against you without his best weapon in hand."

He started as a high, resonant voice behind him complained, "If *some* people would go someplace *else* to talk, *some* people could get some sleep!"

"Salini, Holin," the newcomer snapped, "take care of *her*. I'll manage Xena."

"Ah—Moldawic," Holin ventured unhappily. "I don't think that's such a good idea."

"Why not? You saw her last night, little blond bit of goods, and besides, she's still asleep. Pick her up and toss her overboard. *Then*, if you don't want Niros cutting you two into fish bait when he wakes up, you'll help me with *her*!"

Xena flexed her hands and grinned. "Ya know, that's probably the worst idea you've had yet, Moldawic," she purred. "You got any idea how really mad she's gonna be, those two wake her up?" Before he could reply, she took two long steps toward him, one forearm slapping his sword aside before she brought both down in a slashing arc across his throat. He gagged and tottered back, but didn't fall and didn't drop his sword.

"Get—the—girl!" he gasped, and drew the blade back to stab. Xena's boot caught his wrist, sending the weapon skidding across the deck; she spun into him then, driving an elbow into his gut and whirling back out to bring both fists down on the back of his neck. This time he went down; when he groaned and tried to stagger back to his feet, she swore under her breath and stepped back, waited until he'd made it woozily to his hands and knees, caught the shoulders of his shirt in both hands, and pulled him

26

halfway up, then down, hard, and nose first into her knee. His eyes rolled and he crashed to the deck.

She stepped back, eyes moving around the deck. Niros was groaning but not moving; no one else on the deck moved or spoke. By now, there must have been twenty sailors watching, most from up by the wheel, a few from the prow, the rest braced against the far rail. Back the other way, she could make out the sail of Habbish's *Wode*; it was nearer than it had been, still far enough away she couldn't make out individuals on deck.

Against the near rail, Gabrielle was still a blanketed lump, curled in on herself, only one foot and a little pale hair visible. Closer, a pale Holin was eyeing her cautiously, muttering under his breath and trying to drag the massive, still unconscious Niros aside by himself. Salini had eased back and was partway between Joxer and Gabrielle's sleeping spots, moving with quiet purpose along the rail.

Xena tensed as the seaman bent over the blanketed form and cheerfully snarled, "Rise and shine, darlin'!" and flipped the cover partly aside. Salini blinked and his jaw sagged; Gabrielle's staff shot up, closing his teeth together with an audible *click*, and as he fell, it slammed across the side of his head. Gabrielle's sleep-fuzzed voice mumbled, "Go to Hades. I'll rise but I refuse to shine! 'n furthermore, if you think th. . . ."

The rest, the warrior couldn't make out.

Staff and hand slid back under the blanket; a deep breath, a sigh, nothing more. Gabrielle slept again.

Xena bit back laughter and dragged the hapless Salini over to join his fallen comrades.

It was still quiet on deck. Xena looked around, caught the eye of the sailor holding the wheel, and sent her gaze toward the unconscious men. "You wanna get someone to clean up the mess here?"

Nothing from the captain—though he'd know of the fight within moments, if he didn't already. *Probably egged stupid Niros on himself,* she thought tiredly. Fights like these were merely annoying—one stupid, inept fellow after another throwing himself at her. *Not one of 'em with a tenth of Draco's creative style. Woman's creative juices could dry up, waiting for a decent challenge.* Her mouth twitched: half amusement, half annoyance. *Listen to you. You don't want Draco around, remember?* But when Gabrielle could take one of 'em out without being even half awake. . . .

She stepped away from the mast and settled down close to the sleeping Gabrielle. Several sailors came warily across the deck to help move the still unconscious Niros and Moldawic to the far side of the deck and help a groaning Salini below decks.

So far as she could tell, Joxer had remained oblivious to the entire episode. *Typical.* Then again, he'd been on the move for days now; probably he was at least as exhausted as Gabrielle. Maybe he'd eaten some of his provisions before falling asleep; given Joxer's tendencies to buy whatever was handy and cheap, maybe he wouldn't wake up again. *You wish,* she thought sourly. She didn't really; obnoxious as he could be, often needing a good smacking around; he didn't need more than that. People a lot worse than Joxer (who was merely clueless as opposed to actively bad) didn't deserve to die of bad food.

A glance over her shoulder assured her the *Wode* was sticking close, but not gaining. *Yeah, sure. They don't need to. All they gotta do is stay behind us. Draco, I get my hands on you anytime soon, and . . .* And. She wasn't sure quite what. A grim smile turned the corners of her mouth. Whatever it was, it would be . . . creative.

2

Xena hadn't had as much sleep lately as she'd have liked, she realized. She glanced down at Gabrielle, who lay stretched out on her back, only the top of her head visible, then looked over to where Joxer was still a motionless blob, deep in shadow. Two seamen were reworking some of the rigging straight across from her; a different man stood behind the wheel and only two men gazed out from the afterdeck. A glance in the direction they were staring assured her the *Wode* was still following, but with daylight, the northerner's ship had pulled well back. There wasn't anyone else in sight, and for the moment, things were quiet.

Fine. Take advantage of that. She settled her shoulders against the rail, not far from Gabrielle, and closed her eyes.

She woke some time later to full sun and stifling heat—barely any breeze and that a hot, muggy one. Men ran across the deck and began hauling the sails up, and other men climbed aloft to secure canvas to the mast. The familiar rise and fall of the ship had changed to a jerkier, back-and-forth motion.

It took her a moment to realize why: The wind had died off; the vessel was being rowed. Still something missing—she got to her feet and looked north as Gabrielle groaned softly and began shoving the overly warm blankets aside. The *Wode* was still there—barely visible against the horizon now. But east and south there was land, very close. *Euterpe* had just cleared the long, thick, stone breakwater of one of the smaller islands and was being brought into port. Xena could make out a long pier and, behind that, a steep hillside with whitewashed houses and shops dotting the landscape. And higher up still, thick forest.

Ship like this one would probably have any number of such stops.

Then again, perhaps not. Xena turned as she heard two familiar, angry voices. The captain had come on deck, and Joxer was up there arguing with him.

"*You* said Rhodes was your first stop!" Joxer snarled. It unfortunately still came out as a whine.

The captain's voice topped his easily. "What of it, landsman? Is a landsman about to tell a ship's captain that this isn't—"

"This is *not* Rhodes," Joxer broke in, and when the captain would have shouted him down, he waved his arms. Probably it was the clattering assortment of loose bits flapping around that silenced the fellow—astonishment, Xena thought sourly, that any of it stayed where it had been attached. "No—you could maybe fool some people, but *not* me." He held up a hand and began turning down fingers as he made his points. "One: Rhodes is at *least* a three-day sail aboard a *fast* ship from anywhere

32

between Athens and Sparta. Which, I happen to know, includes Phalamys! Two: Rhodes has a really, really *big* statue of a man standing across the harbor, and I don't see *any*thing like that out there, do you? No. Why? Because he isn't there, and that's because this isn't Rhodes. You ask me, it just *might* be Delos, but I don't think so 'cause it's not big enough. So, probably Menos or Siphnos. You said two things when I paid my way last night." He held up the other hand and began turning down fingers once more. "You said leaving as soon as the tide was right, and we did that. Fine. You *also* said, 'No stops between Phalamys and Rhodes.' Which was why I paid extra, remember?"

"No stops I said and meant," the captain snarled. "*That* was afore y'snuck yon girl aboard, *and* before Xena came on in mid-sea, *and* from yon pirate's ship as still follows us! Some nasty plan of *hers,* I don't doubt! Some 'as say she's changed—well, no one asked *me* what I thought!" The two men glared at each other—well, Xena thought judiciously, Joxer glared as well as his face would allow. The silence stretched. Plice scratched his head then. "How's a landsman know t'islands?"

Joxer shrugged; a pleased grin tugged at his mouth. "Oh," he said loftily. "They don't call me 'Master of Geography' for *nothing*." The smile went. "So—*why* are we stopping in . . . wherever, and are you gonna do this all the way to Rhodes?"

But Plice was already shaking his head. "*Euterpe* is tying up here for good and all—at least until *you* and those women get off!"

Xena settled back down next to Gabrielle as the argument picked up speed and steam once more. Privately, she thought Joxer'd might as well save his breath. The

Euterpe's captain had the look of that kind of stubborn man who would anchor in this harbor until the hull rotted before allowing himself to be persuaded to change his mind.

At her side, Gabrielle shoved hair off her face, yawned, and sat up, groaning faintly as the ship moved jerkily forward. "Ohhhh, this is just *bad*," she mumbled. "Reminds me of that awful little thing you made me row all the way over to Ithaca."

Xena laughed quietly and tugged the small green top straight. "*You* rowed? Seems to me you spent most of that trip flat on the deck!"

"You know what I mean," Gabrielle replied, and stifled another yawn. She sat up a little straighter, shifted around so her back was against the rail, and peered blearily at the raised afterdeck. "You know what I like less than waking up to Joxer making cheerful, 'rise and shine' noises? Joxer having hissy fits at someone!" She frowned at her hands, then eyed her companion. "Did he do that to me this morning? You know, the 'rise and shine' thing? I mean, earlier when it was still almost *dark* out?"

"Wasn't him, Gabrielle."

"It wasn't? Funny . . . I thought I remembered whacking him a good one." She shrugged, then cast the upper deck an irritated look. "Why are they *yelling* like that?"

"Because Joxer paid for passage to Rhodes, and the captain's putting all three of us off here."

"In the middle of the—?" Gabrielle's voice rose to a squeak.

Xena gestured south, where the hillside town was clearly visible.

"Oh." She eased to her knees, looked around, settled

down again. "He's putting us ashore. Okay. And—this is a reason to get angry?"

The warrior laughed. "Not a reason for you, I know. You want some of my bread?"

"With land waiting for us right over there, are you nuts?" She got to her feet as the captain vanished into his cabin, hauling the door to, behind him, and Joxer stalked grandly away, muttering under his breath. He didn't actually fall down the steps, Xena thought—he just missed the last one and went staggering across the deck, caught his balance against the mast— briefly—and went down in a heap. High above him, men laughed raucously. Joxer cast the limp sail and the rigging an injured look, then edged back to his feet and strode over to the port rail.

Fortunately, it was only a few long steps, and he was able to catch hold of the rail as his feet went out from under him again. Gabrielle's lips twitched; Xena laid a hand on her shoulder briefly, then waited until the would-be hero got his backside planted on the deck. He looked extremely irritated.

"I do not believe that man!" he began. "I mean, did you *hear* any of that, Xena?"

"Joxer," the warrior drawled, "I think they heard you down in Tartarus."

He gave her a sidelong, sour glance. "Yeah, well. I can't believe he's taken all the money I had for passage— the dinars King Menelaus gave me, you know? And now he's just—just *dumping* us ashore. I mean, if this is Melos or one of the smaller islands, you know how hard it's gonna be to find a decent ship to Rhodes?"

Silence.

"Yeah, right. Make that, *any* ship to Rhodes, whether it goes straight there, or island-hops for the next moon-season. And you can guess what kind we're gonna find in a backwater like this. If any." He rolled his eyes and sighed heavily. "That's assuming I can dig up enough dinars to *get* there!"

Xena's gaze went beyond him, and Joxer slewed around as heavy footsteps rattled the plank under him. A half-grown boy had come down from the aft deck and hurried toward them, a bit of blue cloth clutched in one hand. Small, slender—his hair all crisp, blue-black curls, his eyes wide set and very brown under thick brows. Unnervingly, he still had the look of Captain Plice. Probably the sister's boy. "Sir, Captain sent this out to you." The cloth was a small bag that clinked as the boy dropped it. "All the coin you paid, he said tell you." He eyed Joxer for a long moment, and his cheekbones turned a sudden red. "Sir—some of us, we heard about your quest. What you're doing for our king. We're—sorry, sir. Seems to us, there'd be honor in taking such a valiant hero on his travels, but m'uncle's that stubborn." He turned and ran back across the deck and vaulted up the steps three at a time. Joxer watched him pass out of sight, through the captain's door, then eased the little bag open and poured the coins onto his palm. He counted them twice, finally shrugged.

"Gee, Gabrielle," he said finally. "Did you hear that? *Valiant—hero.*" Gabrielle sighed faintly. Joxer preened as he stowed the little coin bag in his belt. "Well! Stubborn Captain Plice, huh? Guess I showed *him*!"

"Yeah, Joxer. You sure showed him," Xena said dryly. *More likely, he didn't want Joxer's coins any more than he wanted mine, or Gabrielle's—just in case Poseidon lumped Joxer with me.* No point in even mentioning all that to Joxer. *Leave it be,* she ordered herself tiredly. *A*

36

Joxer who realizes who and what he really is—that's harder to deal with than Joxer the Mighty.

"Yeah." Joxer gave her a smirk. "Too bad I couldn't talk him into taking us on to Rhodes. But I'm not so sure I wanna go anywhere with a grouch like that anyway. Besides, I need to get something else to eat, the flounder sausage that woman sold me back in Phalamys has a really nasty fishy taste, and I almost lost it late last night. It kept coming back up, you know?"

"Joxer," Gabrielle gritted between clenched teeth. "You wanna *die*? Like, right *now*? Just keep talking about food! Or whatever that—that *stuff* of yours is! And, I swear—"

"Hey, you two mind?" Xena broke in flatly. "I'm going deaf, sitting between you. Joxer, we're coming in fast here, you better go bundle up your stuff, maybe."

"Yeah, I guess so," he grumbled. "Be just like these guys not to give me any time once we're tied up, huh?"

"They might *try*," Xena said. "But I'd rather not get in a fight over it, Joxer."

He stopped halfway to his feet and stared at her. "After all that yelling he did last night, and now this, and you—you just—?"

"Joxer," she said patiently. "Think about it, okay? He's got a ship and a lot of men he's responsible for. And he's afraid Poseidon's gonna hold him responsible for me being on board. Because Poseidon doesn't like me on account I helped Ulysses when Poseidon didn't want him helped. And Cecrops broke his curse, and I just happened to be on board *his* ship . . ."

"Picky," Joxer said.

"Yeah, well, these things happen. And because you and I know each other, Plice figures keeping you around might run him the same risk, even if Gabrielle and I go away."

"Huh?"

"She means," Gabrielle put in sourly, "that Poseidon might have reason to hate you, too. And that you're just as much danger as Xena is." The two women exchanged sidelong, barely tolerant looks as Joxer chuckled and swaggered to his feet.

"Well," he said in some satisfaction. "Guess he *does* have pretty good cause for that, doesn't he?" He turned away and squared his shoulders, then strode across to his blankets. For a wonder, he made it without so much as a wobble. Xena swore to herself. Easy to guess why. He was distracted, running new rhymes through his head for yet another verse to "Joxer the Mighty."

Gabrielle sighed then. "I'm afraid to *think* how he's gonna set *that* to music—"

"Don't think about it," Xena hastily advised her. "Not on an empty stomach."

Some moments later, the *Euterpe* eased up next to the deserted pier; two men jumped over the rail and hurried to secure the ship while two others dragged the long plank up from the hold and positioned it. Captain Plice came out to stand by the wheel, arms folded across his vast belly. Xena gave him a brief look, then turned and strode ashore, Gabrielle right behind her. Joxer turned to give the man a long, hard, challenging stare before he stumbled onto the dock. Once there, he dropped his bundle and turned to look all the way around, then shaded his eyes against the early sun and gazed along the island, and up.

"It's Melos, sure enough," he announced with a satisfied smile. The smile slipped as the plank rattled behind him. The *Euterpe*'s men were already back aboard and coiling in the rope. The plank was out of sight, oars dipping into the water as the tubby little ship turned away from shore and headed back out of the harbor. "Do you *believe* that man?" he asked generally. "I mean—"

"Yeah, I know," Xena said; he choked as she clomped him one on the back. "Don't tell me you wanted to stay on board with him snarling at you the whole way to Rhodes, Joxer."

"Well—but I had this *advantage* over all those other guys back in Sparta. I mean, I must have been a whole day ahead of them, and *now* lookit!"

Gabrielle gave him an over-patient look. "Joxer, you didn't have any advantage over anybody, because there is no quest, and there is no holy ewer or—what*ever*."

"Yeah, so you both say," he mumbled. "So—now what?"

"You're asking *me*?" Gabrielle retorted.

"Enough," Xena snarled. Silence. "All right. We need a ship out of here, unless either of you want to stay on Melos."

"Better than taking a ship anywhere," Gabrielle muttered, but fell silent when Xena pursed her lips and narrowed her eyes.

"Yeah," Joxer said. "As a matter of fact, a ship to Rhodes. And no, you and Gabrielle do *not* have to tag after me, if you'd rather not, Xena," he added, stiffly formal.

"Joxer," Gabrielle said. "What *is* it with Rhodes? I mean, what do you think is in *Rhodes*?"

He shrugged; a faint grin tugged at the corners of his mouth. "*I* don't know. It—just came to me, night before last. So, I thought, 'Joxer, after all, Apollo picked you for this quest—'. Did I mention that I had *dinner* with King

Menelaus and his priest?" he added loftily. "After Apollo chose me, that is. In case you weren't aware of that little fact?" Gabrielle cast up her eyes and said nothing; Xena merely cleared her throat. Joxer glanced at her, bit back a titter, and went on. "So, anyway, I thought—"

"You *did* that part," Gabrielle put in.

"Don't interrupt him, Gabrielle," Xena said tiredly. "He just gets confused, and keeps repeating himself."

He frowned. "I do? I mean—yeah. If you didn't keep *interrupting* me, maybe a fellow could think straight! Anyway—there I was, stuck in this—I don't know where, except it was a long ways from those gates or that rose garden, all around the palace. *In* the palace, of course. Still—it was like a servant's room or something, hardly any space, just one window opening, and every time I looked out, I could see. . . ." He shook his head, clutched at the helmet as it nearly went flying. "Never mind about that," he added firmly. "But I was just stuck in there— the door was stuck or something, after this old woman brought in some really awful food, servants' stuff, I guess. You know," he said thoughtfully, as if it had just occurred to him, "maybe they put me in the wrong place—all those servants, you gotta figure orders get mixed up sometimes. . . ."

"Joxer!" Gabrielle shouted in his ear; he winced, stepped back from her, and as she glared at him, he swallowed.

"Sorry! If you wouldn't yell like that, maybe I could remember where I was, Gabrielle! Well," he went on after a clear effort to figure out where he *had* been, "all at once, it just came to me: Rhodes! And—well, if Apollo chose me the way he did—you know, special ceremony, his handpicked priest casting spells and like that? Well, then, why wouldn't the god give *me* a special hint which way to go?"

"Joxer," Gabrielle said. "Words fail me."

"Just came to you to go to Rhodes," Xena said slowly. Most likely, that was purely Joxer, his mind nattering on the way it did. Maybe, just on the off chance it *was* a hint from Apollo or his scurvy priest, it would be a good idea to avoid Rhodes entirely. *Naw,* she thought tiredly. *If Apollo told Joxer Rhodes, Avicus would know about Rhodes, too. Same if Avicus gave him the idea. If Helen was there and god or priest knew about it, it's a good bet they'd've sent anyone but Joxer to Rhodes.* Probably Helen would have been long since hauled back to Sparta and securely locked away so no one but Menelaus could look at her.

It didn't matter. There was no point in trying to second-guess things—the Spartan end of it, or Joxer's supposed thought processes. "All right," she said finally. "We need food, we need to be sure where we are."

"Melos," Joxer said firmly.

"*Maybe,*" Xena told him, as firmly. "I don't know Melos, I never came here when I—yeah. When I spent time at sea. I just know a lot of places this isn't. And I know we need a ship outa here, whether it goes straight to Rhodes or not. So long as it doesn't go straight to the bottom, or straight to Tartarus, I don't care." Joxer opened his mouth to protest, closed it as she scowled at him. "So maybe if *you* talk to some of the men along the dock, Joxer, while Gabrielle and I—"

"Oh, no!" Gabrielle overrode her vigorously. She flashed the would-be hero an icy smile. "Joxer's staying right here with us. All three of us *together.*"

"Gabrielle, it's an island. And there's no other ship in sight. Where's he gonna go—?"

The younger woman shook her head. "I'll tell you where he's gonna *be*. Right where I can lay hands on him if I gotta."

Joxer snickered. "Gee, Gabrielle, I didn't know you cared," he said, then ducked as she swung at him. Xena snarled a warning, then put herself between the two of them and gave Joxer a shove across the dock and into the street beyond.

Melos—for it was indeed the westernmost of the chain of islands known as the Cyclades—boasted only the one small town, and only one main street that crisscrossed the steep slope. It widened slightly for the two main, town fountains, where several women were filling household buckets with water, or washing clothes—or watching a motely of small children playing some kind of touch game while they sat in the shade and gossiped. Total silence fell as the strangers passed, but conversation broke out behind them, louder and more excited than ever. The tree-lined dusty street wound past houses, broadened once more for the tents, canopies, and stone huts of the market, then went on, sharply angling uphill past the last houses. Xena lost sight of the now narrow track as it dove into thick trees and brush.

From mid-market, one could see down to the harbor and the docks, some distance below. The water was a bright, clear blue-green, the stone mole blocking most of the harbor entry as white as the few clouds well to the north—as white as most of the city's walls and houses. Xena could make out the departing *Euterpe*, but no other ship, and the harbor was likewise deserted except for a small fishing boat working its way around the near-circular shoreline. Someone checking his fish pots, no doubt. Her stomach rumbled faintly.

She glanced around. Joxer and Gabrielle were arguing—what else?—about where to go first. Xena took a deep breath, then stepped between them once more and pointed, past a small oil-lamp shop and a girl with a brace of skinny chickens in a woven crate. "That way—it smells like someone's frying eels." Joxer and Gabrielle exchanged wary looks, but dutifully came on after her.

Someone *was* frying eel—a comfortably round, gray-haired woman in a brown dress was turning a pan of sliced eel patties and a few eel steaks, all the while calling cheerful instructions to a girl who stirred a large pot of thick soup. Rolls and loaves were piled high in baskets along a counter, between high-piled wooden platters and pottery bowls towering under strings of onions and garlic and dried peppers. They hung from a woven-branch arbor that kept the sun off but let smoke and steam escape.

It must taste as good as it smelled, Xena thought happily. People filled a long table under an awning; a young couple sat holding hands on a nearby bench, sharing a bowl of soup, while a woman with five children ranging from a gawky youth to a chubby baby occupied a thick red blanket at one end of the counter. The warrior's smile widened as the older woman caught sight of the newcomers, and beckoned them in, shouting to the girl to dip up three bowls of soup.

Some time later, the three stepped back into the open, Gabrielle slowing so she could work two large, cloth-wrapped loaves into her pack. Joxer was looking bored—probably wild to get back to the docks so he could find a ship. *Good luck,* Xena thought. There still wasn't a ship down in that harbor—not even the fisherman, who'd apparently checked his traps and nets, and gone home with his catch.

She thought about this, suddenly. No ships at all. Had Habbish missed the *Euterpe*'s unplanned stop? Or had Draco some agenda—some "hint" of his own about where to look? *Don't try second-guessing him, either*, she told herself. Though, she suddenly recalled, it wasn't likely a raiding ship would sail into a harbor like this on a clear day—unless it intended mischief to the island. Habbish would have good reason to keep his ship out of sight if he hadn't simply gone on after Plice's vessel. Draco'd probably feel the same. "Ship next," she said. Joxer gazed out and down, and frowned.

"*What* ship?" he demanded.

"The one that's eventually gonna come into port," Xena told him. "C'mon, let's get back down there and find someone to ask when that's gonna be."

There were men on the docks now—moving baled goods out of a squat, stone warehouse, or repairing ropes and nets. A small, open fishing boat had been drawn up on shore nearby—the same one she'd seen from above, Xena thought. Several men were gathered down there, picking over a pile of wet clay pots on long ropes, while a white-haired old man squatted on the sand, emptying one pot after another onto a piece of grubby canvas. A small pile of coins gleamed by his bare feet.

Joxer was already moving among the net menders, and apparently not having much luck. One of the men pointed to sea, and another shrugged; someone held up two fingers, another three, and yet another man shrugged broadly. The would-be warrior came back to join his companions; he was scowling. "Fine," he said. "Just great! The next ship out *may* come tomorrow, and *maybe* the day after, but probably it's gonna be the day after *that*, because it goes to every last little hunk of rock out there, and one of them *thinks* there's another ship that sails for Rhodes—eventually, not directly, of course!—but they can't be sure *when* that one's due. . . ."

"And—this is a bad thing?" Gabrielle asked.

Joxer sighed heavily and rolled his eyes. "Gabrielle," he said finally. "For your information, no one *asked* you to come running after me. I mean, if you really did want to be my sidekick—"

"Give it a *rest,* Joxer," Xena snarled. "That's all you got?"

"That isn't bad enough?" he asked huffily. She waited; he sighed. "Yeah, well. They said I oughta talk to Beyro, he's off somewhere just now, but he should be back before midday, and—" He pointed to the far end of the dock, where a small, snugly built hut sat. "And that's his house. He runs things here, keeps track of what's in the warehouse there, what hasta go out and all. So he should know better what ships are due."

"Good enough," Xena said. "Let's go find some shade and wait."

Beyro didn't actually return until very late afternoon, by which time Gabrielle had made heavy inroads on the bread, Joxer had nearly worn a hole through the dock pacing, and Xena had broken up more arguments between the two—and stopped more tantrums mid-tirade on Joxer's part—than she could keep count of. *That's assuming you'd have a reason to want to,* she thought grouchily.

Fortunately, the man was very much in charge of what

went in and out of his harbor, and he was able to let them know the next ship due in would arrive sometime during mid-tide the following morning, that she'd at least provide deck-space for them to sleep, and that her usual route missed most of the smaller islands and—allowing for winds—made Delos in two days.

"From there, it's easy to change ship for Icaria or Chios north, or Carpathos south. Better the last, if it's Rhodes you're wanting." He smiled at Gabrielle as the pale-haired woman sighed deeply and unhappily. "Man'd say you're not much for sea and ships, lass."

"And—you'd be right," Gabrielle said, with a faint smile of her own.

He patted his stomach. "Gets you here, does it?" She nodded. "My old mother—up in the market yonder, two stalls past Marim the potter—she's got an herb shop. Makes a paste y'put on bread afore y'go aboard ship and every bell after, keeps y'so comfortable as if y'was on dry land." He nodded as Gabrielle eyed him in patent disbelief. "Ask old Vorteris, white-haired fisherman yonder with his pots. He'd've sold that boat of his the day his old pa passed it down to him, were not for Mother's herb-brew. Takes his in strong ale of a morning afore he goes out, but y'don't look the type for *that*." Gabrielle wrinkled her nose and shook her head. Beyro looked at Xena. "Tell her I sent you up-along, she'll give you a fair price, not like she would for strangers. Zenipa, she is. She's beds for rent by the night too, if y'please. Or there's place for your blankets just along past my place—no walls but a roof t'keep rain off." He glanced sidelong at Joxer and tipped Xena a grave wink. "Better here, if any of y'fear to miss *Wave Dancer*."

Joxer dropped his bag; his sword tipped out of the

46

sheath and clattered to the stones as he knelt to gather up his spilled things. "Miss—I mean—"

Beyro nodded. "*Dancer*'s captain's proud of his tight schedule; knows the dockmaster at any of his stops, can guess within an hour when he'll tie canvas. He'll not wait here in Melos for anything short of a hard storm or a sea serpent blocking t'harbor entry." He smiled as Joxer snorted, obviously disbelieving. "Oh, m'self, I agree with y'about *them*. Still, one or two men of Melos've seen 'em out to sea, and Captain Plice of t'*Euterpe*—he swears his ship was chased from Andros to Icaria by one of 'em. Says he's never since stinted Poseidon any sacrifice he thinks the god might like, *and* he prays three times a day, just in case."

"We'll stay down here," Xena put in quietly before Joxer could get any words out. *No wonder Plice was so eager to get rid of us!* Though whether he'd actually seen real sea serpents, or simply taken too much ale on the trip in question. . . . *Sea serpents, hah! How long did I sail my own raiding ship? I never saw a sea monster of any kind. Could be there were such things.* They didn't mess with ships, by and large. "We'll pay you, of course—"

"No need," Beyro put in. "It's no cost to me or mine, and little enough to offer when you were set ashore against your own choosing. Plice means well—mostly to his own kind, though. He's a strong man for family, and all else can shift as best it may for all of him."

"Figured that out," Xena allowed, and smiled. "Thank you for your help and your advice; I've been away from the sea long enough it's not a familiar place any more."

He nodded thoughtfully. "Yes. I'd—I'd heard Xena had retired her sea raider's ship some years since. And that these days, she's battling the same kind she used to hire."

47

She merely nodded. "I thought it was you," he added, his color suddenly high. "Not too many women who—"

"Yeah," she broke in as he hesitated. "I know. Gabrielle, why don't you head on back to the market? We'll follow as soon as Joxer gets himself pulled together." Joxer mumbled something under his breath as Gabrielle turned and almost ran down the dock.

3

Xena eyed the misfit warrior sidelong. "What?" she demanded. Joxer's eyes were fixed on Gabrielle; as she started uphill and out of sight, he sighed. He sounded exasperated.

"What!" he said shortly. "What, *my* food isn't good enough for her, she doesn't even want to *talk* about when I'm nice enough to at least *offer* to share, but she'll eat this whatever-it-is . . . *glop*? I mean, I spent a perfectly good bit of coin on that salami, and I— owwwwww!" He broke off as Xena closed the distance between them, one capable fist gripping his ear. He swatted at the fist—in vain. "Ow, ow, ow. . . ."

"Shaddup," she ordered. "And c'mere."

"Ow, ow—you know, I could do this—ow!—easier if you'd let *go* . . . ?" She merely tightened her grip and dragged him over to the edge of the dock. What he could see was suddenly very little wood and lots of water, a good distance down. It looked deep—and cold. "Ah—can we talk about this?" he whimpered.

"What we're gonna talk about," Xena informed him,

49

her voice a low growl, "is you and food. Or whatever that stuff is you call food. Where is it, Joxer?"

"It's—*ow, do you mind?*—it's in my pack, where else would it be?"

"How should I know, Joxer? Get it out." He swatted at her fist again, then staggered and nearly went off the dock headfirst as she let go of his ear. "Quit stalling, and get it out. Now." He gave her a nervous grin, squatted down and fished through his bag. Xena watched him narrowly. *I swear he's got more stuff in there than Gabrielle has in that sack* she *carries.*

With a loud "Aha!" he pounced, shoved what might have been a spare shirt aside, and dragged out two cloth-wrapped bundles. He sat back on his heels, smiling in satisfaction and held them up.

Xena's nose wrinkled. What she could see of the bread through its wrapping was blue-green and furry; the other stuff resembled a length of dark sausage and smelled— *Ya don't wanna think what it smells like,* she assured herself hurriedly. Joxer's smile was fading. She gestured with her head. "Toss them both. Out there."

"You want me to waste perfectly good food?" he demanded in astonishment. "I mean," he looked away as she cleared her throat ominously, unwrapped the bread and eyed it critically. "Well, sure it's kinda—ah, *stale?*—on the outside, but there's a lot more inside that's—"

"Joxer, best thing that'll do is make you sick. You don't wanna be stuck on a ship with me if you're sick, got it? And that other thing—I never smelled anything so disgusting."

"You should taste it, it's really not *that* bad," he assured her, but prudently fell silent as she scowled down at him. His lips twisted. "Yeah, that's how it always is, huh? You know, Xena, you really should try harder to get along with people, it just makes things a whole lot easier when we're all together. I mean, what I'm eating really is not your business, is it?"

"Joxer," she growled, and fixed narrowed eyes on him. He swallowed nervously but didn't seem ready to back down.

"Well, gee. If it's that bad, maybe I shouldn't throw it out there. Maybe it'll kill the fish."

"Joxer," she said sweetly. "You know what the fish out there eat when they can't get things like that?"

He shook his head, baffled.

"Dead, drowned *people,* that's what!"

Silence.

"Get my drift?"

Ahhhh—got it," he stuttered, and began unwrapping the salami.

"All of it, Joxer," she said. "Wrappings, too. That piece of stuff probably smells as bad as what it's wrapped around." He mumbled something under his breath, cast her a sidelong, sour look, but dropped both bundles into the water. "Good. Now, let's go find Gabrielle."

"Um why don't I—?"

"Why don't you stay with me, Joxer? Because the *last* thing I wanna do is get separated again, got me?"

He tittered. "Gee, Xena, I didn't know you cared . . . it was a *joke*!" he yelped and backed as far out of reach as he could. She caught hold of his shirt before he could fall backward into the water.

"Yeah, funny man," she muttered. "Come on."

Gabrielle found the herbalist's stall without any difficulty and wandered slowly between bundles of fresh or dried

51

greens, pausing now and again to smell some particular bouquet or other. The old woman had Beyro's nose but otherwise didn't resemble him at all; she was very short, quite round, and wore snow-white hair in a long, girlish plait woven through with green ribbons. A small bunch of flowers and bits of green—rosemary and forget-me-nots, Gabrielle thought—perched above one ear. At the moment, she was cheerfully passing on instructions to a very pregnant young woman who'd apparently come in to refill her tea box and buy another small pot of skin salve.

"Stay out of the sun on your way home, Ayela!" she called after the woman. "And mind you take a cup of that, double strength, before bed each night!" She turned back to look around her small shop and smiled at Gabrielle. "Now, you'll be from that ship as came in this morning early, won't you? What, I wonder, might I do for a sweet-faced young woman like yourself?" Gabrielle explained; Zenipa beamed the whole time as if the younger woman was her cleverest apprentice rather than a customer who was probably seeking discounted goods. As Gabrielle finished, the old woman nodded vigorously.

"He's right. Winter storms blow up high out beyond our mole, but the men still need to bring in the catch. Some of 'em'd eat nothing but dried salt-fish all winter, did they not take old Zenipa's blend to keep their stomachs calm."

"I can understand that," Gabrielle said, though privately she wasn't sure salt-fish was a great improvement over tossing around on a ship. *Better than raw squid, I'll bet,* she thought dryly. Better than whatever that stuff of Joxer's—but she wasn't gonna think about that. Zenipa had turned away to pluck a small clay jug off the shelf behind her.

"This'll last ye—oh, matter of ten days, calm weather and low seas like it is just now. Now. You take a blob the size of this," wrinkled old fingers made a circle as big as the end of Gabrielle's thumb, "and smear it on bread. Eat that first thing, before you get up even, it should keep you fine the day. Don't worry for the taste, all you'll taste is sweet bay."

"Should keep me fine." Gabrielle pounced on that word. "Should?"

The woman cackled. "That bad for you, is it?"

"Worse," she said gloomily.

"A box of dry wafers to go with it, then." She handed over a palm-sized wooden box tied with red string. "They're small. Take one as soon as you begin to feel queer, and lie down, close your eyes. You shouldn't need another." She put the jug and the box in a small cloth bag and knotted the ends of its thong neatly, before handing it over. But when Gabrielle fished out coins, the woman shook her head. "If it helps you proper, tell others where you got it."

"I'll do that," Gabrielle assured her. "Thank you." She wandered out of the shop as a woman with two babies in tow came in, and claimed Zenipa's attention. *Bread next, I guess,* she thought idly. At the moment, it was very nice to be standing on dry ground, smelling fresh bread and some kind of meat toasting nearby. Nice not having to keep moving, hoping to catch up to Joxer; hoping that Xena would catch up to her.

She found a place nearby where she could see most of the docks; Xena and Joxer were down there where she'd left them, almost. *Why's he sitting down? I thought they were coming up here . . . ?* Maybe they could talk Joxer into a fresh loaf or two. "Yeah, right," she laughed quietly. Meantime, it seemed a long time since they'd eaten. Bread and maybe some fruit. She turned away from the sea and let her eyes follow the road up and out of sight.

I bet you can see all the way back to Sparta, from up there, she thought. Well—why not? She stopped at the baker's for a pair of rolls, and at the counter next to that for a skewer of meat and peppers. Two thick-skinned, sweet smelling oranges went into the bag with the bread; she smiled at the boy sitting behind the mounds and baskets of fruit. "My friends will be coming along in a few minutes," she said. "A woman in leather armor, dark hair, big sword, boots—ahhh, round metal thing hanging from her belt? And a guy—well, I guess you could call what *he's* wearing armor, but it's not in the same class at all. Skinny guy, funny hat, goofy smile." She eyed him inquiringly; the boy smiled back at her, rather tentatively.

"I know," he said. "Everyone knows, the three strangers who came this morning."

"Good," she said. "When you see them, will you tell them that Gabrielle went up there for a picnic? Ahh—I mean, if that's not private or anything?"

He shrugged. "A few goats graze up there. The land is too rocky for anything useful."

A terrific view isn't useful? Gabrielle wondered. But maybe the view wasn't as great as she thought it would be. Maybe these people had enough to do, keeping fed and clothed, and no time for anything else. She gave him another smile and set out.

It was a long, steep, hot climb, and she was too warm by the time she reached level ground once more—but the view all around was easily worth the effort. She stood on the very crest of a rock-strewn meadow and let the wind blow her hair around and dry the back of her neck where it had been plastered most of the walk up. There weren't any goats in sight—no people, either.

The island stretched west for some distance, the ground dropping off gradually into a strip; the strip of land meandered, both sides nearly sheer though she could see pale sand along either side, and the sea all around the long point. East, it looked as though the land dropped straight down, from where she stood. At any rate, there wasn't much visible except the trees on the north face of the island, and to east and south the sea far below.

From up here, she could no longer make out the harbor or the town. And somewhat to her disappointment, she couldn't really make out the mainland from up here, except as a purply smudge along the northeastern horizon. No ships out that way, and none to the south or east. "Almost like I'm alone in the world," she murmured. Her stomach gurgled. "Yeah, I know," she said aloud. "You next."

It took her some moments to find a good place to sit and eat: a spot where the breeze kept the sun from feeling too warm, where there weren't sharp-edged rocks everywhere. One place that looked nice from a short distance turned out to have harbored goats; she wrinkled her nose in distaste, and went on looking.

The bread was still warm in the center when she broke it open and piled the contents of the skewer on it. Once that was gone, she peeled and ate one of the oranges, eyed the second, but shoved it back in her bag. A glance skyward assured her she hadn't been here that long. "Still—I wonder where Xena is?" Probably having trouble with

Joxer. She broke off another handful of bread and absently ate it.

A low chuckle at her back brought her around and halfway to her knees, bag shoved out of the way and the staff in her hands. *Oh, no.* Draco stood there, smiling genially.

"I like a woman with a healthy appetite," he said admiringly.

For a long moment, neither of them moved. Gabrielle managed a breathy little laugh, and got to her feet. "Ah—Draco! What a—a surprise! What—are you doing *here*?"

"I might ask you the same question," he replied quietly. His eyes searched her face.

Xena—where are you? "Ah—right." She managed a smile, shifted her grip on the staff slightly as he took a step toward her. He gave the weapon an amused glance, but stopped where he was. "I asked you first, though."

He gestured behind him. "The ship I'm on always stops here for water. I thought I'd take a walk while they were filling the barrels."

"Ship? Excuse me, but there isn't a ship in that harbor, unless you count the old guy's fishing boat. And you didn't come up through town—"

He laughed quietly. "Why would I do that? Besides, the ship I'm on, the captain doesn't put into the usual ports. Not unless he wants to cause panic, or unless he's making a raid." She gazed at him, baffled. "You should recognize it, Gabrielle. Xena swiped me off it last night and borrowed it to track you down. That's what Captain Habbish told me, anyway."

"Captain—oh. It's that pirate ship, isn't it?" His eyes crinkled with amusement and he applauded her. Gabrielle drew herself up straight and planted the end of the staff against a rock. "I thought you said—the last time we met—that you were gonna try to do good. You call sailing with pirates *good*?"

He stared, and the smile was gone. "I don't—I'm not—" He spun away and slammed a fist into his other palm, drew a deep breath and expelled it in a loud gust. "I'm not a pirate. I bought passage on *Wode*, same as you did on that—whatever it was." He spun back. "People like me don't get passage on ordinary merchant ships, Gabrielle. Frankly, I'm surprised Xena got—" He paused, thought a moment. "That's right. Why're you here up here, all alone? And where's Xena?"

"Xena?" She stared blankly, then managed a shaky little laugh. "Oh, her! She's—around."

"Around." He nodded thoughtfully, eyes fixed on her face. "What about that Joxer?"

"Joxer!" Another laugh; it sounded better, she thought. "Ah—Joxer! Right! You know, I haven't seen him in the *longest* time!" He just looked at her, Gabrielle warily thought, and felt her excellent lunch shift. She swallowed and somehow kept still. The silence stretched.

"Yeah," he said quietly. "That's what Xena said about you, back up in Sparta. You were there the whole time, of course."

"Sparta?"

He nodded.

"There." Another nod. "I—ah—was around. You know."

He nodded again. "I saw you, remember?" He took another step toward her, his eyes suddenly very alert and searching. "What about Joxer? Was *he* there?"

She gaped up at him. "Joxer—? Oh. Him. Well, he wasn't with *me*."

"No? Maybe because he was inside the palace, being

interviewed by the king?" He gazed past her, his face tight. "I knew there was a trick to this," he said quietly, as if to himself. "Had to be." He focused on her again. "That it? He's on this quest for King Menelaus, isn't he?"

Things are getting out of hand, Gabrielle thought nervously. Being alone up here with Draco was bad enough. The way things had gone lately, Joxer was gonna come stumbling into the open any moment now. And then Draco would try to kill him—*what, I'm gonna be able to stop him if that's what he wants to do? Draco* will *kill him!* She suddenly wished she could remember more of the last time she'd seen the warlord, but between the moment Xena'd come out of the temple to untie her and Joxer, until she found herself *inside* the temple with Draco kneeling at her feet and promising to do good—well, it was fuzzy at best. But there was a faint memory of a smiling Draco vowing not to kill the man she loved, and only after he'd learned it was Joxer. . . . Didn't matter exactly what had happened. She only needed to look at him to see he was jealous. *A warlord. Jealous of Joxer. What god did I offend, to have such an "interesting" love life?*

She blinked; he'd just said something, and she had no idea what. She shook her head; he sighed faintly. "Never mind, Gabrielle. I don't think I want to know." He backed away from her, glanced behind and down. "They're just about done, I should go."

"Ah—yeah. Don't want to miss your boat. Not too many of them come around here, you know?"

Draco smiled. "Oh, Habbish'll wait for *me*. I paid good coin—and he'd never want me mad at *him*."

"Good point." Another silence, an uncomfortable one. He seemed to want to leave, seemed unable to take the first step. He smiled then, an uncertain, almost shy look

Gabrielle would have said—if it had been anyone but Draco.

"You're looking good, Gabrielle," he said softly. "Take care of yourself."

"I—yeah, I'll do that." His eyes moved over her once, then he turned and strode off. She could hear a rattle of stones some moments later, far down the slope. When she went to look, finally, she could just make out the top of his head and, much lower and farther out, a sward of pale sand and a sleek raider's ship drawn up and lying awkwardly on its side.

"So," Xena murmured behind her. "I was hoping Habbish was halfway to Crete by now."

Gabrielle let out a breathless, wordless squawk of alarm and flailed for balance; Xena's hands caught her shoulders and drew her back. "Sorry. Didn't mean to scare ya."

"Scared? Me? After being stranded up here alone with Draco, what could possibly scare *me*?" Gabrielle let the warrior draw her back from the steep drop-off and only turned to face the woman once they were where she could no longer see sand or ship down there. "How much of that did you hear?"

Xena shrugged. "Not much. We got up here about the time you stood up, but then I had to flatten Joxer, tie him up and gag him . . ."

"Great," Gabrielle snarled under her breath. "Anything else you can think of that's gonna go wrong today?"

Another shrug. "Not really. What'd he have to say?"

"Not much. Wanted to know where you were. Where Joxer was. Asked me if Joxer'd been picked for—Xena! Don't tell me *Draco's* one of Menelaus' heroes!"

The warrior gave her a wry smile. "Already did, remember? Wanna hear the best part? He's doing it because

59

of *you*. Avicus hinted that Draco finds Helen and brings her back to her heartbroken husband, he'll be sure *you* learn about what a great deed he did."

Gabrielle groaned and sank to the ground. "I don't believe this! I—wait. He told you that, and you didn't—you didn't—"

"Didn't tell him what's really going on? Gabrielle, you know me better than that." Xena knelt next to her and laid a hand on her shoulder. Gabrielle sighed faintly and clasped the hand with one of her own. "I tried to tell him, but I swear, he's as stubborn and hardheaded as Joxer. I did get him to swear that he'd talk to Helen if he found her. That if what she said agreed with what I'd told him, he'd leave her alone, or help her find another place to hide, if that's what she needs."

"And you believed him."

"I know him better than you do, remember?" A faint grin briefly turned her lips. "A *lot* better. He's stubborn, and he thinks he knows a lot more than he does. But he's smart, too. Once he had a chance to think about it, he knew I didn't have any reason to lie to him about Helen. He may still not entirely *believe* what I told him. But he'll do what he said; he won't decide until he hears her side of the story." The warrior shoved a pair of rocks aside and settled cross-legged next to her friend. "Enough about Draco, it's gonna spoil my appetite. You got any of that bread left?"

"Bread—yeah. I ate all the meat, though."

"I figured. Brought my own skewer." She settled a small ale skin between her ankles, took the half-loaf, filled it with meat and peppers, seasoned it with a spicy red liquid from a small clay jug, and folded the bread back on itself. Gabrielle watched. Xena eyed her sidelong. "What?"

"Just wondering—where'd you leave Joxer?"

The warrior scowled. "Where he's gonna stay until I'm done with this. You trying to kill my appetite or something?"

They released the would-be hero on their way back down the road—over an hour later. The sky was suddenly dark, the air sullen, the wind gone. *Storm weather,* Gabrielle knew. Better to be off the heights before it struck. Joxer rubbed his wrists, limped in an exaggerated fashion, and whined all the way down—or he did until both women turned on him. After that, he moved more quickly and quietly, though he still limped and now whimpered to himself instead of either of them.

"Save it, Joxer!" Gabrielle snarled as they reached the first houses. She swallowed hard; even the water in the harbor was all whitecaps, and the little fishing boat was out there again, bobbing wildly. She forced her eyes back to the road.

Joxer snorted. "Oh, yeah, Gabrielle. For your information, I was about to come to your rescue, when—when—"

"When I knocked you flat and probably saved your life," Xena put in flatly. She met Gabrielle's eyes and sent her gaze ahead. Gabrielle rolled hers, and took the lead. Behind her, she could see Xena collar Joxer, and she could unfortunately just make out what the woman was telling him. "Look, Joxer, don't you remember when you challenged Draco, when he kidnapped Gabrielle and you? Well, you made him lose face. Look, I know you couldn't

61

have done anything else, but you got any idea how pissed off he is when he even *thinks* about you?"

"Well—yeah. . . ."

Joxer was thinking about it, Gabrielle realized grimly. *One chance to wipe that complacent note from his reedy little voice. . . .*

"But, Xena, you know if you'd just let me—"

"Joxer, look. There are times you have to back off from a fight, you know that, right? Draco, trust me, is one of those times."

"But—!"

"*Joxer!*"

Silence.

"You're trying to—you're a hero, right? Well, Draco's a warlord. He's good at it. Smart heroes don't go up against warlords like Draco. Especially when the warlord has a personal reason to want 'em dead."

Another silence.

"You gotta pick your fights, Joxer. Even I pick mine."

"Well, yeah," he allowed.

Gabrielle sighed faintly, and picked up the pace. Mercifully, she heard none of the rest of it.

4

An hour later, the three sat in the back of Melos' only tavern—The White Dolphin—watching rain lash the island. Gabrielle jumped as lightning turned the street a brilliant blue-white and thunder crashed almost at the same moment. Xena gripped her wrist briefly, reassuringly, and the younger woman managed a faint smile.

"Sorry. Guess I'm a little jumpy."

"Yeah. Well, after this afternoon, you have every right," the warrior replied softly.

Joxer gave her a sullen look over the rim of his cup. "This afternoon? Oh, yeah, you mean when *I* got *sat* on and tied up?"

She gave him a look, and he eased back on the bench, setting the cup well to the side. A nervous smile tweaked his mouth.

"Joxer, Gabrielle had things under control up there—"

He frowned at his cup, transferred the scowl to Gabrielle, who smiled and shrugged. "Hey, Joxer, what can I say? She makes the rules, remember?"

"Oh yeah?" His mouth twitched. "Maybe that's how it

63

was back when I first met you two. These days, everybody makes the rules but *me*." His gaze flicked resentfully over Xena, resettled on Gabrielle. Silence, broken shatteringly by more thunder. This time Joxer started violently, sending his cup flying. Liquid puddled on the table and dripped onto his pants; he mumbled something under his breath and tried to slip backward off the bench, but succeeded only in losing his balance and upending the whole thing. Momentary silence in the tavern as everyone turned to stare. Joxer reddened, forced a wide, embarrassed smile, and waved.

Xena sighed wearily, but got to her feet and held out a hand, which he took. "Ahhh—seem to have run out of ale," he stammered. "You—need anything, Xena?"

The warrior picked up her cup, eyed the contents, then shook her head. Gabrielle drained her cider and shoved the mug within his reach. "That's *plain* cider, remember," she warned him.

It was Joxer's turn to sigh—exasperatedly. "Gabrielle. This is me, remember? I know you—and I know what you drink." He turned on his heel and strode across the tavern.

Gabrielle shook her head. "He's in a hissy fit again! Did you hear him just now? And—well, just *look* at him!"

"Yeah, I know," Xena drawled. "Best way to get him to walk across a crowded room without tripping over people and dropping things."

"*Tell* me about it! Did I tell you he made it all the way from camp up in Thessalonika without tripping once?"

"No—but I'm not surprised." She settled on the bench across from Gabrielle. "Did you get your paste—that whatever stuff from the harbormaster's mother?"

Gabrielle nodded. "Some wafers, too. The stuff that

goes on bread is in a really neat little jug—here, wait."
The younger woman dove into her pack and brought out
the pottery vessel. "It's not like any pottery I've ever seen,
have you? Lookit! It's white with black. I really like the
pattern, it looks like—oh, I don't know, twigs on snow?
Maybe? What?" This last more sharply as the warrior
picked the jug off her hand and held it close to her eyes,
turning it slowly all the way around, then back again.
"Xena? Since when did *you* get *that* interested in pottery?"

Xena shook her head absently; her eyes were fixed on
the bands of wavy black lines. "It's not that. . . . I've seen
something like this before. The colors—" She blinked
rapidly. "Most pottery you see around this end of the
world is red and black, orange and black."

Gabrielle considered this. "Well—yeah. With heroes'
tales on them, or foot races or something like that. So,
someone got bright and decided to do something different,
that's all. What's the big deal?"

Silence. Xena set a precautionary palm of one hand
over the stopper and upended the jug. Her eyes glinted.
"Thought so." She handed it back, casting a cautious
glance toward the taverner's counter as she did. Joxer was
telling some tale or another—probably a "Joxer-the-
Mighty" that made him look both heroic and ridiculous.
The way he really was, actually. Whatever he was up to,
he had the tavern's attention. Two old men were laughing
at something he'd just said, and the taverner was refilling
the would-be hero's cup. "He'll be there a bit longer.
Look at the bottom of the pot, Gabrielle."

"I don't see—oh." She turned the little piece toward
the uneven light of a nearby torch. "You mean those fancy
scratch-marks?"

Xena nodded.

"I know all about those; that's the signature of whoever threw this particular pot. They all do that, so you can identify who made it, in case you want more of one person's stuff—say, because they don't explode when you fill them with cold stream water and then hang them over a fire. Anyway, I know that because the woman who made all the water jugs and cook pots in Poteidaia marked hers with a sign of crossed sticks and a fire—just five or six lines, but you could tell that was what it was. And, no one else in all the region used just those strokes to mark his or her pottery." She turned the pot one way, then the other. "I can't tell what this is supposed to be, can you?"

"It's a swan," Xena said quietly, then put her hand over it as Joxer stepped back from the bar. Gabrielle glanced that way and immediately pulled the pot into her lap, but he was apparently deep in some story or another and, after another raucous laugh up that way, he leaned back on the wooden counter and took a deep swallow from his cup. Xena growled under her breath. "Joxer the Well-Mannered. Joxer the Easily Distracted. You bet. Good thing neither of us was very thirsty, isn't it?"

"Yeah." Gabrielle stowed the pot back where she'd put it earlier—padded by her blanket and the bread she'd bought—so it wasn't likely to get broken. "Swan? Wait a minute!" she said sharply. Xena shushed her vigorously; Gabrielle clapped a hand over her mouth and glanced both ways. No one was interested in their conversation, and Joxer couldn't possibly have heard with all the noise around him. Still, the bard lowered her voice prudently. "You mean—*swan* swan?"

Xena nodded.

"You mean—*Helen* makes pottery? Helen of Troy?"

"Hey, Gabrielle." Xena spread her arms in a wide shrug. "Noble women don't have a lot of choices how to keep themselves amused while their men are raiding neighboring kingdoms or whatever. Taking off to fight Troy for ten or more years, say."

"Well—sure. But most of these women weave, Xena! Like Penelope. Or—well, okay, some don't. But they compose music or sew instead. Plant flowers. Sing—or make masks for the theater, or compose lines some male bard gets to claim as his own." She considered this, wrinkled her nose. "Okay, that last doesn't happen so much any more. But pottery's messy. And it's hard work."

"All I know is, that's what she did. Oh—sure, she didn't make village cook pots and water jugs, just things like this: little jugs for her cosmetics and for scented oils. You know, specialty items. And she had servants to manage the hard stuff. I only know about Helen being a potter because of the time Menelaus invited me to Sparta. I saw some of her things—small things, like this. White with black. And the mark on the bottom."

"Okay, but how'd you know they were hers?" Gabrielle shook her head. "I don't know . . . this makes about as much sense as Joxer getting picked to go quest."

"I didn't know about pottery at the time—I just paid attention. I heard some of the servants talking about the pots; some guest had knocked over an oil lamp she'd made, Menelaus had it set out for some reason—"

"Probably because it was something else he could brag about," Gabrielle put in sourly. "You know: Look what *my* woman can do."

"Yeah. Maybe. You and I are *not* gonna disagree where Menelaus is concerned, Gabrielle." The pale-haired bard grinned ruefully; Xena chuckled and riffled her hair. Gabrielle snarled aloud, and slapped the warrior's hands aside so she could comb tangles from the base of her neck. "Menelaus. Yeah, what a jerk. Anyway, the women were complaining about the fuss he made when the pot got broke. Tiny little thing, probably Helen had made a dozen of 'em. So it doesn't make a lot of sense to me, either, Gabrielle. Why he cared about her pottery. Any more than why one of her pots would turn up on Melos. Only thing I'm certain of is that they didn't come from Troy. Paris never let Helen do anything in Troy except look beautiful for him. A pottery kiln—yeah."

"I can just imagine. But—wait." Gabrielle leaned forward, her eyes bright. "You don't mean," she whispered, "that you think Helen is *here*? On Melos?" But before Xena could say anything, the bard shook her head. "No, that doesn't follow, either. This place is so small, it's like Poteidaia, a stranger moves in and everyone knows everything about them." She thought about this. Shook her head. "Of course, if she *was* here, and everyone knew she was hiding, they could keep the secret."

"True, Gabrielle. But think about it. Melos is one of the closest islands to Sparta—"

The young bard was already shaking her head impatiently. "But that wouldn't matter! Don't you see? Because it *is* so close, so he wouldn't expect her to be *here*. Right under his nose." She considered this, then finally sighed quietly. "But maybe you're right, Xena. Because if she *was* here, she wouldn't be making and selling pottery that could get picked up by accident by some Spartan. Or by some idiot like Joxer." She thought some more. "Al*though* . . . if there was any more pottery in that shop like this—white with black—I didn't see it."

Xena drained her cup. "There may have only been the one piece. You know, one pot."

"But—it's not making sense! Xena, she's not some village woman who'd *have* to support herself, she's Helen! You can't feed yourself one little pot at a time—especially if the herbalist gives them away. Either way, it just doesn't work out." She settled both elbows on the table and leaned forward. "You know what *I* think? She's staying out of sight in some palace somewhere, and whoever's hiding her is letting her live there as an honored guest." She glanced toward the counter, eyes narrowing briefly as they fixed on Joxer. "You know, a woman could die of thirst around here . . ."

"I know. But we need to talk about this while he's not under foot; he's *still* not convinced the quest isn't real, and I don't want him to know we're looking for Helen ourselves. Not just yet, anyway. Keep that in mind, will you?"

Gabrielle gazed at her close companion blankly, then nodded sharply.

"You may be right about her, Gabrielle. There are plenty of kings and rulers around who don't count themselves as Menelaus' allies. They'd have no reason to betray Helen to him.

"But remember, when she left us, outside Troy, she didn't *want* to be known as Helen. She wouldn't let herself be announced as queen. Maybe she found she liked that kind of life. And maybe she found that she could support herself by making and selling her pots, and she liked that, too. And keep this in mind: A pot like yours coulda been traded half a dozen times since she made it."

"Or more, I know," Gabrielle said tiredly. "So she could still be just about anywhere."

Xena smiled at her. "That's all right, Gabrielle. If we can't figure out where she is, certain other people can't figure it, either. And that should keep certain royal and priestly types—*and* Joxer, in the dark!"

"Dark?" A familiar, reedy voice asked. Joxer had fetched up against the end of the table, three mugs slopping over and leaving a liquid mess on the tray—part ale, part cider. Gabrielle leaned across to snatch up her cider and swallowed deeply. "Gee, I guess you two have been so busy talking, you didn't notice the storm's moved off like us guys did."

Gabrielle slewed partway around on her bench; there was pale blue sky breaking through the clouds, and sun reflected blindingly from wet paving stones. She shielded her eyes and turned around once more.

"How long have you been standing there?" she demanded. Joxer shrugged and settled with a tooth-rattling thump on the end of the bench.

"I just heard one of you use my name, that's all. And something about dark—"

"Except! It's not. We know!" Gabrielle said quickly.

"What'd you do, get lost over there?" Xena asked, her voice flat.

"Well—" He spread his hands. "You know. We got to talking about—ah—things. You know. Things. All the same, when they found out it was you who was helping me out, Xena, Jedius thought he'd better send an extra ale for you. In case, you know?"

Gabrielle made a face at her cup. "This is *not* plain cider," she said flatly.

Joxer shrugged. "I told him plain, Gabrielle," he said as flatly. She gave him a look and scrambled to her feet, taking the cup over to the counter with her.

Xena drew the cup to her, tasted the liquid and set the cup aside, then smiled at the taverner, who was watching her anxiously. Gabrielle got his attention then, and the warrior turned to gaze narrowly at Joxer. Thoughtfully. "What'd you tell that poor innkeeper, Joxer?" she demanded softly. "To get him so scared? Tell him all the old, bad stuff I did?"

"I—didn't? I mean—maybe just a little, you know, couple of times we went up against Callisto, and—" He leaned back with a complacent smile, but spoiled it with a loud hiccup. He clapped both hands over his mouth and eyed her sidelong; the warrior chuckled. "I mean, you know how it is, Xena, when you start trading war stories, and—"

"Spare us," Gabrielle put in quickly as she slammed her refilled cup down on the table and settled back on the bench. "Please."

Joxer gave her a sour look, but said nothing.

A short while later, the three left the tavern and walked down a road stained brilliant reds, yellows, and purples as the sun broke through a last band of black cloud before it set. It was much cooler than it had been, now that a light breeze had sprang up. Gabrielle wrapped her arms around herself as they came onto the dock. "I'm gonna be glad for shelter from the wind tonight. You want to keep watch?"

Xena shook her head. "No reason for it," she said. "Any problem we had around here is long gone, don't you think?"

"Problem?" That, inevitably, was Joxer. Gabrielle laughed.

"Problem? That woulda been the rain, Joxer. *And* that stupid ship's captain who dumped us here this morning."

"Huh?" Joxer removed his oddly shaped helmet and scratched his head. "Oh, yeah. Him. But—wait a second, why would *he* come back tonight and—?" Brief silence. "I don't get it."

"Nothing to get," Xena assured him. "Except some sleep."

The would-be hero stopped so abruptly, Gabrielle nearly ran into him. "Sleep?" he demanded. "This early? I mean, if I'd known you were coming down here to *sleep*, maybe I woulda stayed back at that tavern! You know, some of those guys were *really* interesting to talk to—"

Xena sighed heavily, silencing him. "You mean they were listening to *you*, right?"

"Well—what's wrong with that?" Joxer asked. "It's not like I'm telling them fake stuff like *some* people."

Gabrielle snarled under her breath and started for him; Xena's arm stopped her.

"Gabrielle. Nothing against all your bard stuff, but most *real* men I know like to hear other men's stories about *real* things they've done."

Silence. Gabrielle was mumbling under her breath; Joxer stood his ground and met Xena's gaze defiantly, though the corners of his mouth were threatening to twitch. The warrior finally chuckled throatily; Joxer caught his breath in a squeak and took a step back.

"Joxer?" the warrior said softly. "It means that much to you to entertain a buncha guys up there, you go right ahead."

"Thank you," he said with heavy dignity; he jammed the helmet back on his head—not very straight—and strode off, back toward the heights.

Xena watched him out of sight, then wrapped a warm arm around her companion's shoulders.

"Come on, Gabrielle." The younger woman held back a moment.

"You *sure* that's such a great idea?" she asked finally, and her voice was still sharp with anger.

Xena laughed. "Hey, Gabrielle! Calm down! It's an *island*. Where's he gonna go?"

"If there's a way," the younger woman gritted out, "he'll *find* it! Maybe that pirate friend of yours is still hanging around—"

"Gabrielle, you don't really think Joxer's gonna ask for a ride from Habbish—with Draco on board?"

"He might." Gabrielle cast her a dark look. "I mean, what if this Habbish comes to that tavern, and—"

"He's a *pirate*, Gabrielle," Xena replied patiently. "Probably well known around these islands. But even if his face isn't familiar, his ship isn't in the harbor. If it's not there and he just shows up, the locals *know* he's a pirate, okay? Because he had to leave his ship hidden somewhere else."

"Yeah, right. Maybe. Or maybe, Joxer goes wandering all the way up that hill and down the way Draco took back to the ship, and—"

"And falls and breaks his neck. I looked that way, remember? Gabrielle, you heard those men around Joxer, back in that tavern. Get real! Where else is he gonna go, with *that* waiting for him?"

Gabrielle muttered to herself a moment, then sighed as all the fight went out of her. "Yeah. I know. Open ground and bad footing against an adoring audience—and the chance to teach a whole new buncha guys his 'Joxer the Mighty' song. Xena, did I tell you what he added to that—to that—?"

"Spare me," the warrior said hastily. "C'mon, Ga-

73

brielle. Let's get you out of this wind. Joxer can sleep on the ship tomorrow. I'd like my sleep tonight."

They boarded the *Wave Dancer* two hours past sunrise the next day. At least, Gabrielle *thought* it was past sunrise; it was hard to tell with the clouds so thick. The water of the bay was iron gray and the wind rippled it first one way and then the other. Water that had gently *ploosh*ed against pilings the previous morning now slapped them. And beyond the stone mole, where the sea lay . . . she swallowed hard. The water was all sharp-edged waves, peaked in white foam.

Part of the queasiness, she unhappily realized, was due to that paste she'd smeared on her bread. *Maybe doubling the dose wasn't such a good idea,* she thought. Adding one of the wafers just as she went up the plank might not have been the right way to go, either. Still—it didn't *feel* like the kind of sick she got from being on a boat. Nerves, maybe.

Or maybe anger. She'd slept heavily the night before— until Joxer had come tromping into the warehouse, humming under his breath and tripping over everything—and everyone—in sight. Of course, *he* claimed he'd tripped because it was so dark, he couldn't see anything. Or anyone—including Gabrielle, whose backside was bruised from where he'd tripped over Xena's sword, and fallen across *her*. Of *course* he hadn't shed any of that crummy armor of his first.

One of these times. . . . She turned away to gaze back up at the neat market town half hidden in trees. Not that there was anything to see, but it was better than gazing at the open water beyond the bay. Or Joxer, who was alternately whining about his aching head, and looking inordinately pleased with himself for some reason. *Whatever it is, I do not wanna know.*

She nodded as Xena paused on her way up-deck to pat her close companion's shoulder. *No. I'm not gonna be sick.* She thought it, but for some reason, couldn't get the words out. Something about her must have reassured the warrior. Xena smiled and moved on to find a corner of the deck to stake out.

Delos was their next stop. Another island on an in-and-out path between Siphnos, Paros, and Naxos—and a few others that were uninhabited, including some that were mere outcroppings of rock above the tide. Some of those, Gabrielle knew, had been islands once. Bardic tradition: When Ares and his spoiled sister Aphrodite got in an argument over which of them "daddy loved best," they decided to take the fight to the people of Samos to settle. Being sensible people, they'd decided *not* to decide—at which point, Ares had thrown a tantrum, Aphrodite had backed him, and the main peak of the island had blown sky-high. Most of the islands had come through all right— a little extra ash to improve the grape harvests, a few stones falling from the sky—but on Samos there was a new harbor where part of the mountain had collapsed and a few pieces of ground all across the sea had sunk while others had risen.

"You gotta be nuts to live on one of these things," she muttered, and turned away from Melos as two sailors dragged the plank in, and others ran to set the sails and still others to man the oars below decks. "Gods," she whispered as the ship plunged awkwardly around and the oar drummer set the pace, "who'd live on one of *these* things, either?"

She licked dry-feeling lips—this despite the coolness

of the morning and the constant spray that assaulted the open deck as the ship wallowed toward the sea. Xena had picked a spot for the two of them forward, just past where the lines were tied off, and where they'd be out of the way of the ship's company. She managed a tight smile as the warrior looked up from spreading out their blankets to wave, drew herself up straight, and managed to stalk in a nearly direct line across the uncertain footing.

"Where's Joxer?" she asked as she dropped gratefully to her knees; the rail was high enough on this particular seagoing torture machine that she couldn't see water from this position.

"Over there." The warrior pointed straight across. "He's gonna want to sleep all day, and I don't want him bothering either of us."

"You got that right," Gabrielle mumbled.

"Gabrielle." The warrior laid a hand on her hair. "You took that stuff, didn't you?"

The younger woman sighed heavily. "Xena, you put the stuff on the bread *for* me, remember?"

The well-muscled hand drew back. "Hey—Gabrielle, just checking, all right?"

"Yeah. Fine. Whatever." Her stomach felt distinctly *odd,* Gabrielle thought. And her mind was chattering at her, little of it making sense. She glanced sharply beyond Xena, then over her shoulder. "Where's Joxer?"

"Straight across, remember?"

Gabrielle could see the woman frown, and barely resisted the urge to yell at her. *I'm okay, fine, all right? Leave me alone, quit—quit pestering me!* Somehow, she kept that behind her teeth. *That's Xena, you—you chattering idiot!* she told herself angrily. *You don't mess with her!*

Still, it could be so maddening! Because now and again, Xena did things—just. . . . *Yeah. She just decides that's how it's gonna be, and that's how it is! And whatever I want? Well, that's too bad, isn't it? Like back in Thessalonika, when stupid Joxer took off on me, I coulda gone north with her, spent a little time with Iolaus and Herc, but oh, no! Xena decides I gotta follow Joxer south! So what happens? I do, and he gets away from me and. . . .*

"Gabrielle?" Xena's voice broke the inner rant; Gabrielle caught her breath sharply and looked up at the warrior. "Are you *sure* you're all right?"

You don't mess with Xena, Gabrielle managed to remind herself. No one with any sense messed with Xena. And there were things between the two women, recent events that might get out of hand, as they once had. . . . *Don't!* she ordered herself fiercely. Why was she even a *little* angry with Xena? *She's your best friend, and she's worried about you, that's all!* Gabrielle offered a faint smile and nodded. "I'm fine. Kinda nervous about whether this stuff is gonna work, that's all."

Xena's eyes were warm as she stroked long blond hair and tucked it back behind her close companion's ears. "I don't blame you, Gabrielle. Remember your earlobe, pinch it, just in case the stuff doesn't work. And I won't let you eat anything except plain, fresh bread." Gabrielle nodded, and the warrior drew her close to lightly kiss the top of her head. "Trust me on that one."

"I do trust you," Gabrielle replied softly. She sighed very faintly as the tension and anger suddenly left her. "I think—maybe I should lie down. Just in case."

"I think that's a good idea, Gabrielle," the warrior replied. "Sleep, if you can. I'll be right here."

"Thanks." The younger woman settled her shoulders on

the familiar blanket and drew a corner of it over her shoulders, then closed her eyes. Below decks, the thump of the rowers' drum and the constant creak of oars in their locks seemed to match the beat of her heart.

5

Gabrielle woke some time later, hot and disoriented, hair plastered to the back of her neck. Sun lay across the deck now, and only the shadow cast by the sail protected her. It was still much too warm; even the wind that rattled the sail was a hot one. Spray plumed high over the bow, soaking everything at that end of the ship; the bow rose, runnels of water coursed down the deck, puddled, then ran back the other way.

"Ohhhh," she groaned. "This is bad. This is just—this is really bad." She closed her eyes once more, but sleep wasn't going to return. Not with her stomach demanding food and her mouth so dry. Her head pounded—no, that was the drum below decks? Except—except it wasn't. *I don't know a lot about ships, but I do know you don't row them when there's high wind.*

She rolled cautiously to one side, levered herself up on an elbow, and hauled the pack over so she could rummage through it. Water bottle first; fortunately, it wasn't buried under everything else. One careful sip—another. "So far so good," she mumbled. Bread next. It had gotten stuffed into a corner, along with the little box of wafers. "Glop once a day," she reminded herself. "Wafers anytime. Bread first." She sat up slowly and got her shoulders more or less comfortably braced against the rail before tearing off a chunk of bread; she rewrapped the rest and put it back before eating. "Yeah. Bet it would taste *wonderful* sopping wet." The way the deck looked just now, it was a good bet *she'd* be sopping wet in no time.

The headache eased as she ate, and for the moment, she didn't feel seasick. "Don't trust that," she ordered herself gloomily. "Eat a wafer." She fumbled the little box open and fished out a wafer—two stuck together, actually. She shrugged and popped both in her mouth. "Rough as it is out there, what can it hurt?"

Xena was up on the high aft deck, near the wheel. Talking to someone, but Gabrielle couldn't see who. It wasn't Joxer, though; *he* was clinging one-handed to the rail across from her, swaying back and forth—and singing. Gabrielle's jaw muscles tightened. "Joxer the Mighty, is it?" She felt a little light-headed all at once. Too awake, too alert, something like that. "Nah—doesn't make sense," she mumbled and held out a hand. It trembled slightly. "Let's hear it for ship travel," she snarled, and got cautiously to one knee.

Hot wind blasted the hair back from her face, then wrapped it around her throat. She gripped the rail hard with her left, wrapped the flying stuff around her right, drew a deep breath, and looked out.

Small islands here and there—most looked too small to hold anything but a few birds, and others were merely piles of wet rock. Everything else was blue sky and waves; steep-sided, whitecaps. She groaned as the ship dropped into a trough and wallowed through it, then eased her way back down. "Did I ask for this?" she snarled under her breath. "No! Was it something I did? I haven't got a *clue* what it might have been! Except I just *had* to follow Joxer all the way from Thessalonika to Sparta and out to the water and then *on*to that ship!" *Joxer.* Her eyes narrowed as she contemplated him.

There weren't any sailors in sight—just whoever was up on the wheel-deck with Xena. "*They* probably have more sense than to run around the deck in weather like this. But Joxer . . ."

The wind slacked briefly; just enough for her to hear his triumphant, ringing, ". . . he's Joxer! Joxer the Mighty!"

The wind picked back up as the ship lurched to one side; he flailed for balance and clung to the rail with both hands. Gabrielle fell back into the rail, her head slamming into the damp wood so hard she saw stars. Anger boiled over all at once; she'd had enough. "Joxer the—I'll Joxer the Mighty *him*!"

He couldn't possibly have heard that, but something brought him partway around; his eyes met hers, and he grinned cheerfully. "Hey, Gabrielle! Have a nice nap?" He righted himself with care, let go the rail, and staggered toward her.

"Right!" She smiled grimly and fished the staff from behind her, surged to her feet and met him mid-deck. "Joxer!" She had to yell to be heard above the flapping of the sail. "You have *finally* done it!"

He slowed, gave her a puzzled look. "I have? I mean—oh, yeah right!" He smiled happily. The smile faded. Silence as she stopped within arm's reach. "Ah—Gabrielle? What have I done?"

"You've finally made me *mad,* that's what!" And she

brought the staff around and jammed the end down, hard, on his toes. He yelped and fell back into the mast.

"What are you doing?" he demanded furiously. "That *hurt*!"

"It was supposed to hurt!" she snarled and went into fighting stance. "Well, come on, Joxer! Let's you and me *do* it!"

He drew himself up, wincing as he put weight on the bruised foot. "Gabrielle, this is no place to practice—"

"Practice?" she demanded. "Joxer, I am going to—" She drew a deep breath. "I am going to mangle you! I am going to turn you into one gigantic *bruise*! And *then* I am going to *hurt* you!"

He stared at her, his mouth agape, then dodged behind the mast as she swung at his elbow. "Gabrielle, what's the matter with you? I'm your friend, remember?"

"Friend? Friend?" She snapped the staff end at his head, then began stalking around the mast; he swallowed hard and kept it between them. "Friend, hah! Joxer, you may be a *lot* of things—including the most maddening, irritating, *maddening*—!"

"You said that already," he put in helpfully, then yelped as her staff cracked down on his forearm. "Gabrielle, will you cut it out!" he shouted. "I am not gonna fight with you, all right?"

"No!" she shouted back. "Not all right! And furthermore—"

"Hey!" Xena's voice broke over hers; the warrior had come up unnoticed behind her. "Gabrielle, what's the problem here?"

"No problem!" Gabrielle said brightly, through gritted teeth. "There won't be one, anyway, once I've killed him and tossed the body overboard. Any objections to that?"

"Ah—I object," Joxer began hastily; he swallowed the words and cowered behind the mast as Gabrielle slammed her staff into it, just missing his head.

"*You* don't get a say. Xena," Gabrielle added sharply, "you stay outta this, you already said I get to mangle him this time!"

"Yeah, sure. Not like this, okay?" But as the warrior laid a hand on her friend's shoulder, Gabrielle snapped the staff overhand into the mast and back; hard wood slammed into Xena's forehead, sending her staggering back—as much out of surprise as anything. Before she could recover, Gabrielle had stalked Joxer halfway around the mast, reversing their positions. Xena felt her brow gingerly. No blood. A bump, though. "I don't believe she did that," she said softly; a proud grin spread across her face. "All right, Gabrielle! She's getting good!"

She stiffened as a familiar, soft voice spoke against her ear. "You know, Xena, your little friend's getting to be quite a warrior."

The smile was gone; her mouth twisted. "Ares," she said flatly and sent her gaze sideways. The god of war gave her a mocking bow. "What're *you* doing here?"

He raised an eyebrow and smiled at her. "Always looking for new talent, Xena; you know that." His eyes followed hers, up to the rail of the wheel-deck, where five or six sailors were following the one-sided fight with evident relish. "Oh, and don't worry about *them*; you're the only one who can see me right now. You're bad for my reputation these days, remember?"

"Too bad, Ares. And I know about you and your talent searches. Leave Gabrielle alone."

He laughed shortly. "Oh—believe me, Xena, that's one you *definitely* don't need to worry about. You know? I *still* don't understand how you put up with her. All that chatter—"

"She's a friend. *You* wouldn't understand something like that, Ares." Her eyes narrowed, and she turned to face him. "So you just 'happen' to show up here, is that about it? So of course, *you* wouldn't just happen to know anything about that?" A gesture took in the pair circling the mast; from the sounds of things, Gabrielle had just landed another blow, and Joxer was starting to get angry.

He leaned back and folded impressively muscled arms across an equally impressive chest, scarcely concealed by the ornately worked, sleeveless leather shirt. "I'm shocked. You actually think that I—? Xena, you've got the most suspicious way of looking at things—"

"When you're around? Funny how that works, isn't it?" She caught hold of his collar. "What've you done to Gabrielle?"

"Me? Do something to her? What's the point?" He removed her hand. He glanced at the one-sided battle and chuckled. "Using her to get rid of *him*—sure, that might be interesting. Then again—" He looked down at her, visibly amused. She cast her eyes up and waited, wincing as Gabrielle's stick slammed into Joxer's cap so hard the metal rang. "Hey, it was an accident! Your little friend there did it all to herself, actually. All I did—"

"You did *what*?" She closed the distance between them and bared her teeth.

"It's a long story—"

"Then shorten it!" she snapped.

"Fine," he snapped back. Silence, broken only by the delighted yells of the sailors and the rhythmic *clack* of Gabrielle's staff, punctuated now and again by Joxer's howls of pain. "You know, every single time, I tell myself

I'm not gonna let you get to me, and every—"

"Ares," she warned, "just—tell—me!"

"Whatever." He began to pace, two steps away, two back. "That stuff your little friend got for her seasickness? That old woman didn't exactly come up with the recipe for it on her own. She—ah"—he preened—"had help."

"You?" He nodded. "Why?"

"Because there was a nice little family feud going on between some fishermen from Melos and another bunch from Delos. I knew if I worked it right, I could start a—really nifty little war."

She considered this, eyes fixed absently on Gabrielle, who was feinting with her staff, and Joxer, who was yelling at her, all the while dodging her blows and trying not to get slapped by a flailing length of rope that had come loose from the yard overhead. She shook her head finally. "Nice try. But the old woman is known for the stuff. People in Melos use it. For seasickness."

"Oh—it does cure that. But if you take more than you're supposed to, it has an additional effect, Xena. It makes you *really* angry." He grinned. "Anything can piss you off, just about anything at all. Get you mad enough to kill." He grinned as his eyes were drawn to the fighters; Joxer had pulled out his crossbow and was using it to deflect Gabrielle's staff as he backed around the deck; Gabrielle was yelling at him—Xena couldn't make out the words for the wind. Joxer looked too winded to do any more yelling. "Ya know?" the god of war remarked cheerfully, "she's actually kinda cute like that!"

"Nice," Xena remarked; her backfist caught him squarely on the nose, hard enough that he yelped in surprise and fell back from her, clutching it two-handed.

"What was that for?" he demanded in an aggrieved

voice. Xena gave him a look; her lips twisted.

"That's a stupid thing to say to a woman."

"Hey! I didn't say *you* were cute when you're mad, did I?"

"If you're smart, you won't even think it, Ares. But Gabrielle's my friend. You don't say things like that about her, not around me. You got it?"

"Got it!" he replied mockingly. He gave his nose a final tweak and glared down at her. "You know—I remember when you used to be a *lot* more fun." Before she could say anything, he vanished.

Xena bit back a sigh and strode over to Gabrielle's bedding, one eye on the battle mid-deck as she knelt to rummage through the other woman's bag. Clay jug— there. And the box . . . good. *She still gets the goo, and the wafers, but from now on I decide how much she takes of both.* She shoved both items deep into her own pack, then strode across the deck to get between Gabrielle and Joxer.

Gabrielle still looked angry—but not nearly as furious as she had been. She still *sounded* as furious, though. "Xena, get outta my way, this time I'm gonna—"

"Gabrielle. Enough. I said you got to mangle him, not kill him." She clamped a hand down on the staff and glanced over her shoulder. "You mangled enough, Joxer?"

"Ahhh—yeah," he panted. The crossbow fell to the deck with a clatter and started to slide aft; Xena's foot shoved it back in his direction. "Think so. Thanks."

"He's mangled enough," Xena said blandly. "C'mon, Gabrielle, you two've entertained the crew long enough, they need to get back to work."

"Xena! I—" Gabrielle sighed heavily as the warrior took the staff out of her hands and rested one end on the deck. The fight went out of her abruptly. "All right." A heavy thump; she leaned around Xena to look down at Joxer, who'd collapsed to the deck and sat cross-legged, holding his head in his hands and moaning softly. "Thanks for the workout, Joxer," she said, mock-sweetly and turned away. A groan answered her.

She stopped abruptly as her eyes took in the dozen or more men leaning on the rail of the high-deck, staring down at them. "Xena!" she whispered urgently.

"Smile and wave," the warrior replied softly. The younger woman eyed her in disbelief; Xena nodded. Gabrielle brought up a bright smile, spread her arms wide and bowed; the crew erupted in loud yells and applause until a sharp order from someone behind them sent them running "C'mon, sit down with me. We gotta talk."

"Ah—we do?" Gabrielle frowned as Xena handed her back the staff; she turned it over in her hands thoughtfully. "You know, I really can't think why I went for Joxer like that. I mean, not that he didn't deserve it, but . . . You know, I was really, *really* mad all of a sudden!"

"Yeah, I know. Let's talk."

They talked. Xena left Gabrielle alone with a small hunk of bread, and went back over to kneel next to Joxer, who hadn't moved, though he seemed to be breathing easier. "You all right?" she asked softly.

He nodded without removing his head from his hands. "I—yeah. I think so. I'm bruised all over my body, but hey! If Gabrielle's—"

"Joxer, you gotta trust me on this one. That wasn't Gabrielle, all right?"

He glanced up at her briefly before cradling his head once more. "Xena, you know, I realize I'm not exactly the cleverest guy who ever lived, but—I think I know Gabrielle when I see her?" He drew a deep breath and let it out in a shuddering sigh. "I just wish," he went on, his voice muffled, "that I knew what I did *this* time. Because I really didn't mean to get her that angry, and—"

"Joxer, will you just shut up and listen to me?" she snarled. He sat up straight, met her gaze squarely and waited. "The stuff she got for seasickness—you take too much of it and it turns you into a berserker."

His mouth twisted. "Yeah, sure, Xena. Try again, okay? I mean—" he frowned, then winced, and clutched carefully at the bright purple bruise swelling his right eyebrow "—that doesn't even make any *sense*!"

"Yeah, it does. Trust me. I talked to someone right here on this ship, just now," she said flatly. "Someone who knows about the stuff. You take the right dose, you just don't get sick. You take a lot more—well, Gabrielle did just that."

"She did?" he asked. Xena nodded. "So—what if she does that again? Because, honestly, I'd rather not—"

"I understand, Joxer." Xena laid a hand on his shoulder, withdrew it gingerly as he winced again. "You did a real good job, not letting her get you mad and fending off her blows."

"Yeah." He gave her a sidelong, disgusted look. "I'm really good, aren't I?"

"I'd say so," she replied, and shoved hair off her forehead. Joxer gazed at her blankly. "She's getting pretty fast with that 'little stick'." She got to her feet and held out a hand, dragged him up, handed him his crossbow. "Go on back over to your blankets, I got some stuff that'll help the bruises."

"Sure. Except—" He dithered, gazed at the deck, his

hands, the crossbow. Finally shrugged. "Look, tell her that—if it was something I said or did, well, I'm sorry."

"Joxer, it's fine. She said to tell you the same thing. G'wan, scram. I'll bring the stuff over. You got enough bread?"

"Yeah. I'm fine." He staggered, righted himself, and made the opposite rail without actually falling down. Xena went back over to join Gabrielle, who had finished her bread and was recorking her bottle.

"Ah—is he all right?" she asked quietly.

"Pretty bruised," Xena said as she fished through her pack for her healing supplies. Gabrielle groaned.

"I—how'm I gonna face him, after that?"

Xena separated the salve out, then turned to clasp her friend's shoulder; her eyes were warm. "Gabrielle, it's Joxer. You know how he is, he expects—"

"I know." The younger woman didn't smile back. "That's what makes it so bad. I mean—yeah, sometimes he deserves that. But that's what he got from his mother and his brothers, and then I—"

"Gabrielle, just don't worry about it. You apologized. Just go on like it never happened. Anything else, and you'll only make him more uncomfortable."

She sighed. "I—yeah, I guess." She winced as wind shrieked across the deck and the sail cracked sharply. "How much more of this until we reach Delos?"

Xena shrugged. "Way it's blowing? I'd say we'll be there *well* before sunset, instead of an hour after."

The waves began to smooth out not long after mid-afternoon, and the wind lessened a little—enough that the sail bellied out evenly. The ship passed between two large islands—near enough Naxos to the east that Gabrielle could make out sheep and a shepherd high on a grassy meadow. Paros to the west was mostly in shadow with the sun behind it, but she could see small fishing boats on either side of the steep-sided island. Straight ahead, a misty, purply shadow between water and sky that Xena assured her was Delos.

"How's the stomach?" the warrior asked, as Naxos fell behind and Delos began taking on shape.

Gabrielle smiled. "It's fine. All the same, I'll be glad to get off this boat for the night." She settled both elbows against the rail and leaned comfortably on her arms. "You know, I could go for a *really* good meal tonight. Meat— maybe chicken. No fish—and no squid," she added hastily as she caught Xena's sudden grin. "Meat," she repeated thoughtfully. "Yeah. Did I tell you about that meal I had in Katerini? I mean, even with the landlord yelling at his help, it was still the most incredible—"

"You didn't tell me," Xena put in as Gabrielle sought words. Her smile widened. "We haven't had much time to talk about any of that."

"*Most* of it wasn't worth talking about," Gabrielle said flatly. "You know, though. . . ." Her gaze went distant. "I wonder what happened to the landlord's son. Briax."

"Thought I told you, Gabrielle. He showed up at Sparta, and they sent him questing. He was still in Sparta when we left."

"So he could be anywhere." She sighed. "I hope he's okay. I mean—he just isn't the sort of person you'd want wandering around this end of the world looking for something valuable. He's—well, he's young, and he's never been out of Katerini."

"I know. I heard him when Menelaus and Avicus tested him." Xena kept the other thing she'd learned to herself:

Gabrielle would feel responsible—and terrible about it—if she learned that Briax had taken on the quest in hopes she'd somehow learn of it. *For love—she's right, he is young.* "Remember, when you left Poteidaia, *you* were young and naive, too."

Gabrielle laughed and cast her companion a warm glance. "Yeah, I was, wasn't I? Briax doesn't have you to keep him safe until he can learn how to take care of himself, though."

Xena ruffled golden hair. "Well," she drawled, "just maybe he's a faster learner than you are. Maybe he doesn't like taverns with 'atmosphere.' "

"Yeah, sure, rub it in, Xena. I still say places like that have some of the best food."

"Sure. All you gotta do is fight for it."

"Which is why you don't catch me going in places like that any more." She glanced over her shoulder, then turned quickly back to gaze at the sea, her color rather high. Xena turned as Joxer came staggering toward them, caught his arm and shoved him against the rail with herself between him and Gabrielle. Silence. Joxer handed over the box of salve, and glanced sidelong at Gabrielle, who cleared her throat, opened her mouth to say something, and shut it again.

"That stuff help?" Xena asked him. Joxer nodded, then turned partly away from her, apparently intent on the view. Gabrielle glanced at him, then turned the other way, apparently fascinated by the trail the *Wave Dancer* left behind her. Xena looked at one, then the other, rolled her eyes, and reached out to grip a shoulder of each, and turned them toward each other. "Enough, already," she snarled. "Gabrielle, Joxer knows you weren't responsible, Joxer, you know Gabrielle didn't mean to clobber you like that. *Deal with it!*" She scowled impartially at both, until Gabrielle held out her hand; Joxer's mouth twitched as he shook it. "Fine. We need to decide if we're going on to Chios on this tub, or looking for something else in Delos." Silence. She glowered at Joxer, then at Gabrielle.

Gabrielle's eyes widened and she spoke quickly. "Depends on what we find in Delos, doesn't it?"

"Find?" Joxer asked. "What're you looking for—ah," he took a step back, hands flapping. "I know, not my business, right?"

Xena gave him an astonished look. "But, Joxer—we're helping you find Helen, remember?" Silence. Gabrielle stared at her; Joxer gaped. He finally shook himself, shut his mouth, and gave her a sidelong, wary look.

"Xena," he said with as much dignity as he could manage. "I didn't get enough sleep last night, and I think it's done something to my brain. Because I thought I heard you say that . . . Never mind. I'm—gonna go take a nap now. If that's okay with you?" He looked from her to Gabrielle, back again, nodded once. "Fine. I'll be right— over there." He turned and walked back to his blankets, settled with his face to the rail, and stretched out, helmet tilted sideways over his head.

6

It was dark inside the Spartan palace—particularly stygian in the king's reception chamber, Menelaus sat rigidly, back straight against his throne, his hands clutching the polished, black arms, his eyes fixed narrowly on his priest's back. Though they flicked, now and again, toward the bowl of water that rippled despite a complete lack of moving air and which flashed bits of light, reflecting where there was nothing to reflect.

Avicus's back was as stiff-looking as his king's felt, Menelaus thought angrily. *As it should be, after the dressing down I gave him! He serves the god Apollo—but he also serves me, and he had best not forget that again, anytime soon!*

The priest's suddenly sagged, and his color was bad as he turned away from the suddenly dark and still water-mirror. "Majesty," he said; he sounded very tired. "The dread god Apollo bids you to patience—"

"Patience! *Patience?*" Menelaus's howl of rage filled the chamber. Avicus merely waited until the echoes died away, then inclined his head.

93

"Patience, majesty. He bids me remind you of the patience you showed during the battle for Troy—"

"That was *not* patience!" the king gritted out between clenched teeth. He tugged at his moustache and swore under his breath. "That was—that was necessity . . . !"

"*And*—!" Avicus overrode him, though the priest's voice carried no emotion whatsoever, "it is the same now, and so the god bids me tell you!"

Dead, unpleasant silence. Menelaus broke it with another oath. "Patience—have I not been patient these past years, since Paris stole *my* Helen? Have I not patiently born the smirks of my fellow kings, because of that?" He nearly spat.

Avicus inclined his head; his face was expressionless. *Which of his fellow kings would have dared such a thing?* he wondered, then put it aside as unimportant. "You have, sire." The king eyed him narrowly. "There can be no one in all Sparta who does not admire your strength of will, sire. Including your humble priest."

The king's voice rose a notch. "As it should be." He cleared his throat, leaned forward, and when he spoke, he was clearly striving to control his temper. "Avicus, you know me. You have served me long and faithfully, since well before the day I acquired Helen. Did I ever once lose my temper when she giggled and played with her maids, behaving like a child when I wanted to school her in the behavior required of a queen of Sparta?"

"Sire—?" But the king was caught up in his tale; he swept on.

"And during the war, did I not do each thing Apollo asked of me, however foolish it seemed at the moment? However unlikely to get me Helen back? And yet I *still* must be patient? Does he intend that I embrace her only

94

on the other side of death?" He growled under his breath.

A corner of the priest's mouth twisted, but since he was turned partly from the king, Menelaus did not see it. Though it was gloomy enough that Avicus doubted his earthly lord would have seen anything short of a broad smile. *There is nothing of humor in this.* "Majesty, it was never the god's intention that you forego Helen in this lifetime." *My intentions, however . . .* "He simply tells me to remind you that you have set forces loose that will find her, wherever she presently hides from you. And that, through this, you and she will be together again. Soon."

"Soon." Menelaus spat the word. He indicated the gazing-bowl with a vicious sweep of his arm. "Have you finished there?"

"For tonight, Majesty."

Menelaus clapped his hands ringingly, and when two of his household guard pushed the main doors open, he shouted, "Bring light here! And food!" He threw himself back in his chair as one of the guards came in with a lit torch, waited in silence until the man had touched it to two oil lamps and another torch which he jammed in a niche in the wall above the priest's bowl. Menelaus waved the man off impatiently as he bowed. The silence stretched, even after the door was pulled quietly to behind him.

The king shifted his gaze; Avicus stood still under it and waited him out. "I *have* been patient," Menelaus said finally—mildly for him. "And what have I to show for it, Avicus? A wife—somewhere—who is more than ten years older, and less lovely, than when I saw her last." The muscles in his jaw flexed. "Not even a *glimpse* of her in Troy! Avicus! Can your cold soul even begin to comprehend the pain that causes me, even yet?"

If only because I hear of it every single day, the priest thought flatly, but he inclined his head. "I can understand what it is to face great loss, Majesty."

"Can you!" Menelaus leaned forward to touch one of the oil lamps—a long, slender thing of black-glazed clay, a fan of white incised lines its only decoration. "Pottery is an even more fragile thing than a woman's beauty, Avicus. This lamp and one other I keep in a safe place—all I have left here to remind me of her. All the other things she wrought—"

He sighed deeply, and for one horrified moment, the priest feared he might break into tears. Silence, broken by another sigh; this one trembled. Menelaus managed a faint, bleak smile, and shrugged.

"All broken, save two." The smile went; his eyes were suddenly chill. "And Apollo bids me to have *patience*!"

"But, Majesty," Avicus said quietly. "Your searchers have been gone only three days! That is hardly time enough to get beyond the regions you yourself have searched for Helen. And I *have* asked the god if he would see her for you—he cannot. Which means another of his kindred somehow protects her."

"Gods," Menelaus muttered. "Squabbling, taking sides against one another over minor slights. We humans have spoiled them, Avicus, and they show it."

The priest swallowed past a suddenly dry throat, and glanced back at his bowl. "Ahhh, sire? Majesty, I would humbly suggest that if you are asking a—"

Menelaus snorted angrily, silencing him. "Yes, I know! So you remind me so often, that to gain what *I* want, I must flatter, toady, and pander; accept every rule laid upon me and offer no restrictions in return!" His nostrils flared as he sat back with a thump. "I wonder, Avicus—

what if you reminded your other master of the *other* gods? Gods who do not dwell on Olympus, and haven't the family ties—?"

Avicus closed the distance between them. "Majesty, I beg of you, this is *not* the time and place to bring up such a matter! Of course the god is aware of others of his kind: Isis to the south, as well as Thoth; to the east, Kali; to the west, Quetzal—"

"And to the north," Menelaus broke in flatly, "Dahak." He smiled grimly as the priest eyed him glassily.

"Where did you hear that name?" Avicus finally whispered.

"I heard it." He shoved himself upright and strode across the dais to gaze down at his priest. "And if a god may be—exchanged, shall we say? for another? Then, what of his priest?" He brushed past Avicus and stalked out of the Reception room.

Avicus watched him go; Menelaus slammed the door against the outer wall, bellowing, "Where is the food I ordered? Have it brought to my rooms—at once!" The door banged into place. When the echoes finally faded, the priest briefly closed his eyes. "Dread Apollo," he murmured finally, "you cannot even begin to think this is my fault, the man is out of control—mine, yours, anyone's!" His voice rose briefly; he bit his lower lip, drew a deep breath, and after a moment, tried again. "I ask so little for myself. But if that—that *man* does not find Helen soon, then he *will* seek out priests serving Dahak the Destroyer. . . ."

Silence. And then, suddenly, another was at his elbow. Avicus blinked, then took two quick, long strides back as he realized this was not Apollo—but Ares. The god of war smirked at him, and Avicus managed a lips-only smile in reply. Inwardly, he was praying the most basic of invocations, the only one he could remember at the moment. But Apollo wasn't listening.

Ares's smile widened—very white teeth between very black moustache and neat beard. "Sorry." He didn't sound it. "My brother's off whining over his lost dryad. The tree he's in love with, remember? You know how it is." The voice was soft and low—unexpected in a deity who urged men to kill one another, the priest thought. Ares sketched him a bow and, unnervingly, replied to the other's unspoken remark. "Your King Menelaus has it all wrong."

"Has . . . he?" Avicus wondered at his bravery—or maybe his tongue was running away with him, as it had when he was a child. *Be still!* he ordered himself. *Here, that will get you killed!*

"Sure. He bellows like the Minotaur." The smile widened. "You wanna get someone's attention?" He leaned close to the priest's ear; Avicus just managed to avoid jumping back as garlic-scented breath tickled the hairs inside his ear. "You whisper," the god of war breathed. "Know why? 'Cos it sounds *scary*. Besides, they gotta shut up to hear what you're saying."

The priest swallowed, then managed a smile of his own—the bland turning of lips that didn't reach pale eyes that usually got Menelaus to shut up, however briefly. *If only because he believes it means I've come up with a new and more nefarious scheme to get him what he wants.* To his surprise—and satisfaction—it seemed to have the same effect on the god of war. Briefly.

It gave him courage. As Ares eyed him, the priest drew a steadying breath. "Everyone has his little secrets, including the god of war," he murmured.

"Really!" Ares said. "Tell."

"Oh—that *you* are contemplating a change of pantheon—?"

Ares chuckled. "Hey, what can I say? Family's what you get stuck with. And some of my family is downright—annoying. *Alliances,* on the other hand—sometimes the right alliance is what keeps you alive. Get me?" He sketched a brief bow with one arm—and vanished.

The priest stared at the place he'd been; he could feel anger warming his face. "Things are getting—complicated," he managed finally. "And I—am—heartily—*sick*—of complications!" Silence. The priest strode over to his bowl, and drew a finger's worth of herb from an inner pocket to sprinkle over the water. It turned a vibrant, deep blue. "Dread Apollo," he intoned, "I really *do* try not to be much of a bother—but if you have the *least* suggestion on how to deal with your brother Ares, I would *really,* and truly, appreciate it?"

Silence. He was about to turn away from the bowl when a tearful, drunken voice brought him back. "Ares? What do I care about *Ares*? Whuh—why should *you* care about Ares, priest? What does that have to do with finding my lost love?"

"My honored lord, there will *be* no lost love, and not much of anything else!" Avicus shouted him down. *Ares's advice be damned to Tartarus,* he thought furiously. "If Olympus loses its hold on these people!" Silence; the priest held his breath and closed his eyes—and fully expected to be fried by lightning at any moment. The moment passed, and the next moment. "I'm sorry," he added in an exasperated voice. "Really! I apologize! But I really do wish you could recognize that things are getting out of hand!"

Then. "You realize that, do you, my priest?" For a wonder, the voice sounded utterly sober.

"I see the danger," Avicus replied steadily, and wondered at his nerve.

Momentary silence. Then. "You need assistance, my priest."

"Here?" Avicus snorted. "Send another priest, and Menelaus will merely dismiss me if I'm lucky, or kill me if not. Is *that* your intention?"

"No, my priest. Assistance—elsewhere. Especially since Xena has removed my Eyes and Ears from two of the Chosen."

"I know she did. She knows entirely too much."

"She is not your business, priest."

"I know that. I have no intention of fighting Xena. But *you* know where they are, even if I do not . . . ?" Avicus asked finally.

"I do. They are not far from Delos. At sea."

"That's little use to us. Menelaus has searched Delos, twice since Troy," the priest began.

"They seek more eastern ports—Rhodes, I think. . . ." The voice faded, and was gone. For good, Avicus thought. But it returned briefly. "Another—yes. I have someone in mind . . . to the east. . . ." He waited, but this time Apollo really was gone. Avicus cast up his eyes and strode from the hall.

The *Wave Dancer* pulled into Delos harbor just before sundown. Xena, Gabrielle, and Joxer leaned on the rail, out of the way of the crew, and watched the town grow larger.

"Funny," Gabrielle said. "The island is a lot larger than the last one, but the town's smaller. And look at the dock—there's barely room for one ship to tie up."

Joxer cleared his throat. "Um, well, that's because Delos is poorer. They have a couple of olive groves, some skinny sheep that turn out so-so wool, and what food they *do* grow, mostly they keep."

"Oh." Gabrielle considered this, then eyed him warily. "Hey! How'd you know all that?"

His mouth quirked. "I'm Master of Geograhhh—" He froze as both women gave him a look, tittered nervously. "I know geography, okay? It was one of the few things I got to study that I actually *liked.*"

"Oh." Gabrielle glanced at Xena, who shrugged. Moments later, the ship slowed, then turned awkwardly against the low harbor-waves as someone snugged it to the pier, fore and aft. "So—if you know all *that,* where'd be a good place to *eat*? Because I'm really hungry."

Joxer sighed faintly. "Geography doesn't get into that kind of detail—" Gabrielle's spluttered laughter silenced him.

"It was a *joke,*" she informed him cheerfully. She looked around for Xena, who was over by the plank, talking to two of the sailors. She looked up and beckoned. Gabrielle glanced at Joxer and gave him a courtly bow. "After you," she said.

He leaned back against the rail. "Ah—you know, Gabrielle, I was thinking about maybe just staying here, getting a little extra sleep? You know, maybe you could bring me back something—?"

"Joxer? Does the phrase 'Fat chance' convey anything to you?"

Joxer smirked, started across the deck in front of her, but as they passed the mainmast, he swung around it to face her. "Gee, Gabrielle, I didn't know you cared so much." And as she swatted at his head, he jerked it out of reach; the smirk widened. "It was a *joke,* Gabrielle." And he set out ahead of her once more. Xena was already down the plank and across the narrow pier, where she waited for them.

"Answered one question," she said. "There won't be another ship here for days. We go on to Chios, maybe all the way down to Rhodes with them."

Joxer shrugged. "Sounds all right to me. Of course, I don't have a say, exactly, but . . ." He subsided as Xena raised an eyebrow.

"Fine," she said. "I also found out about a tavern, near the town's edge, that way," she pointed vaguely north. "Okay food, lots of it and cheap."

"Sounds like *my* kinda place," Gabrielle said. "Ah— wait. No 'atmosphere'?"

Xena's mouth quirked. "No atmosphere."

Some time later, dinner behind them, the three came back via the small garden market in search of fresh bread and fruit for the journey to Chios. Gabrielle slowed as they passed a combination fruit, jugged drinks, and pottery stand, then tugged urgently at Xena's leather dagges.

The warrior glanced where Gabrielle's chin gestured; she caught up with Joxer, who was ambling along in front of them, humming under his breath. "Hey, Joxer," she said, "do me a favor, all right? That awning over there, see it? The guy on ship told me he's got good knives. Check it out for me, will you?" The would-be hero looked startled, then wary at this unusual request.

"You—you want *me* to . . . ?"

"You. Go for it."

"Well—sure." He gave her another slightly puzzled look, but went.

"Nice work," Gabrielle muttered behind her friend.

"I don't know that it's necessary for us to keep things from him right now," Xena said. "But I'd rather not take any chances. Another pot?"

"Another pot." Gabrielle went back to the fruit stand and began haggling with the proprietor—an elderly man with a strong stutter—while Xena perused things, picking up an apple, then a pear, a small painted wooden jug marked "cider," and another—this time a leather bottle with the word *cider* carved into the neck. Finally, she moved down to the small collection of pottery. *A varied bunch,* she thought. Some of it looked used, a few pieces were definitely chipped, and one or two had been repainted. Several small pieces were clustered together: a nest of shallow, bright red cups; a two-handled, footed, toasting cup. Cosmetic and herb pots. Off to one side of these, an iridescent, black, slender jug capped with a matching plug, and marked with a spray of incised white lines.

The warrior picked it up to look it over, removed the plug and peered inside, and then casually turned it over. *Swan,* she thought in satisfaction. *I thought so. Gabrielle's got a good eye to pick it out from so far away, and after seeing just one of Helen's pots before.*

The things next to it were unusual, too. *Children's toys, likely,* she thought. A clay hut, about the size of her hand, with three windows and a doorway, all hung in scraps of yellow cloth. And in the same shallow basket with them, four little clay figures.

Gabrielle, her bargaining done, came over with a cloth bag clutched in one hand. "What?" she asked. The warrior pointed, and the younger woman's face lit up. "Oh, *look* at them!"

The stall owner leaned across to see what she was looking at. "Ah," he said. "Th-that's from east-like. B-b-belonged to a child as d-died, t'man as sold it t'me s-s-said." Gabrielle scarcely heard him; she was studying the figures, carefully lifting each to the torchlight and turning them.

"Xena," she said suddenly. "Look." Her eyes were very bright, all at once, her voice tight. "It's—it's just like Perdicas, when he was a boy."

Xena laid a hand on her arm, then turned to the old man. "Would you sell just the one?"

He looked at Gabrielle for a long moment, and smiled. "If sh-she wants it so b-bad, it's hers. N-n-no charge." Xena closed her friend's fingers around the little figure.

"C'mon, Gabrielle. Let's get back to the ship."

The bard looked down at the small clay figure, wrapped her hand around it again, and gave the old man a brilliant smile. "Thank you. Thank you *so* much."

They collected Joxer—who'd bought himself another small boot dagger. "I don't know who told you about that guy, Xena," he said, moving slowly and awkwardly as he tried to shove the knife in place while he walked. "But, let me tell you, most of what he—oww!"

"Joxer, wait until you get back on the *Wave Dancer*, will you?" Xena demanded sharply. "You're gonna bleed all over the street." As he bent over again, she grabbed his near ear and tugged. "I said, *c'mon*," she growled. "We need to talk."

• • •

104

It was full dark, the ship quiet when they got back aboard, the only lights at the plank, in the captain's cabin, and a small oil lamp that flickered up by the wheel. Xena dropped to the deck and got her shoulders more or less comfortable against the rail; Gabrielle settled next to her after shoving her bundles over with the rest of their gear, though the warrior noted she still clung to the little clay figure. Joxer landed cross-legged on the deck with a thump that must have rattled his teeth; he let out a muted yelp, then began muttering to himself. No doubt he would have gone on grumbling, but Xena cleared her throat and he was quiet.

"All right," she said quietly. "Joxer, it's time for you to let us in on things."

"Ah—things?" he asked warily. "What things?"

"I saw you get picked back in Sparta. I didn't see anything before you got in to see the king, or after you left him. So— why'd you leave early, and why Rhodes?"

Silence. "You know, Xena," he said finally, "I could probably get fried just for *thinking* about telling you anything about it."

"I heard that part," she said patiently. "Secret word, right? They can say it to you, you can't say it first. I don't care about that part, Joxer."

"Ah—" He grinned nervously. "Xena, if you heard all that, then you probably —ah, I mean, there's this . . . ? I mean, they've got some kinda way they can . . . ?" He grimaced.

"Don't worry about it, Joxer. You had something of the priest's stuck to your shirt. I pulled it off that first night."

"You—you did *what*?" He stumbled to his feet, waving his arms. "Well, great! I mean, that's just *fine*! I get this chance to—to do something really important and heroic,

105

and you just—you—" His mouth twisted. "My friends," he said sarcastically, and turned away from them. Xena and Gabrielle exchanged an exasperated look; the warrior got to her feet and went after him.

"Joxer," she hissed. He stopped, mid-deck, but wouldn't turn around. "Joxer, will you just listen to me?"

"There's no quest," he said, even more sarcastically. "I already heard. You done, now?"

She gripped his shoulder. "No, I'm not. Just listen to me. There was a thing on your shirt that would let Menelaus and Avicus hear everything you said and did—everything anyone around you said."

Silence.

"Think about it. What if you just happened to find Helen, and what if there isn't this thing Avicus claims he needs back from her? And what *if* in the meantime, they were using your priest-thing to follow you, and take her back to Sparta?"

"Well—but, you could see he loves her—couldn't you?"

Xena shook her head. "I was there when you weren't, remember? I heard it all. I know about him anyway. He *wants* her. That's not the same thing." Silence as he considered this. "I've spoken with Helen, keep that in mind, Joxer. She doesn't want him."

"But—"

"Look," she interrupted him. "If we—if you find her, you can ask her. Fair enough? But I know what she'll say. And then you'll be glad you didn't lead Menelaus right to her."

Silence again. Joxer finally turned, drew the helmet from his head and looked at her. "Just—tell me. How many other guys were there? That you saw?" he asked finally.

She shrugged. "I didn't count. A lot. Twenty or more." He sighed deeply, stared down at his feet.

"Yeah. I really shoulda known. I shoulda guessed." He looked up at her; she gripped his shoulder. "That was why I left in the middle of the night, instead of waiting for sunrise, like we were all supposed to. Only, when I first got back from looking in that bowl of water, I thought it was only *me*. Then I kept seeing—all these other guys, like they'd opened an inn at one end of the palace. And I figured, the only way I could prove myself—"

"Joxer," Xena said quietly. "You don't have to prove yourself to me. I know there's a lotta good in you, and I've seen you do some pretty brave things. Don't worry about what's happened. We'll find a way to make it come out right."

But his eyes were still bleak. "Yeah. 'We.' " He stepped back from her, managed a faint smile. "I'm gonna go get some sleep. Oh—yeah. Rhodes." He shrugged. "It's one of the farthest islands from Sparta, it's big— seemed as good as anyplace." He turned away and walked off. Xena waited a moment to make sure he'd gone to his blankets instead of down the plank, then went back to Gabrielle.

The younger woman was admiring her gift in the uncertain light. Xena wrapped staff-strong fingers around it and held them a moment. "Take good care of it, Gabrielle."

"I will." There were tears in her voice. "It's—amazing. How anyone could make a statue that tiny, and make it look—look just like . . ."

"Yeah," the warrior said, as her close companion fell

silent. "It would take a really *good* potter to do something like that, wouldn't it?" She could feel Gabrielle's eyes on her. "I looked at the bottom of it while you were getting your cider. It's Helen's."

7

The journey to Chios was uneventful, the storms gone for the time being. Even the waves smoothed out, and the wind died back to the point that *Wave Dancer* often needed to be rowed. Xena spent a good deal of her time honing her sword and various of her hidden daggers; Gabrielle was usually somewhere under whatever shade she could find, putting the finishing touches to yet another of her scrolls, or working up a new batch of quills. Joxer slept or dozed on deck most of the afternoons, but when he was awake, he was most often well across the deck from the women, staring at the islands they passed, or on his back, gazing up at the clouds.

Gabrielle finally emerged from beneath the blanket shelter Xena had rigged for them against the heat of the day, a long scroll dangling from her fingers. "Ta-da!" she announced.

"All done?" the warrior asked. "Good for you, Gabrielle."

"Well—it's nice to have the time to just sit and get caught up like this."

"It's a good thing you've got something worthwhile to do," Xena replied. "Ships can be pretty boring if you don't."

"I've never had the *chance* to be bored on a ship, remember? Not until now. Too busy being sick, or trying not to be. Which reminds me. How much of that goo have I got left?"

"Plenty of the wafers, and enough of the other stuff to get you well past Rhodes." The bard frowned. "Never mind, Gabrielle. I'm willing to wager that if one herbalist figured out how to make something like this, another one has, too. We should be able to find something in Rhodes." She smiled. "Something without the side effects."

Gabrielle tested the ink on her scroll with a cautious finger, then rolled it up and tied it closed. "You know, that's just so *weird*. I mean, that some of it just makes me okay on a ship, and more of it . . ."

"Well, I got that from the source."

The younger woman's mouth twitched. "Ares. Yeah, right. Figures he'd have something to do with a mix like that."

"Well, he *said* he did. He coulda been lying, Gabrielle."

"You think so?"

The warrior shrugged. "Hey—his lips were moving." Gabrielle laughed, Xena chuckled.

Gabrielle glanced beyond her close companion then, and sighed. "Is he *ever* gonna come out of it? I mean, not that he hasn't got reason to be in a mood, but it's almost three days since I went for him—and I didn't hit him *that* many times or that *hard*, you know."

Xena raised an eyebrow. "You sure about that?"

"Well—I don't *remember* hitting him that many times."

"Don't worry about it, Gabrielle. You got him a couple

110

good ones but he did a pretty good job of keeping the mast between you. But it's not just that, think about it. We've both been trying to tell him that his precious quest is a hoax, but just before we left Delos, I think he finally accepted it. And he's—well, disappointed."

Gabrielle considered this, finally nodded. "Yeah. I can understand that. I mean, wanting to prove yourself to someone, show them how brave and strong and tough you are? Remember how long and hard I tried to prove myself to you? I guess it's no surprise Joxer's doing the same thing. He wants you to admire him, and . . ."

Xena ruffled her hair, silencing her. "Yeah, I guess so. But I think we both know *I'm* not the reason he left for Sparta. Maybe a little, but not the main reason." Silence—a companionable one. Gabrielle sighed faintly and nodded again.

"It's like I said back in Thessalonika, if I hadn't pushed him so much, picked on him, maybe he wouldn't have . . ."

"Gabrielle, that's not it either, and you know it." She glanced across the deck. Joxer lay on his back, fiddling with his crossbow. "Gods, I hope that isn't loaded," she murmured, then turned back. "You know how Joxer feels about you—"

The bard winced and briefly closed her eyes. "Yeah. I do. Just like I know it's not gonna ever happen, Xena. Not in this life."

"And he knows that, too, Gabrielle. Oh, sure, he'd change the way you feel about him in a heartbeat if he could. But since he can't, he's willing to take what he can get. And if that comes down to being—"

Gabrielle laughed mirthlessly. "Yeah. Comes down to being picked on like a stupid little brother."

"Hey. He's used to that, remember the family he comes from?" Xena's mouth quirked. "At least *you* don't hang him up by his Joxers."

"*Not* going there," the bard replied hastily. She stared over Xena's shoulder. "Wait a minute—what's that?"

"What's what?" The warrior turned and looked where her companion pointed. "I don't see any—wait. That line of water?"

"Like something's moving out there, yeah," Gabrielle said. "Shallow enough it's leaving a track, but deep enough that you can't quite make out—listen! Those sailors up by the wheel, they've seen it, too!" The two women gazed off to the west, where late morning sun glinted on the spray thrown up by something large and very fast-moving. Joxer, alerted by the excited voices above him, clambered to his feet and peered uncertainly across open water. Xena stood very still, watching. A flash of dark gray or near-black just above the water and perhaps a darker fin as the thing dove.

The men on the aft-deck were chattering, so many at once, she couldn't make out a word of it. Gabrielle clutched her arm; her face was pale. "What—*was* that? I—thought it was—like an eel, ex—except a *whole* lot bigger?" She was still staring intently out to sea. "That wasn't a *sea serpent*, was it?"

Yeah. Nothing wrong with her eyes, Xena thought. She'd seen much the same thing. No point in saying so and scaring Gabrielle. "Sea serpent? Gabrielle, get real! What I saw wasn't much like an eel. It's probably a dolphin. Or a bunch of them; they swim in packs."

"Oh. Oh? Dolphins?" Gabrielle's eyes shone and she moved across the deck to stare eagerly to sea. When Joxer came over to join her, Xena could see how tense he was

112

at first. When he found out it was likely a dolphin instead of some kind of sea monster, he shrugged and went listlessly back to his blankets.

She could make out the men on the aft-deck, now—and the captain. Apparently *he* had the same idea *she* had had. Some of the sailors weren't going for his explanation of dolphins, or a mass of fish, but others were. It would make for an interesting mess this evening, she thought in amusement.

The amusement faded as she gazed all around what sea could be seen from her vantage. *That* was *one of Poseidon's pets, had to be.* Surely the sea god wouldn't endanger an entire ship of men, just to see her drowned? *He might,* she decided. *He's arrogant, like all of them. And self-centered. Almost as bad as Aphrodite.*

Then again, he'd badly miscalculated if he thought one lousy sea serpent was any match for *her.*

Chios was a major stopping-off port between Athens and the Hittite coast to the east, but aside from a large, deep harbor and two long piers, there wasn't much to the island. Gabrielle looked around as she paused at the head of the plank and sniffed. "This is *it*?" she asked. "I mean—all that traveling, for *this*?"

Xena came up behind her. "Well? Would *you* wanna live all the way out here, at least two days from anything else except another island?" Gabrielle wrinkled her nose in distaste. "Neither does anyone else. Hardly. There's a few shepherds on the back side of the island and the guys down here at the docks who sell barrels of water." She shrugged. "An old seer somewhere around—"

"Oh?" Gabrielle glanced at her.

"Yeah. Was the last time I sailed through Chios harbor.

He came here to get away from people, though."

"I can understand that. I mean, if every time you got around people, you *saw* things . . ." She shook her head. *Like I did in Athens,* she remembered suddenly, and shuddered. Xena's arm went around her and drew her close.

"You all right, Gabrielle?"

"Yeah, sure. Just—thinking."

"Well, don't, if it does that to you." The warrior gave her a brief squeeze and a gentle shove toward the dock.

There was one short, narrow street between tall stone houses and other buildings, a decent-sized pool and fountain where a young woman washed clothes and a handful of children played. They went silent and still as the three strangers passed them, then broke into excited chatter.

Gabrielle tested the air and sighed happily. "Mmmm. I smell fresh-baked bread, and somebody's roasting a bird."

"There's a small bakery and tavern at the end of the street," Xena said, and led the way.

There was no market, except for two elderly women who leaned against the baker's outer wall; both were busily spinning dark gray wool. The blanket under them and their wares was the same dark stuff, and all around them, small piles of fruits and vegetables, and a shallow basket that held little jugs of cured olives. If there was a dealer in pottery, leather, or anything else, they weren't in the open. Gabrielle smiled; the women smiled back shyly. Xena tapped her arm. "Food first," she said. "Then supplies."

Gabrielle took another deep breath. "Good idea," she decided, and went inside. The warrior gestured Joxer in ahead of her; he cast up his eyes, but went.

• • •

The next evening saw them in Samos; Gabrielle looked around, visibly fascinated by the near-circular harbor and the jagged slope north of it. Xena was up talking to the captain, and Joxer had, Gabrielle decided, finally come out of his sulk. Mostly, anyway. *Remember, this time he has cause to feel put out,* she reminded herself; his voice was the same reedy whine that had set her off back in Thessalonika, when she'd been trying to build a fire with wet wood.

"... I mean, it's a harbor, Gabrielle. Just like the one in Chios, or the one in Delos. What're you gonna do, make a song about it?"

She looked at him. "Maybe." He shrugged, his lips twisting as he turned away. "You don't get it, do you, Joxer? Haven't you ever heard about the feud between Ares and Aphrodite?"

He laughed mirthlessly. "Sure. Because things are one endless feud between them. Right?"

"This was special." She explained.

He eyed her in disbelief. "Where do you *hear* these things? I mean"—he gestured toward the steep, north face and the few straggling trees clinging to its stony wall—"around this part of the world, you get volcanoes all the time, why couldn't it just be one of those?"

Gabrielle bit back a sigh. "It could've been," she allowed. "But what kind of a story does that make?" She went into declamatory stance. 'And then, once day, the mountain erupted, and half of it fell into the sea!' *Boring!*"

"Not," Joxer replied evenly, "for the people living here when it happened."

"It's a point," she agreed, then turned to gaze around once more. "Yeah," she said thoughtfully. "If *my* ver-

115

sion's the right one, at least if you lived here, you'd know *something* might be about to happen. If it just blew . . ."

"Boom," Joxer said gravely. "And there goes your house, and your goats, and *probably* your boat, because when all that stuff falls into the water, you get a *big* splash." She glanced at him; he shrugged. "*Really* big."

Gabrielle closed her eyes and shuddered. "You mean to tell me, people would still *live* here, after all that?"

"Maybe they don't have any choice." Xena had come up quietly behind them. "The ship is just putting in here for an hour, get fresh water, leave off some stuff, and pick up a couple crates. The captain doesn't like staying in Samos harbor any longer than he has to."

Gabrielle glanced at the aft deck. "Yeah, well, you ask me, he's got sense. But where do we stop next, then? And when?"

"Rhodes—unless there's a flag out at Cos, which is halfway between. He says there seldom is, the Cossans are pretty self-sufficient. So, two days from now, probably just after midday. He's sending two of the men ashore for food. How's our bread?"

"It's all right. Two days from now, it'll be really hard, though. Ah—how's my goo holding out?"

"You'll make Rhodes," Xena assured her. In fact, though Gabrielle didn't know it, the warrior had been cutting back on the amount of paste she smeared on her close companion's bread each morning—gradually enough that Gabrielle didn't notice the difference, or she'd have said so. *Yeah. She's still half-asleep when I give it to her; as if she'd notice anything short of a sea-serpent wrapped around the mast.* "And Rhodes is almost as big as Sparta, Gabrielle. If there's replacement stuff there, we'll find it."

Gabrielle nodded absently; she was watching a fisherman lower a string of clay jars into the water. "And—we're leaving ship at Rhodes, right?"

"Right. This one stays in Rhodes harbor a couple days, then goes back the way we came. So we should have time to look around, listen—see if there's anything to learn."

Joxer sighed heavily. "You know, I'm beginning to wonder if this isn't all just a—a big waste of time, and we're . . ." He swallowed the rest of his words as Gabrielle rounded on him, and stared at the finger leveled at his nose.

"Joxer, the *last* thing I want to hear out of you, *ever,* is that I have been on a ship for—how many days? Never mind, don't tell me! And you think you've made a mistake!"

Xena drew her back. "Gabrielle, take it easy. It isn't a waste of time. Helen needs to be warned that Menelaus is looking for her again."

The bard laughed mirthlessly. "Again?"

"Oh, sure. He's had people looking ever since Troy fell. Not like this. And if one of those guys I saw back in Sparta gets lucky—well, it won't be so lucky for Helen. Here—we'd better settle down, get outta the way," she added as two sailors tossed ropes down to other men on the pier. "Short stop like this, the open deck is no place for us to be."

Joxer went back to his own corner of the deck; Xena settled down next to Gabrielle, under the shade cloth, and closely watched the men who came on board to help unload and load crates and bales, take empty water barrels ashore, and return them full. *Not likely I'll run up against someone I know in Samos—but if I do, I want to see them first,* she thought. Now and again she glanced at Gabrielle, who seemed fascinated by the traffic across the deck.

It *was* amazing, really. At least twenty-five men swarmed between the holds and the plank, across the deck, and up and down the steps to the aft-deck, some of them at a dead run, while others staggered under heavy and awkward loads—and not one collision.

"It's like a dance," Gabrielle said finally. She considered this, laughed. "Well, not like the last dance we had in Poteidaia. You wouldn't *believe* how bruised my feet were by the end of the day. Still—look at them. It's like everyone knows the steps and the music." She glanced at her companion. "Or like a battle—"

"More like a dance," Xena assured her with a faint smile. "No one's supposed to get hurt out there. Goronias has a good crew. Experienced."

"Yeah, they look it." Gabrielle watched as the last of the landsmen went ashore, and the ropes were hauled back in. The ship lurched, then turned in a series of jerks as men worked the oars to bring her around and head her back out to sea. "Too bad his cook isn't. Experienced, that is. I wouldn't mind a hot meal tonight—"

"You wouldn't want one *here,*" Xena said. "Whatever he does to food—well, it smells worse than *my* cooking."

"Pass."

"Me, too. But Goronias said the bakery he buys from here also makes meat pies. When I asked his boy to get us bread, I told him to bring us each one." Her stomach rumbled, and she got to her feet. "I'll go find 'em while they're still hot."

They were still hot from the oven—*and* from whatever had been added to the thick sauce that coated cubes of meat and vegetables. Joxer picked through his, washed it down with several mugs of water and two of ale, then leaned against the rail, panting. "I think my *tongue's* been burned off!" he said. Xena glanced up at him, chewed and swallowed a final bite.

"Nah, we'd never get *that* lucky," she drawled. She glanced at Gabrielle, who was smiling as she ate, clearly savoring the meal.

"I mean, it was *good,* and all," Joxer went on after a moment. "But—hey." He stiffened. Xena stood and gazed in the direction he was staring. The sun was nearly down, and long shadows lay across the water from nearby islands—these mostly small and uninhabited—and the waves themselves cast shadows, making it hard to tell what might be out there. Anything smaller than a ship, at least, she thought. And there wasn't another ship anywhere around them.

"I don't see anything," she said after a moment. "What'd you see?"

"I don't know," he said; his eyes searched the water some distance from the ship but well short of the horizon. He finally shrugged. "More of those dolphins, I guess. It—"

"Wait." Xena gripped his forearm. She saw it now; a long white wake, cutting across the waves, moving parallel to the ship. She leveled a finger, and when Joxer froze and would have said something, she gripped harder, met his eyes and faintly shook her head. A sidelong glance at Gabrielle, who was licking gravy from the tip of her thumb. Joxer glanced that way, then cautiously nodded. The two watched the wake until it shifted direction, away from them, and finally vanished. Though whether it dove or just disappeared into deepening shadows, Xena couldn't be certain.

Joxer looked at her, questioningly. She shook her head, mouthed, "Later," and he nodded.

"Mmmmmmm." Gabrielle sighed happily. "That was incredible. Too bad there was only one each." She looked at her fingers, sucked the tip of the littlest, and got to her feet. "So, what's out there that's so interesting?"

"Rocks," Xena said. "Islands. Water."

Gabrielle glanced around. "Yeah. Really exciting." She settled cross-legged against the rail again, leaned back, and closed her eyes. She opened one as a board creaked under Joxer's foot, let her eye close once more.

Xena caught up with Joxer at the mast. He turned, his face grave. "So," he said quietly. "What's out there you don't want Gabrielle to know about?" He considered this, swallowed. "Or do *I* wanna know, if it's that bad?"

He's right, the warrior decided. *He doesn't wanna know.* "I didn't get a good look the other day, and you saw as much as I did just now. Anything that swims near the surface could leave a line in the water like that."

"Okay. Fine. Ah—like what?"

"Lotta things. Most of them couldn't care less about a ship."

"Even a ship with *you* on it?" he asked.

She gave him a baffled look. "What does that—? Oh. That ship we caught out of Sparta. Some people listen to the wrong kinds of stories. I guess he's one of them."

"You mean—Poseidon doesn't have a grudge against you?"

"Joxer, why would he?"

"Why—?" He dragged the helmet off, scratched his head. Finally shrugged. A corner of her mouth went up.

"Exactly." *He looks convinced. Mostly.* The creature hadn't come after the ship either time, anyway. No point in having Joxer worried about something that likely wasn't going to happen. She clapped him on the shoulder and went back to Gabrielle, who had fallen asleep where she sat. Xena gave her a fond smile, then leaned against the rail to watch as sunlight slowly left the water and the sky turned a glorious orange.

All around she could hear familiar sounds: the splash of water against the hull, the creak of wood against wood, the faint snap of the sail as wind gusted and slacked. The sound of bare feet slapping against boards as someone ran along the deck and dropped down the ladder. A groan from the ship's wheel as it was turned to port, where apparently it hadn't been properly greased. She inhaled mixed odors—like a once familiar perfume— compounded of tar, saltwater, fish, wet wool, and the oil rubbed into the deck and the rails. It wasn't a life she wanted back—commanding her own ship—but there had been moments. . . .

She turned to glance at Gabrielle as the younger woman mumbled something under her breath—talking in her sleep, apparently. She'd slumped to one side and looked uncomfortable. Xena eased the younger woman down onto her side and pulled the shade blanket across her knees, where she could pull it around her shoulders if she got cold. "Sleep well," she whispered, then went back to her study of the water—though by now, it was dark enough out there she could only make out the occasional white where water rolled over nearly submerged rocks, or the wind blew caps off the waves.

Some distance away it was even darker, but the small stone shrine was windowless and a thick, black length of wool blocked the only entry. Helen uncapped the small, warm, oil lamp and blew on the smoldering wick to relight it, then set the lamp on a black, polished-stone table in the center of the little chamber.

She stooped to retrieve a narrow clay pot the size of her hand: white with a black sheaf of wheat incised into both sides. She set it next to the lamp, then set two cloth-wrapped bundles on the edge of the table. The first—long and slender—held sticks of incense. She selected three, lit them, and placed them in the small jug before rewrapping the remaining pieces and setting the packet on the low shelf where the pot had been. She eyed the second bundle for a long moment, her face expressionless, then opened it. A pedestaled plate—white with black patterns, like the incense jug—held three shining, silver fish. This she left on the corner of the table, away from the incense and the lamp, hesitated, then drew a deep red flower from the sash at her waist and laid it on the opposite corner from the fish.

Before she could do anything else, light flared, and an impressive female with long golden curls and a body scarcely contained *or* concealed by lengths of pale pink fabric leaned back against the wall opposite the door. The light remained strong as Aphrodite tossed her hair back from her shoulders and gazed questioningly at Helen, who gazed steadily back at her.

"You know," the goddess said finally, "I've been expecting to hear from *you* for a long time. A *very* long time." Helen simply looked at her. Aphrodite stepped away from the wall to examine the table and its offerings. "Nice scent to the smoke," she commented. "Nice pottery, the flower's starting to fade and—you know, I simply *do* not understand what this thing is with *fish*! You touch it, and your hands simply *reek* of fish—!"

"I want to know what Menelaus is up to," Helen said evenly. The goddess stared at her, then burst out laughing.

"And you think *I'm* interested in *him*?"

"You should be. After all, you're the reason I left him."

"I—? Oh. That." Aphrodite waved a dismissive hand. "As if you would've stayed with a man like that, anyway."

"I might have. That doesn't matter, though. I need to know if he's still—" She turned away abruptly. "That was foolish, of course he's still looking for me. I need to know if he's close to finding me." She turned back to meet the other's eyes. "Enough men have died because of me. The people who've taken me in are good, I won't see them hurt." Silence. "You owe me, Aphrodite."

"Owe you? Owe *you*?" Aphrodite wrinkled her nose.

"You used me. Used my youth and ignorance."

"Honey, what I *used* were your looks. You don't think Paris woulda looked at you twice if you hadn't been—" She leaned forward and peered closely. "Is that, like, a *line* between your eyes?" She flounced back against the wall, grinning like an urchin.

"I wish it were," Helen said bitterly. "Enough of them that Menelaus would give up."

"Sorry," the goddess chirped. She didn't sound it. "Can't do anything for you *there*."

"I know. I didn't ask that." Her mouth twisted briefly. "Nothing to put you out. Just—tell me what Menelaus is up to, so I can use my own wits to avoid him."

Aphrodite's eyes narrowed. "Yeah, right. I am *so* like, you wouldn't ask if you thought I'd deliver. But, it's not like I haven't helped, you know?"

"I know. I'm sure he's used every seer, mystic, and gazing-bowl in Greece to search for me."

"Maybe." The goddess had lost interest. Helen simply

waited, and Aphrodite gave her a discontented scowl. "Oh—all right. You know," she added, "if you'd put those fish somewhere else . . . it is getting a little thick in here, if you know what I mean."

The once-queen smiled faintly and shook her head. "I know the rules, Aphrodite. I break the seal around this shrine, even by putting a finger past that doorway, and you're gone. Nice try. The sooner you help me." She left the rest unspoken.

Aphrodite muttered something under her breath and closed her eyes briefly. "There's this problem, you know?" she complained. "Menelaus by himself—sure. But he's still got that priest of my brother's."

"Avicus," Helen said flatly.

"Whatever. But my brother's still helping him, and you know what? I am so *not* getting on Apollo's wrong side, because he is so totally a bad loser. We are talking nettles in my sheets, thank you!" She drew a deep breath and rearranged her neckline with finicky little gestures. "That do you?"

Helen sighed quietly. "I suppose it has to. Thank you." Aphrodite eyed her warily.

"Look," she said abruptly. "Deal, okay? I'll see what I can see—later, when my brother's out cold or something. So he stays clueless about all this. If there's anything you should, like, know—" She vanished before Helen could say anything.

Helen stared unseeing at the spot where the goddess had been; her shoulders sagged momentarily. "Thank you for everything," she murmured flatly, and began clearing the small table.

8

Rhodes, Gabrielle decided from her perch along the port-side, high, aft-deck rail, was a *lot* more interesting than any of their previous destinations. They'd just passed the smaller southern port of Lindos, which, according to one of the sailors, mostly traded with Egypt and other tribal people to the east and south on the mainland. What she could see of Lindos *looked* exotic—almost Amazonian. Massive wooden masks topped the poles marking the harbor entry, and there were as many thatch-roofed huts as there were whitewashed houses.

Too bad the ship wasn't shallow-drafted enough to sail into Lindos. She'd like to have seen the village—and, privately, she thought, if there was anywhere so far she'd seen that might be Helen's hiding place, this was it. No way for warships to get in. No reason for Menelaus to suspect it as Helen's hideout, since there weren't any royal or noble households here, and no mention in bardic tradition of half-gods, *or* gods, ever visiting Rhodes's smaller city. Artsy-craftsy village, actually.

Plus, if there was anything Amazonian about Lindos—

even a tradition among the local women—Helen wouldn't have to worry about being betrayed. Well—maybe not. She watched as the archaic pillars slowly vanished behind the ship. Even the Amazons hadn't been all for or against Xena; or herself, for that matter. Not even all for or against one another, unless it was that they'd side with women against men any day. Still. *They're people, like everyone else.* Fact was, wherever Helen went, she would probably find at least one person willing to betray her to Sparta.

"Which," she told herself quietly, "would explain why you and Xena haven't heard anything about her since Troy."

She glanced down at the whitecapped water spilling from the side of the ship and smiled briefly. The queasiness hovered in the back of her mind like a bad dream; reminding her it hadn't gone away. Still: *Bless that man on Melos for his mother's seasick recipe—and bless Xena for taking charge of the stuff.*

She was still shaky on what had happened when she'd thought a doubled dose would be better. Like another bad dream, or something that happened to someone else. All that anger she'd vented all over Joxer—just like the time she'd been stuck in one of Ares' little "adventures," and the least thing that hadn't gone her way had been enough to turn her into a Fury. *Well, it wasn't your fault, and it wasn't entirely Ares' fault. Sisyphus stole Ares' sword and that made him mortal, which meant anyone not a warrior went nuts—like I did. Still, I wish Xena had let me thump the god of war a hard one when I had the chance. For what he did, changing her and Callisto, if nothing else.* Not that she remembered much of *that* one either—mostly what Xena had told her. Xena in Callisto's body. . . .

Gabrielle shivered elaborately. "Yeah," she told herself quietly. "Tell yourself *that* little happy story whenever you think things are getting out of hand here and now!"

She straightened to peer eagerly along the length of Rhodes. All at once, she could make out the easternmost tip of the island: the city of Rhodes itself, with its white-washed houses perched on the highest points of the surrounding hillsides, facing the southern sea. Wildflowers made an orange, white, and deep-pink carpet of the land beyond the farthest houses, and she could just make out the distant shapes of a herder and his goats perched high on a slab of rock.

She leaned her elbows on the rail, cupped her chin and watched. The island had slowly come into sight over the course of the morning —because unlike Samos or some of the other islands that were single mountains with worn down shelves or bays where people could live, this island rose at an even incline from surrounding water. It was at least four times the size of Samos, and huge compared to Melos. And it wasn't just one peak, but a variety: everything from rolling hills to a couple of unclimbable rocky peaks. It was longer than it was broad; one of the crew said it would take a day and a half to cross east to west, half a day across its narrow, north-south angle. That was, if you could find the right place to cross at all. In places, the island was deceptively, incredibly steep, and the footing treacherous thanks to loose rock and scree.

"But, why would anyone want to cross by foot," she asked herself, "when you could take a ship around?" She considered this and laughed quietly. Apparently, the old woman's goo-for-bread worked better than she would ever have thought.

She caught her breath. All at once she could make out

sun on polished metal, high above the hillside behind it. Cup-shaped—no, a lamp, with bronze flame curling straight into the sky: the Flame of the Colossus! She caught her breath on a shaky gasp; blinked rapidly. *There really is a statue! Oh, gods—look at—look at that!* It really must be huge to be seen from here. Now she could see a metal tip and a curved surface, which turned out to be the back of the god's head. *I can't believe what I'm seeing!* To know about something as exciting as this for so long, and to finally see it. . . .

She swallowed salt and blotted the tears rimming her eyes, managed a smile and a wave as Xena on the lower deck glanced up at her and pointed out the statue. The warrior smiled back, then turned away and began to point out things of interest to a blase-looking Joxer. Gabrielle gave the back of *his* head a sardonic grin. *Yeah. Sure. Like he never saw anything to give him the groobies.* He probably had them right now, but was determined not to let Xena see him as excited as a boy on solstice morning.

She bit back laughter; the nearby crewmen would think her nuttier than they doubtless already did if she simply started giggling. But—groobies! She'd forgotten all about them: the little imps who supposedly came around villages where hardly anything ever happened, and created trouble. Not major things—just hiding tools or sandals, or sneaking into the fields to take part of the harvest as soon as it was ripe and before the farmers could get at it.

Of course, they weren't real. She and Perdicas had made them up, back when a few irate village farmers noticed missing fruit, or corn. *We couldn't'a done it, we weren't anywhere near the corn. But the groobies, now—* It was still funny, how many of the older men had accepted the story and taken to using the special warding-sign against the little mischief makers. Then again, Perdicas was the one who'd had the original idea—but it was Gabrielle who'd embelished it. Eventually, Poteidaia had come to think of groobies as what you felt when you saw something incredibly impressive or something that scared you silly. *Scared the groobies out of you.* She smiled at the memory.

More of the statue had come into view as the ship neared the port entry. She could now see a well-muscled metal back and crisply curled golden-looking hair, the bow and quiver of arrows hanging across one shoulder. A stone and wood fort blocked everything from shoulder down. Gabrielle sighed and glanced around the aft deck. It was getting crowded up here with so many sailors getting the ship ready to turn into the harbor, slacking the sails, readying the ropes to tie *Wave Dancer* off. Not the place for a landswoman, for certain. She waited until the stairs down were clear, and went down them.

Xena looked up as the younger woman came across the deck, her smile warm. "See much up there?"

"I can't wait to see all of it," Gabrielle replied; she went up on her toes to peer toward the harbor. The warrior laughed.

"You will—but not from up close. Not just yet."

"Huh?" Gabrielle's eyes were fixed on shore.

"Looks like we're about to head in, Gabrielle, but we aren't."

"We're not?" That was Joxer. "Why?"

"Look at the shore." Xena pointed to where water broke over jagged rocks. Some were near enough Gabrielle could make out individual cups, edges and markings on the stone—one was draped in slimy-looking seaweed. "We'll make a wide pass out and around all this, turn once we're past the island to the east, then head straight in."

"Fine with me," Gabrielle said. "I can't see Helios up close if I'm on my way to the bottom—" She broke off and shuddered elaborately. "*Not* going there," she finished firmly. Xena wrapped an arm around her shoulder.

"Hey, Gabrielle, I've sailed these waters before. If I'm not worried about how the *Wave Dancer*'s being handled, you shouldn't be."

Gabrielle eyed her sidelong. "Yeah. Sure. But you'd *tell* me that, so I *wouldn't* worry."

"So? Either way, why are you worried?"

Time wore on. Xena pointed out landmarks she remembered from her own days as a ship's captain, others she knew about from other sailors. The mainland was very near, and in the clear, mid-morning light, looked almost as if a strong person could swim it. Xena smiled faintly. "Not a chance; it's as far as you and I travel a day, most days. Water's too rough, anyway." She gazed about as the ship wallowed slightly. "We're coming around, heading back in. Should be inside the harbor by midday."

"Good," Gabrielle said. "Can't come soon enough for me."

The harbor entry was a narrow opening between two in-curved man-made spits of stone. The wooden fortress stood on the seaward of these and Helios on a matching stone platform across from the fort. Gabrielle cast her close companion an accusatory look. "*You* said—" Xena raised an eyebrow and gave her that "what?" look. Gabrielle sighed and turned back to rest her chin on one palm and gaze up the massive body. "You said he *straddled* the harbor. Oh well. I guess it would be awfully hard to build a statue like that, across a harbor."

"Well, sure," Joxer put in. "One good earthquake, and *blam*! No more statue, probably no more fort. And any ships going under it—well, forget them."

"Wasn't so much that," Xena said. "I heard the man who designed it wanted things that way—but the locals felt Helios wouldn't like ships full of people looking straight up his—"

"Ahhhh, right," Gabrielle agreed hastily. Her eyes fixed on the torch Helios bore in his outstretched right hand. "But—you really *can* get up inside it, right?"

The warrior shrugged. "Sure—if that's your idea of a good time." She smiled at Gabrielle. "I know. If there's time, I'll climb it with you."

Gabrielle smiled back. "Thanks."

Joxer eased in between them, eyebrows puckered together. "Is it just me," he asked, "or is there a *lot* of traffic around here for the outer edge of a port?"

Gabrielle sighed. "Joxer—du-uh! Something like that"— she gestured toward the magnificent head and shoulders, high above them—"draws a crowd? Maybe? You think?"

He gave her a discontented, sidelong look. "Sure. Maybe. But—"

"Will you two quit?" Xena put in evenly. "I see what you mean, Joxer. Way too many ships out at this end of the harbor, too many small boats where they don't belong—and those people on the steps aren't sight-seers."

Gabrielle looked where the warrior's eyes were fixed. There were men—at least twenty of them, all dressed in somber, ankle-length robes with identical white scarves hanging down the back. These were bunched on the lower steps of the platform where the statue stood, many of them shaking their fists or walking staffs. Facing them, a barrier of young women holding babies, a few young men, some half-grown girls, and even a white-haired woman who supported her frail body on one stick and shook another at the men.

It had seemed a fairly quiet group, but as *Wave Dancer* was rowed past, everyone was apparently shouting all at once, including women somewhere high above. Gabrielle's gaze moved up the statue, one hand shading them.

"Look, there are people up there! In the openings for the eyes!"

"Yeah. And everyone *I* can see or hear up there is a woman," Xena corrected her absently. The ship was inside the harbor then, and all Gabrielle could make out was the back of the statue, and possibly another small opening in the back of the head. No one was visible through that opening, but from this angle, all she'd be able to see was the inside of the top of the god's head. "That's odd." Xena was staring at the back of a bronze calf without appearing to see it. She shook herself, then. "Guess we'll find out what's up when we get to port. C'mon, you two. I want to get off this boat and get something *done*."

It still took a while. Too many unnecessary boats manned by too many gawkers taking up too much space in the small harbor had delayed ships that had come in before their own. But eventually *Wave Dancer* approached its regular dock, and the sailors were ready to toss down the ropes to make it fast.

Odd, Gabrielle thought as the ship maneuvered to its berth. There wasn't anyone about to take charge of the ship's ropes down on the docks. In fact, there seemed to be no one on the entire dock except two wrinkled, white-haired women clad in identical bright pink dresses—sleeveless, unfortunately, *and* low-cut across what must once have been impressive territory. At this late date, however. . . . Gabrielle dragged her stunned gaze from the pair and fastened her eyes on a whitewashed building partway up the low slope.

The old women were talking—gossiping, by the sound of it—as they peered nearsightedly toward Helios' back and the hysterical crowd now encircling the statue's left foot.

The two women must have been at least partly deaf, they didn't even twitch as the captain began bellowing orders from his place on the high aft deck. His words were still echoing off the warehouses and other dockside buildings as his two rigging boys clambered onto the near rail and leaped ashore to catch ropes tossed after them, so they could tie the vessel off.

Xena tugged at Gabrielle's hair to get her attention, and when Joxer continued to stare blankly toward bronze Helios, she rapped hard on his helmet. "We really want to be last behind everything in the hold?" she demanded. She almost had to yell to be heard above the distant noise at the harbor entry, the shrill, birdlike voices of the old women, and the captain's barked orders, as well as the screeching and rumble of crates being shifted belowdecks.

"It's a point," Gabrielle said, forestalling whatever Joxer might have said, and she was first down the plank. It wobbled; she used her staff for balance and ran onto dry land.

Well, solid wood, anyway, she reminded herself, and tried to ignore the fact the pier had probably been built over water deeper than she was tall. Ten or so paces north or west, and she'd be on real land. *Can't come too soon for me.*

Xena drew her aside, then, beckoning Joxer to join them so they'd be out of the way of the crew as they unloaded. The two old women exchanged looks, smiled at each other brightly, and bore down on the newcomers. Xena cast her eyes heavenward. The skinnier of the women cackled delightedly and clapped her hands together.

"*Told* you, Merlinas!" she exclaimed. "It's the same woman as came here years ago!"

"Isn't t'same ship," the other objected waspishly.

"So? Is the same woman, 'member all that dark hair and them eyes?" Washed-out blue eyes narrowed and were lost in a maze of wrinkles. "Not wearing half as much as she did then, though. And let me tell *you,* you hussy," she snapped as she leveled a finger at the warrior's nose, "you were ill-clad enough *last* time you came through Rhodes, you and your nasty pirates!"

"Oh, yeah?" Xena drawled quietly. "Well, I can always put on more clothes. But *you* two will still be a pair of annoying old gossips!" Gabrielle eyed her in astonishment. "Yeah. I remember you both, and you know what? I'm not any happier to see you than you are to see me. Get over it." She gazed toward the harbor entry. "What's going on out there?"

Gabrielle had decided the women were offended enough to storm off—*they* certainly seemed to think so—but they conferred with eyes and gestures, and finally one of them shrugged broadly. "Seems," she said in a would-be confidential, low voice that still carried across the docks, "that a new religious leader's come to Rhodes. All his following, families, village worth of people and such. Claims he's

134

found some promised land for 'em, but since they stopped over here, he made a longer stop of it, so's to preach, filch coin from t'soft-witted, make converts—"

"—and convince 'em to hand over *all* their dinars once they convert, Merlinas," the second butted in. "Apollo's Seeress told us 'bout that part," she added, narrowed eyes disapprovingly moving over Gabrielle's garb—or lack of it.

"Spare me," Xena overrode her tiredly. "I know all about men like that. What's the problem over there?" Her eyes moved toward the Colossus.

"Well, yesterday he's got his ship and all, supplies, bags of coin if t'Seeress is right about *that,*" Merlinas put in. "And all at once, there's no women and such on ship. Flat vanished, and their leader's blaming our Seeress, Apollo, the governor, everyone in sight. *Then* they turns up inside t'statue, and swears they isn't coming out, 'cos they ain't a-goin' across t'sea to Hittite lands. T'leader's argued with 'em, t'men've threatened. They still won't have it."

Gabrielle gazed wide-eyed at the mob around the base of the Colossus, and swallowed. *Who can blame them? Life in some of those religious communities can be hard enough, but a sea away from anyone you know, no one around you even speaks your language. . . .* She touched Xena's arm. The warrior's gaze slid sideways to meet hers, but Xena shook her head minutely.

"Gabrielle," she said softly.

"I know," Gabrielle murmured. "We have our own major problem to deal with. But—"

"Gabrielle. Believe me, it would be different if we came across them in the desert, not a situation like this. But this is Rhodes. Those women don't want to leave here, that's their choice. All they have to do is appeal to the governor; by law he has to let them stay."

Hagris sniggered. "Tell their men *that*. They claim no governor has any say above their god, and t'women got no say in anything but how t'wash is done and suchlike."

Brief silence. The two women eyed Xena warily, gave Gabrielle a disapproving scowl, smiled coyly at Joxer, and scurried back down the dock. Xena watched them go and sighed heavily. Gabrielle nodded.

"We had a couple women like that in Poteidaia when I was little. All they cared about was gossip—the worse the better, especially if it hurt someone."

"People like that everywhere," Xena said absently, her eyes fixed on the statue. She came back to the moment. "Gabrielle, I think Joxer and I will stay down here and find out what we can about a ship. You go on up to the market—it lines the main street, not too far up the hill from here." She pointed. "Get food and—well, you know."

The pottery, Gabrielle knew; they were still keeping it from Joxer, who couldn't be turned loose down here alone. If they had to split up, this was probably the best way to do it. She eyed the Colossus. "Xena," she said abruptly. "Those women. Kids. Can't we—?"

The warrior laid a hand on her shoulder, silencing her. "Gabrielle, we have our own problems right now. And those women are doing the right thing. The governor won't let them be dragged out of there and onto a ship if they don't want to go."

"I hope you're right." Gabrielle turned away and strode up the narrow, warehouse-lined street. A few paces on, she glanced back. Xena was already talking to someone from another ship that had just come in. *She's not wasting any time. You want a decent supply of bread and the like,* she told herself, *you'd better get going.*

Pitch-coated wooden docks gave way to dirt and loose stone, then well-set paving stones; the warehouses were left behind, replaced by the kinds of housing the very poor could afford—and that gradually turned to rows of shops, small, neatly whitewashed houses, and finally the farmer's market: row upon row of neat stalls or blankets piled high with fruit, vegetables, meat, and prepared products of all three, as well as imported goods and crafts from local artisans who also sold things that came in from the ships. It was warm and windless in this bowl, protected from the usual west winds—Gabrielle decided this would be a useful thing come winter—but at least the sun wasn't much of a factor. Every single stand or stall was neatly covered by a striped canvas awning.

It was oddly quiet, too. She was used to merchants bellowing back and forth, exchanging good-natured banter or insults, trying to draw custom from each other. *Better than being half torn apart by competing fish cake sellers,* she decided, and moved slowly along the rows of stalls, choosing bread, jerked meat, wine for Xena and cider for herself, bottles of water the stand owner claimed (with a straight face, yet) to have come from the well nearest Apollo's shrine. Sour ale for Joxer. She resisted the temptation to buy their inept companion a box of dried fruit and meat cakes that, to her, smelled worse than that salami stuff he'd bought in Phalamys. *Waste of good dinars, and he'd never get the joke,* she told herself firmly, and spent a portion of that coin on a box of spiced honey cakes that smelled as good as the ones her mother'd made.

To her disappointment, there were only two pottery stands in sight, and one sold only the unglazed ware made by the stall keeper, while the other's goods were the kinds of things poor families bought for cooking and eating—chipped, scorched, indifferently scrubbed, but extremely cheap. She showed her small figure to both stall holders, but neither recognized the work, and neither recalled having any of the white and black, or black and white ware with the swan glyph carved into the bottom.

Gabrielle climbed above the last of the awnings and let her head fall back so the breeze could cool her face. It was shady here at the moment—a few fat, white clouds rather than the bulk of the island to the west that would darken this street by late afternoon. From this vantage, she could clearly make out most of the harbor—everything but the feet of the Colossus, the port entry just beyond that, and the fort opposite. There were now four ships tied up around the *Wave Dancer*, and men everywhere shifting crates, boxes, and bales of goods. No sign of Xena or Joxer, but she'd have been surprised to make out either from this far away.

A glance at the sky assured her she hadn't taken much time in securing her purchases. She eased out of the way of foot traffic and turned slowly in place, taking in her surroundings. "Yes!" she whispered in sudden exultation as her eyes fixed on dressed stonework not much farther uphill. The small combination theater/arena/temple that served Rhodes was so close, it would be a shame to miss it. *I don't know about anything else, but the theater—Master Docenius at the Athens Academy told me—the Rhodes amphitheater had accoustics to die for. Well—just maybe you can get a chance to try them out.*

Maybe she wouldn't be able to get inside, maybe there

would be some stupid rule to keep people from just wandering in and declaiming.

Then again—maybe not. She smiled happily, dug her staff into the dusty cobbles, and headed uphill.

9

A narrow doorway, half ajar, led to the amphitheater. The entry then dove immediately down a flight of cracked steps and along a tunnel, dimly lit by barred windows overhead every few paces. It was still fairly dark, and Gabrielle kept one hand on the wall, the staff clutched in her other to make sure she wasn't about to trip over a fallen stone or disappear into a hole. The staff hit a low step perhaps twenty paces on and she began climbing again, to emerge into a brightly sunlit area. She blinked, shaded her eyes.

The familiar bulk of the west hills served as a backdrop for a well-worked, if small, arena. Stone block steps rose sharply from level ground in a near circle, surrounding a low platform. This latter was swept clean at the moment, the only indications that it was a stage were its location and the tall wooden framework across the back, where curtains would be draped during performances to hide actors not on stage and also conceal any worker of effects such as flying gods and the like. Gabrielle sighed happily as she strode forward.

"Nice size," she murmured; the whisper echoed briefly, and she stopped. "Gosh," she added aloud. The single word hung in the air as if it had been shaped by a well-cast bell. She looked around. There was a small shed or building off to one side, but no sign of occupants, and no one anywhere about the amphitheater or what she could see of the grounds to either side. *Well,* she thought, *why not?* She crossed the dusty grounds, stepped onto the platform, and faced the central seats.

Now—what to say? Even alpha, beta, gamma would probably sound great, but . . . She shrugged, drew a deep breath—and let it out in a squeak as a hand gripped her near shoulder. "I wouldn't do that," a low voice said.

Gabrielle whirled, staff still in one hand but ready to strike. She relaxed slightly as she looked into the face of a woman no taller than she. Short black hair wafted from under a priestess' hood in a sudden gust; dark brown quizzical eyes studied her, then glanced down at the staff. Gabrielle let out a held breath and shoved the end of the stick into the wooden platform. "Sorry!" she gasped. "You startled me."

"I could say the same," the priestess replied. "You must have come in on one of the ships, or you'd know. The head priestess doesn't like unnecessary noise out here, which means any noise at all when there's no play or readings."

"Oh? But you—I mean—"

"I'm just her novice," the woman went on with a faint smile that warmed her eyes. "Saroni, at your service," she added.

"Gabrielle." The bard turned on one heel to gaze around the amphitheater. "This is such an incredible place, I am really impressed. I mean—listen to how good it sounds when we're just talking. I don't supposed there's going to be anything happening here this afternoon? A play? A reading? Poetry, anything? Because we're probably leaving as soon as we can find a ship, and—" She came back around to find the woman now staring at her, slack-jawed.

"Gabrielle? You—you're not *that* Gabrielle, are you? I mean, the bard who travels with Xena, writes all her adventures, and—?" She clapped a hand over her mouth. Gabrielle felt her cheekbones flushing as she nodded. "I've *heard* about you! It was—let me think." She shoved the hood partway back over short-cropped hair. "It was— yes, about this time last year, a couple of the fresh graduates from the Athens Academy came through here, wanted to give a reading. Not a lot of people showed up, I'm sorry to say—"

"Sure, that happens to all of us," Gabrielle said.

"Well—but this one, nice young fellow, lovely voice. . . . Twickenham—that's it!—he said he had a tale by the bard Gabrielle, and he told us about you and Xena rescuing that baby from the stream and meeting Pandora and . . . Well, he had such a wonderful, powerful voice, but besides that, it was such a terrific story," she finished with a sweep of one hand, as if she'd run out of words. "And ever since then, I've been collecting your tales—as best as you can someplace like Rhodes."

Gabrielle smiled. "Well—thanks. I'm really glad to hear Twickenham's doing so well. And I'm glad you like my stories." She felt suddenly shy. "But—you know, they wouldn't be nearly as entertaining if I wasn't traveling with Xena."

"You would have found something or someone else," Saroni assured her firmly. "Talent always does, I know." She stepped closer, suddenly and laid a finger across Ga-

143

brielle's lips, gesturing with her chin. Gabrielle peered into the shadows before the small hut. Movement—? Someone was standing there, watching. A white-swathed figure, the hood pulled low over its face—Gabrielle couldn't even make out whether it was male or female, but somehow, the stance was ominous.

Saroni sighed faintly, then, and made some complicated gesture with her free hand; the woman responded in similar fashion, and turned to walk away. Loud, clonking sounds echoed across the bowl until she vanished inside the little building. Gabrielle frowned, then turned to eye the younger priestess. "That was Krista," Saroni said. "Head priestess, and The Seer."

"Oh. All right," Gabrielle allowed. "But—I'm confused. Because, was she wearing shoes? Wooden shoes? Because"—her eyes took in Saroni's bare feet—"I thought an Apollo-priest was supposed to go barefoot—?"

"That's only if you're reading the steam—you know, doing visions for people. Except we don't have a steam vent here, like they do at Delphi, we have to use a brazier. But—well, Krista goes her own way, she always has. I guess she's pure enough or whatever, the god indulges her. Because even when she's reading, she wears those clogs," Saroni said. "She claims the stones hurt her feet." She grinned suddenly, and Gabrielle realized the woman was no older than she. "It's handy, you know. I can always tell when she's nearby."

Gabrielle laughed. "No kidding! You could probably hear her halfway to the pier! So—well, I guess if she doesn't want noise out here, I'd better go. Xena sent me for supplies and things while she looks for a ship."

"Another adventure?" Saroni asked eagerly, and as the

other woman hesitated, she added, "I understand, you don't have to say a word, not if it's something secret you and Xena are doing. We'll all hear about it in a year or so when you can set it in verse, anyway, won't we?" She seemed to come to a decision. "Ummm . . . one thing, if you *can* tell me, though. Did you really punch Ares out?" Her face was suddenly quite pink. "And—and is he really as gorgeous as they say?"

Gabrielle stared blankly. "Ares? Ahh—oh. That. No, I never did punch him. I wanted to. And he had it coming, believe me. But—no, Xena stopped me."

Saroni's eyes were wide. "Gosh—you're really *brave,* going after the God of War!"

"Well, he wasn't God of War right then, thanks to Sisyphus—but that's a long story. And gorgeous? Well—I guess he could be good-looking to some people," she added with an apologetic smile, "but he really isn't my type."

"Oh." Saroni sighed faintly, then shook herself. "Sorry. Of course, he isn't *my* type, either," she said hastily. "After all, I'm sworn to Apollo. Though," she added in a much lower and less carrying voice, "I'm not so sure that's for the best, either. Ahh—" she glanced toward the small hut, where Gabrielle could see a wisp of smoke rising from the vent in the thatched roof. "Listen. Do you have a minute?" Gabrielle nodded. "Well, then . . . Can we go back out into the street? There's something I think I should—" She turned and started across the amphitheater grounds without waiting for Gabrielle's response. Gabrielle took a last wistful look at the small theater, then followed the dark woman back through the tunnel. Saroni drew her back against the wall, next to the tunnel entry. "I am probably speaking out of turn here," she said, "and it may get me into trouble, but honestly I don't care. Because, I didn't know *you* were involved here. Or Xena. I hope you won't feel like I'm interfering, or anything . . ."

"That's all right," Gabrielle nodded as Saroni hesitated.

"I just—sometimes I wonder if I'm doing the right thing, serving Apollo. I mean, he's the god of light and things, and that's what I always wanted to serve. It's not like being a Hestian virgin, or anything, and it's certainly not like serving Hades. Or Ares. But sometimes—there are just these—*undercurrents,* around here. Like something's going on that I can't quite get hold of. Like I— you probably won't understand, it's as if I hear things in my sleep, or just barely overhear things when I'm going about my own duties." She shrugged helplessly. "I—you don't know me; you only have my word that I'm not mad."

Gabrielle shook her head and smiled. "You don't look *or* sound mad to me. But I know a little about Apollo."

The priestess gave her a long, measuring look, and abruptly nodded. "Well—it's just that Krista had some kind of vision in her seeing-bowl two or three nights ago. I was outside, working on one of my lessons, so I didn't *see* anything. I wouldn't have anyway; I'm not tuned to her seeing-bowl. And I didn't hear everything she said, I wasn't listening at first, you know how that is? But all at once, something caught my attention. I'm sure I heard her talking—not to dread Apollo, she sounded more like she was talking to another priest, if it's possible to do that— talk to another priest with the bowl." She shook her head, visibly frustrated. Gabrielle shrugged. "*I* thought it was only for communicating with Apollo, or the other way around, but I only know what *she* teaches me; I'm too untrained yet to speak with Apollo directly. The thing is,

I'm almost certain I heard Xena's name and then Helen, maybe—then something like, "joker," or "huckster"? That sounded odd, because we don't have any people selling things on Rhodes unless they live here, and they have to obey all the market laws if they want to keep selling things, the governor's got strict laws."

"Joxer?" Gabrielle ventured.

The priestess frowned; after a moment's silence, she shrugged. "Could be. I'm not sure. Anyway, it sounded like Krista was supposed to watch out for them and find a way to keep them from getting onto a ship leaving Rhodes." She gave Gabrielle a worried look. "I didn't hear *your* name, I would have remembered that. But I did clearly hear her say she'd keep me completely out of it."

Gabrielle bit back a sigh. *Figures, doesn't it?* she asked herself. She patted the novice priestess' shoulder. "Thanks for telling me," she said quietly. "That may just keep us out of of some serious trouble."

Saroni considered this, then blurted out, "You—if you could tell me anything about it, maybe I could help? After all, I feel almost like I know you, and—"

But the bard was already shaking her head. "Too dangerous for everyone, especially you, if Krista found out," she said. "But, maybe you *could* help, a little." She fished in her bag and drew out the little clay figure. "Have you ever seen anything like this before?" The other woman studied it carefully, then shook her head. "Or this?" The signature glyph got the same result.

"Is it important?"

"We don't know, Saroni. It just may be. Anyway— thanks. For the warning."

Saroni smiled. "I'm really glad you came here. Maybe someday, if you come to Rhodes again, we can talk. Next time, let the governor know ahead of time if you can; you'll have as long as you like in there to tell your stories." She held out her arms; Gabrielle gave her a brief hug and let the woman pat her shoulder.

"I'd like that," she said. "Thanks again." She turned and strode back into town. When she looked back, Saroni was still standing on the street, watching her, but the woman waved then and vanished into the tunnel.

"Odd," Gabrielle murmured to herself. Over the past couple of years, she'd run across plenty of Xena's wide-eyed fans, but this was a first for *her*. She bit back a grin as she passed the first market stalls. *Imagine, a priestess of Apollo with a huge crush on Ares! That really has to be a first.*

Partway down through the market, she remembered the dwindling box of goo to keep off seasickness. It took several inquiries, but as Xena had suggested, one of the locals had what she claimed was a similar substance. *Let's hope it works,* she told herself as she pocketed the little jar. This stuff was a liquid and smelled a bit like rosemary— not even a little like the other. And, of course, there'd be no way to test it until they were at sea. Too late to get her dinars back if the shopkeeper had sold her herb-scented water. *Remember that a lot of people fish off these shores and come home to Rhodes every night,* she told herself. *And that other people on ships come through here now and again.* A local merchant would be foolish to pull a stunt like that. She got a small, flat loaf of black bread from the baker's next to the herbalist's for eating on her way back down to the wharf.

The crush of men around the base of the Colossus seemed to have grown, if anything; now she could hear men bellowing at one another well up the street from the wharf. She emerged onto the dock nearest the *Wave Dancer* to find Xena standing in the shade, talking to a couple of men; Joxer sat cross-legged on the dock, fiddling with his pack. Now and again he eyed the warrior or her companions with a sour look and a twist of his mouth, but mostly he seemed to be doing his best to ignore them. He glanced up as she came into the open, sighed elaborately, and went back to fiddling with something in his bag.

Gabrielle ignored him. *Joxer in a mood is something I do not need today,* she told herself firmly.

Xena turned as she came close—alerted by the movement of the boards underfoot, no doubt. And beyond her, one of the men uttered a glad, wordless cry and came into the open, hands extended.

Gabrielle stopped short. "Briax?"

"Gabrielle! I was—I—that is, I mean—"

"He's been looking for *you,*" Xena murmured dryly. The village youth gave the warrior an alarmed glance.

"Well—I have—I mean, that is . . ."

"Briax," Gabrielle broke in; undoubtedly, he would have gone on in like fashion for the rest of the afternoon. "I'm really glad you're okay." She extended her hands and he gripped them; his fingers were slightly damp. "But, Briax, I thought—I honestly hoped you'd stayed in your village. And, when I found out you were in Sparta—well, I couldn't help but hope that by now, you'd have gone back home."

"I understand," he managed, a little more normally. "And I know you said there wasn't a quest. But—Gabrielle, I couldn't help myself, after you left, and then my father was bellowing the way he always does, and—well, something just snapped. It was—was as if your coming

149

to Katerini was what I needed, to get me out of my rut. Make me go out and *do* something. Prove myself. You know?"

Gabrielle bit back a sigh. "I know," she replied quietly.

"So I took one of our boats down the coast to Sparta, and the king and his priest were really very nice to me. Even though I hadn't really been chosen, except for that priest coming to Katerini and talking about it. Well—" he waved that aside and smiled at her. "The priest agreed to give me the test, and he and the king gave me the right to search, and . . ." He drew himself up, letting go her fingers. "But there really *is* a quest, there must be! Because, after all, *you're* here, aren't you? You and Xena? And—" He glanced doubtfully at Joxer, then turned to beckon his companion forward. "Gabrielle? This is Bellerophon, from Corinth. He's come from Sparta, too. We met in Phalamys, while we were searching for a ship, and Bellerophon said it was a good—I mean, he decided I could come with him."

Gabrielle's eyes widened. Briax's companion looked like he'd stepped straight from old legend. Tall, superbly muscled, golden skin and golden hair. Even the outdated armor that looked cut down from a larger man's pieces couldn't detract from his beauty. *And doesn't he know it,* she thought dryly. He gave her a casual, cold glance, waved a hand in greeting and slightly inclined his head. *Bellerophon—wait.* The name was familiar. She couldn't remember; maybe later.

Briax caught his friend's elbow as the taller man would have retreated into shade. "Bell, this is Gabrielle—you know, I told you about her? She's the one who's a warrior *and* a bard—"

"Bard?" Bellerophon caught at the word; the corners of

his mouth turned in a smile, then suddenly, his whole face warmed, and he gave her a neat, proper bow. "Of course, I remember, Briax. I hope to hear some of your tales—to lighten our journey, Gabrielle."

Wow, the bard thought; that smile was enough to dazzle anyone, especially coming as unexpectedly as it had. She pulled herself together, and smiled back. "Well, it kinda depends, you know. How long we have here on the docks, and—"

Briax broke in eagerly. "I already found us a ship, Gabrielle. And when I found out from Xena that you and she were here, I went back and made sure the captain'd take you, too. And Joxer, of course," he added as a snarled, wordless noise came from along the dock.

Gabrielle glanced at Xena, who gazed back at her impassively. "Well, you know, we might not be going the same—"

"The difficulty," Bellerophon put in neatly, "is to find a ship going from Rhodes that isn't making a circle of the main islands. We two arrived four days ago, just before those—" a distainful gesture took in the near-riot at the end of the harbor. "We've been seeking a ship ever since."

"Going where?"

"Egypt!" Briax said. "It stops other places, of course, but we were thinking—" Bellerophon cleared his throat gently; Briax blushed and fell silent.

"I understand," Gabrielle assured him. "You don't have to tell us. Xena?"

The warrior shrugged. "I got no problem with it myself," she said evenly.

No, Gabrielle thought as the situation came clear, *but Joxer sure does.* She nodded and thought for a long moment. Joxer in a sullen, jealous fit—that could be bad, especially on the confines of a ship. But infrequent ships could be a bigger problem. Especially if Apollo's priestess was communicating with that priest in Sparta. Xena would have to know about Krista as soon as possible—obviously not right here and now, though. "Well," she said slowly. "I got everything we need just now: food and drink and the like. So if we can get off Rhodes, we probably should."

"Sure," a voice behind her mumbled, "all of us in a happy little bunch, isn't that just—swell?"

Gabrielle ignored him; her eyes were focused on Xena, who knew her well enough to realize the other woman wanted to talk.

"Fine," the warrior said. "Briax, if you and your friend want to go on ahead, let the captain know we'll be there. Gabrielle and I have a few things to talk about. We'll meet you down there within the hour."

"No longer than that," the village youth warned. "*Yeloweh* is supposed to sail as soon as the tide's full."

"We'll be there, okay?" Xena said. Gabrielle moved to Xena's side and the two women watched them go, Briax tugging at the sleeves of his dark-red tunic and trying hard to keep up with the longer-legged Bellerophon. The two men veered around a pile of crates and up the ramp of a medium-sized merchant ship—to Gabrielle it looked almost as wide as it was long. Much nearer to hand, Joxer had apparently run out of things to fiddle with, but he was still mumbling. Fortunately, the bard thought, he was doing it quietly enough, she couldn't hear anything he said.

"Well?" she said finally. "You think traveling with them is the best way to go?"

Xena shrugged. "No. But it gets us off Rhodes. What'd you find up there?" She listened while Gabrielle made the shortest and most coherent tale of it she could. "Great. Good idea for us to get out of here, before this priestess finds out we've been and gone, don't you think? Especially since there's no trace any of Helen's pottery's ever been here."

"Which means, probably Helen hasn't either," Gabrielle said. Her eyes went beyond the *Yeloweh*, which rocked gently side to side as men swarmed into the rigging and onto the spar; several of the sailors seemed to be mending the sail where it attached up there. "You actually think that thing's *safe*?" she asked in a smaller voice.

"I've seen her before," Xena said. "Her captain's got a reputation for taking good care of his ship. She's all right."

Gabrielle sighed. "And, all right is as good as safe? Never mind," she added hastily. "I'll take it. You know though . . ." Her gaze went beyond the ship to the Colossus. Sun shone on the back of the massive head and shoulders and seemed to spark a flame in the torch. The crowd had moved back from the base of the statue. She could make out steps, and near that foot, a half circle of armed guards. "You know, it just seems wrong, leaving those women. I mean, if we could *do* something . . ."

"Gabrielle." Xena touched her arm to get her attention and smiled at her. "I know how you feel. But we've already got something to do, and right now, we're no closer to Helen than we were back in Sparta. At least knowing where she is, and how close they are to finding her. And those women are doing all right for themselves."

Gabrielle gave her a startled look. "You're kidding, right? I mean, if half what those old gossips said is true—"

"Then they're part of a cult, they aren't allowed any rights or freedom, and their men are trying to take them

153

as far from other people as they can. I know that. But they haven't exactly gone along with that, have they, Gabrielle?" Silence. "Look at them. They managed to grab their kids and get inside the statue, barricade the entrance so the men couldn't drag them out. They've got other people out there trying to keep the men away from them, and the governor's sent troops down to protect them."

"I suppose," Gabrielle said doubtfully. "But what if he decides the men have the right to haul the women out of there?"

"Then they're gonna have a hard time getting through that door," Xena replied evenly. "But this is Rhodes. I don't know what'll happen, but that's the least likely thing I can see."

Gabrielle considered this, finally shrugged. "I—well, I guess you're right. If there's a way to settle it by fighting, I can't see how—and nobody out there could hear either one of us talk."

"This is one for a government, Gabrielle. Sure you got everything you went for?" she added, in a clear change of subject.

"All of it."

"Good. Then let's go." She nudged Joxer with one booted foot as they passed him. "Joxer, c'mon," she said.

He looked up, his mouth twisted and his eyes sullen. "Feel free," he said finally. "You just—go right ahead, Xena. I'm sure that—those two—" He sighed deeply. "Yeah, maybe that's better anyway; you lead them astray, and I'll—"

"Joxer," Xena growled warningly.

He fell prudently silent.

"I said, c'mon!"

"Hey, Joxer," Gabrielle said cheerfully as she grabbed

his near arm and dragged him to his feet. "What, you giving up that easy?"

"Giving up? Hah!" he replied loftily and bent to grab up his pack. When he would have bowed the women ahead, Xena gave him a look and Gabrielle propelled him forward, between the two of them. "Sheesh," the would-be warrior grumbled under his breath.

"What?" Xena asked dryly. "You afraid of competition like *that*, Joxer? A half-grown village kid and a snotty Corinthian noble?"

Joxer wouldn't welcome *any* competition, Gabrielle knew; he'd never have enough real self-assurance to think he could overcome it. *I hope we aren't gonna have to listen to him sniveling all the way to Egypt,* she thought unhappily. To her relief, Joxer glanced at Xena, drew himself up straight, and snorted.

"Competition? *Those* two? Xena, for your information, I—"

"Yeah, yeah, we know, Joxer," the warrior cut him off hastily. "Let's go before we get stuck here, all right?" She waved a hand toward the Colossus. "All that noise is giving me a headache."

10

The ship rocked at anchor, making even walking up the plank an exercise in balance. Gabrielle staggered aboard, brushed past Joxer, and tapped Xena firmly on the arm. "Wafer first," she said. "I haven't had any of that stuff all day, and this is—this is bad, okay?"

The warrior gave her a dubious look, then shrugged. "If you say so." She fished a wafer from her belt, where she'd apparently shoved one or two for emergencies, and handed it over. "Save half of it, if you can. In case it's rough out there."

Gabrielle closed her eyes and groaned faintly.

The warrior laid a reassuring hand on her shoulder. "Gabrielle, it'll probably be just fine. You find us a good place against the rail, will you? I gotta go talk to the captain myself. Make sure there won't be any trouble."

Gabrielle merely nodded; she opened her eyes and began nibbling on a portion of the dry little cracker as she turned in place, seeking out a likely spot. Briax had settled his blanket near the foremast, close to the small boat that hung over the side. Clever of him, she decided, but she didn't care for the way his mind worked. *In case the ship starts to sink, he's close to a way off . . . brr!* Might not be that, of course.

She gazed his way a moment longer. *Poor kid. Did he bring anything with him but one blanket and that big old sword?* The sword looked like it belonged to someone twice his size—probably his father. Great. That would give the obnoxious innkeeper something *else* to yell about. Besides his son being gone, of course. *I swear, I had him convinced!* Well, there wasn't anything she could do about that now. Unless she could persuade him to turn around and go home sometime during this voyage.

"Sure, you could," she told herself, and bit back a chuckle. "Just like you woulda stayed in Poteidaia instead of following Xena, if someone had just talked sense to *you*." At least, *she* hadn't had a parent like Briax's father, yelling abuse at him all the time.

Bellerophon was almost exactly opposite him, a little nearer the ramp on the starboard side, unfolding a woven mat. Joxer mumbled something peevish-sounding under his breath, and stomped off. She turned, ready to tackle him if he was trying to head ashore, but he had apparently picked out his own spot, where the high aft deck overhung the lower and at the moment, there was the least bit of shade. His shoulders were hunched and tight, sure sign he didn't want to talk to her, or anyone else. *Fine. I don't wanna talk to him, either.*

His choice of location seemed like a good one, she thought. But unless she and Xena wanted to rub elbows with him, there wasn't much other room over there. Boxes and crates and a few nasty-looking damp bags were piled against the starboard rail, and on his other side, coils of rope were piled high next to the water barrels. On either side of the barrels, doors led into the space below the aft deck: crew's bunks and mess, most likely.

She turned some more, shielding her eyes against the glare of sun coming off the harbor water. Best bet seemed to be about the same location they'd taken on the *Wave Dancer*. Nearly midships, a little farther back, away from any of the rigging. She walked slowly up and down, pausing every few paces until she found a place where there seemed to be less movement back and forth; she doubted anything could be done about the side to side rocking and could only hope it would go away once they got into open water once more.

The sun was suddenly very hot and blaring off the water into her eyes, the sky cloudless and what breeze there had been was gone. Ropes creaked on tackle high overhead; the ship slammed into the dock, then wallowed sluggishly side to side as a heavy net of goods dropped onto the deck. High on the aft deck, a gravelly voice began bellowing curses; this was answered by someone deep in the hold and other men she couldn't see, down on the dock. Men came running down the deck from above, the net swung barely off the boards and was guided into the hold where it again landed with an unnerving thump. Gabrielle was already braced, fortunately; the ship rocked in earnest this time, but apparently it was all right—by the captain and crew's standards anyway. No one was yelling this time, anyway.

The echoing cries of men bellowing at each other around the base of the Colossus was overlaid by shrill women's voices, all of it nearly overwhelming, coming at once. Gabrielle cast up her eyes, and unsteadily knelt against the rail to spread the under-blanket on the deck, then rigged the covering cloth between the rail, her staff and Xena's small pack. She crawled into the sliver of shade this provided, drew her knees out of the sun, and closed her eyes. The wafer began to work—suddenly as they always did—and as her stomach calmed, the outside noise seemed to fade.

She woke some time later, by the feel of the air and the position of the sun. The ship rocked less than it had when it had been tied; a faint breeze ruffled the shade cloth over her head. She opened an eye and could just make out a bit of dark blue sky beyond the rail and, re-assuringly close, a dark leather boot. She yawned and be-gan easing her way out of the little shelter. "Gosh," she murmured. "That felt good. What time is it?"

Xena settled down cross-legged next to her. "Almost sunset. You all right?" Her companion nodded. "If you want to look, you can still see Rhodes from here."

Gabrielle waved a dismissive hand.

"Next stop should be Carpathos, then probably Alex-andria."

Gabrielle considered this. "The library? Really?"

Xena smiled over at her. "That would mean a lot to you, wouldn't it? It would probably be a good place to ask after Helen, too." The warrior uncorked her water bot-tle, drank, and passed it on. Gabrielle swallowed, passed it back.

"Thanks. So—who's this Bellerophon? I mean, the name's familiar, I think."

Xena shrugged. "Don't know, except what I overheard in Sparta. He might be the king's son—"

Gabrielle stared at her. "What—you mean Menelaus actually—?"

"King of Corinth," Xena corrected her. "Then again, he may be the son of Poseidon."

"Oh." Gabrielle considered this, then smiled suddenly. "Hey, if we've got Poseidon's son with us, Poseidon's that less likely to sink us, right?"

"Good point, Gabrielle."

"Maybe *that's* why the sea's so calm?"

"Maybe. More likely, that's just how the sea gets around here, this time of year, this time of day," Xena said. "Briax, though . . ."

Gabrielle sighed. "I know. Xena, I swear I did everything I could to convince him—"

"Hey, I know you did. I don't think there was anything you could've done. At least, he seems to have made friends with our young hero over there. Maybe that'll keep him alive, until he learns how to take care of himself."

"You think?" Gabrielle glanced up the deck; Briax was on his feet, leaning against the rail and staring out to sea, but she thought he was very aware of her, and just doing his best not to stare, or at least not to be caught glancing her way. The look he'd given her this afternoon, when she'd first walked onto the dock . . . her eyes closed briefly. It was the exact same look that Hauer fellow had given Xena—pure, blind, dumb adoration. Funny when Hauer'd followed Xena around like a puppy hoping for a pat on the head. Now it was *her* turn. . . . *I don't need this,* she thought unhappily. Especially with Joxer at the other end of the ship, glowering at her. And Bellerophon . . .

She touched Xena's arm to get her attention, sent her gaze across the deck. "So," she asked quietly. "What's *his* problem? I mean, the way he looked at me when Briax introduced us. He's not one of those women-hating types, is he? Except, no," she answered herself with a little frown, "because if he's out looking for Helen . . ."

"Gabrielle," Xena broke in dryly. "He wants to be a hero. A *classic* hero. You know—the pure and noble kind? If Briax hadn't told him you were a bard . . ."

"I—oh. I get it," Gabrielle said. "Pure and noble, as in, no women of any kind, right? Unless there's one to adore him blindly, and spread tales of his heroic deeds for him?" Her mouth twisted. "Yeah, right. And I'm supposed to just—he smiles pretty and I fall for that."

The warrior raised an eyebrow. "Well? It's a pretty package, isn't it? Some women would."

"I guess," Gabrielle allowed. She shrugged that aside. "Look, let's forget it, okay?"

"Fine with me. Anything else you learned from that priestess that you didn't tell me?"

"Don't think so." Gabrielle turned down individual fingers. "No Helen. No pottery with a swan glyph. No little people. The head priestess—well, she seemed weird and a little scary to *me,* even without Saroni saying so. And then that conversation she overheard—"

"Thinks she overheard," Xena corrected her absently. "Though I don't see why it *couldn't* be Avicus."

Gabrielle was fishing bread out of her pack; she hesitated, then set the pack aside and swung around to face her close companion. "You knew about those bowls, that they could be used that way?"

"I don't know anything, Gabrielle. But Avicus definitely has more ways than one of finding things out. That *rhodforch* we found early on; the patches he put on—" She fell abruptly silent. Gabrielle cleared her throat.

"Patches? What patches?"

It was Xena's turn to stare. "I told you about those." Gabrielle eyed her sidelong, then shook her head. "I didn't tell you? There are these—wait here, okay?" The warrior rose to her feet and strode up-deck to talk to Briax. The young man started as she said something, then smiled faintly. Gabrielle couldn't make out a word of any of it, and, was slightly surprised when Xena laid a hand on the youth's tunic. Some moments later quietly, she moved the hand and pointed something out. As Briax turned to look, Xena eased the hand out beyond the rail and shook it, hard. She clapped Briax on the shoulder then, and walked over to talk to Bellerophon.

The Corinthian youth was visibly less open to the conversation—wary of Xena, which didn't surprise Gabrielle, since most people were. After some moments, though, Xena's hand rested casually against the fellow's armor and came away as if clutching something. She said something else; Bellerophon shrugged and the warrior turned away to walk back across the deck. Her hand was now a white-knuckled fist, and when Gabrielle would have spoken, Xena silenced her with a look before moving over to shake her hand over open water. She scrubbed her palm against the leather straps of her skirt and settled next to the rail.

"Sorry," she said finally. "You got some of that bread? I'm hungry."

The two women ate in silence for some moments; Xena finally wrapped her share of bread and let Gabrielle stow it away. "Do you mind telling me what that was all about?" the bard finally asked. "And—what's all this about patches?"

"I meant to tell you in Sparta." The warrior glanced at her and shrugged, a faint smile tugging at her mouth. "We never got the chance, right? When Avicus chose each of his heroes, he put a patch on them."

"But, I didn't see—"

163

"You *couldn't* see," Xena said. "Some kind of god-thing, like the *rhodforch;* it lets him see where they are, like he was right there. If I got it right," she added, mostly to herself. She glanced at Gabrielle. "I got Draco's first thing; and I grabbed Joxer's as soon as I got my hands on him, just out of Phalamys."

Gabrielle was eyeing her narrowly. "Wait a second," she managed finally, setting her bread aside. "You're telling me that Avicus—that he could *tell* where we were, like on that lousy ship out of Sparta, because Joxer had on some stupid patch that—?" She stopped, apparently searching for words. "But, that means that, now he knows where we are!"

"He knows where we were, as of a few minutes ago," Xena replied.

"Is that supposed to make me feel any better?" Gabrielle retorted. "Because, frankly, it doesn't."

"He might already have known which ship we'd be taking," Xena told her. "If only because that head priestess might have already found out we'd come in aboard the *Wave Dancer* and maybe had her own ways of learning we went out on the *Yeloweh*. But we weren't exactly hiding back there. And there were only three ships leaving port today. So . . ."

Gabrielle let her eyes close. "You know," she said finally. "I wish just *one* thing could go straight and normal. Because, I swear, nothing has since Joxer talked to those Spartan soldiers back up in Thessalonika."

Xena wrapped an arm around her shoulders and drew her briefly close. "I know. Look, I'm gonna go talk to Joxer, see if I can't get him out of this mood."

"Great, go for it," Gabrielle mumbled. "I think I'm gonna take another nap, while it's still calm." She forced her eyes open long enough to return the bread to its wrappings and store both her and Xena's loaves to their corner of the pack, then stretched out again under the canopy. The ship rocked gently, ropes creaking softly high overhead, and her last glimpse of sky before sleep claimed her was a dark blue canopy with one faint star.

She woke some hours later to a sickle moon and scudding clouds; wind hissed across the deck, snapping the sail.

Xena slept heavily at her side. The bard eased quietly down the rail and into the open, then got to her knees; Xena murmured something in her sleep and was still and quiet again.

To Gabrielle's surprise, the water still looked fairly smooth, and the ship was still plowing evenly along. An occasional whitecap rolled past, and once, she thought she made out the shape of a vast fish—maybe even one of the fabled dolphins, just behind the sweep of water that curled away from the bow.

Tantalizing thought. *I wonder if they really do swim with people—or rescue people when boats go down.* The latter thought wasn't a good one. The first, though . . . *Wonder what that would be like?* She edged a little farther forward to gaze out and down, but it was just too dark for her to tell what might be moving out there. The moon was in and out of cloud, and the only lights aboard ship were ones that glowed steadily back where the wheel was and another high on the main mast, flashing out only now and again.

She was just as glad the light up above wasn't a steady one. *No sense hanging out a beacon for another ship to find us.* From what she'd gathered the past days, listening to the crews of the ships they'd been on thus far, they were far more likely to meet another merchant ship than anything else. Still, there were pirates about. And foreign raiders, either of whom might be drawn to such a light. *If I were gonna attack a ship, I'd think about doing it at night. An hour like this, when no one would expect it. You could probably round up the whole crew without anyone getting hurt.* Not the way pirates thought, if the tales were true; they didn't care who got hurt, including their own kind. Still. . . .

She dismissed pirates and raiders alike. Nothing she could do about them. Xena wouldn't be sleeping so peacefully if there were any chance of them being boarded. Gabrielle eased down to peer into the rigged-up shelter, smiled faintly. The warrior slept flat on her back and the chakram was still hooked in its usual place on her belt, not up by her shoulder where it would be ready to catch up and throw. *No pirates,* she reiterated to herself, this time with relief.

Of course, there was always the possibility of a ship carrying King Menelaus and his pet priest, who would know what ship to seek out thanks to those patches. . . .

I wish Xena'd remembered them earlier. It wouldn't have mattered, of course; Avicus would certainly have been aware that Briax and Bellerophon were in Rhodes earlier, that they had met up with Joxer, Xena, and Gabrielle. No way Xena could've gotten to them sooner. So Xena was right about that, too. No way they could have prevented Avicus knowing what ship they were on.

She swallowed past a dry throat. Was it likely king and priest were already at sea, staying close on the heels of certain of the heroes in hopes of nabbing Helen? Gabrielle considered the notion briefly, then tried to dismiss it. Anything was possible, but as many men as had been sent out from Sparta—no way they could follow all of them at once.

Of course, that might be extra. Maybe Menelaus had focused on Xena to begin with, assuming she could find Helen, and the rest weren't important. Yet—once that ship had left Sparta, they could have gone anywhere. Xena could have commandeered the *Euterpe*, and how would Avicus have known, with Joxer's patch gone?

If Saroni was right, Avicus had been communicating with that spooky-looking head-priestess. Which, again, should mean he was back in Sparta still, keeping an eye on all his questors.

She clutched her head. That didn't mean he wasn't aboard a ship; there wasn't any reason *she* knew of that the priest couldn't have brought his bowl along. Or something else that would let him stay in touch with others of his kind.

Give yourself nightmares, why don't you? she told herself. She glanced around the ship. It was very quiet out here at the moment. Men were talking softly far overhead, above the mainsail. She couldn't make out what they said, even if there were two or three of them. *Or one, who talks to himself,* she decided with a faint smile. The smile faded. Or one, talking to Avicus. "Cut it out," she whispered sharply, then clapped a hand over her mouth as Xena stirred. Silence. The warrior sighed deeply and slept once more.

Joxer seemed to be asleep—quietly for once. If he was lying awake and sulking, she didn't want to know. She couldn't make out where Briax was, or Bellerophon—the deck was simply too dark for that. *You can't see anything,* she told herself. *So, be sensible and don't bother. Go to sleep.* She eased back between Xena and the rail and closed her eyes. It seemed like a long time indeed before she actually slept.

At her side, Xena lay still, breathing deeply and regularly until she was certain Gabrielle was again asleep. *I wonder if she saw anything out there?* There didn't seem any point to getting up, herself. Even if she weren't getting sleep, she was still resting, and that was nearly as useful. If Gabrielle was awake, or if she woke her close companion, she'd just worry.

She'd have reason to worry if she'd seen what I saw, just before full dark. Two long, matching wakes well behind the ship, and off to the south. Poseidon's sea serpents hadn't given up. She didn't think they'd come close tonight. First night out from this port, generally captain and crew kept a close eye out because of the half-submerged rocks and islands all around Rhodes, and because at least two different ships of freebooters liked to prey on merchants in the triangle between Rhodes harbor, the Hittite mainland, and Egypt well to the south.

With luck, Gabrielle wouldn't ever need to know that. Or how treacherous sailing could be along the sea southeast of the big island. *If the chunks of rock stayed put, up or down—but they don't.*

She briefly opened one eye; Gabrielle was curled on her side, head close to the warrior's shoulder, golden hair spilled across her face. Xena smiled, settled her shoulders, and fell asleep.

Some distance behind the *Yeloweh*, another ship followed—staying as near the horizon as it dared for the dark night, barely keeping the faint, occasional flicker of light in view. A few crewmen worked the lines, hauling in sail as the wind stiffened. This vessel was longer and sleeker than *Yeloweh*, and could easily pass her.

High on the aft deck, a vast, ruddy-haired man worked the wheel with thumb and forefinger, eyes fixed on the ship ahead, making minute changes in direction as it did. At his side, a slightly shorter and much darker figure peered into the gloom. The captain glanced at him, finally cleared his throat. "Y'said ye'd decide by middle night, man and t'is past that. D'ye follow Xena or no?"

Draco sighed deeply. "What point? You win, Habbish. I think you were right all along, Xena doesn't know where Helen is. Or, if she does, she's making certain no one learns by following her."

"She's a clever one," Habbish allowed. "And y'won't trick a thing like that of *her*."

"Or anything else she doesn't want me to know," Draco admitted. "All right, Habbish. I've run out of ideas; we'll go where you suggested."

"Good man," Habbish replied. "G'wan then and get y'self some meat. There'll be fresh mead in my cabin, or wine if y'd rather. Get some sleep, if y'can. T'is gonna blow up rough later in t'day tomorrow, I think."

"Thanks for the warning," Draco said. His eyes strayed to the ship far ahead of them, a faint smile moved his mouth and warmed his eyes. *Sleep well, Gabrielle,* he thought, then turned and left the deck.

It was dark all across Rhodes at this hour of night. A torch fluttered aboard the *Wave Dancer*, casting odd shadows over the deck, and another pair burned on the next ship down. Beyond it, torches cast ruddy light against a well-muscled metal calf. Two Rhodsian soldiers paced back and forth between the legs. No one else was in sight anywhere around the statue, and only the faintest gleam of light high above through the eyes—and the least sound of a whimpering child—showed the statue was still occupied.

The market was deserted, tables and stalls wiped clean, canopies taken down and stored for the night. Wind whistled in fitful gusts across the stone paving.

Some distance away, the stone steps of the amphitheater gleamed briefly as the moon came from between thin clouds. The small priestess-hut was dark, and anyone standing just outside the doorway could have made out faint, whuffling snores. The high priestess, her day's duties concluded, slept.

Moonlight slid across the open courtyard and was gone. A small figure muffled in a dark cloak slid from the hut and stole quickly across the open, stopped just short of the tunnel, and edged along the wall to a place behind the back of the theater. There was a well here, and a pool, visible only as the merest gleam of reflected stars; and another brief glimpse of moon.

Saroni listened intently for a long moment, then eased the hood away from her face. A moment later, she cast the cloak aside, knelt by the pool, and drew water into her cupped hands. Murmuring under her breath, she hesitated, then gently blew on the liquid. It rippled, seemed to steam, and when it cleared, a pale face with intense blue eyes gazed into hers. "Honor Avicus," she said quietly.

He smiled, though his eyes remained wide and cool. "Yes, Saroni. I am aware of your success." His mouth quirked. "You will hold yourself ready, for when the time comes."

"Of course, Honor."

"In the meantime—well done." He was gone. Saroni drew a deep breath and let it out with an exultant smile. It had worked. And he still needed her. One day soon— very soon—Rhodes would be behind her. She opened her fingers to let the water spill back into the pool.

Good-bye to Rhodes . . . It couldn't come quickly enough for her, poor, dull town, dull people—the dull, hourly progression of a priestess's rounds. She caught up the dark cloak and prudently covered herself again as she stepped into the open, though by now she could hear the chief priestess' faint snores. Her mouth twisted in amusement. A famous bard Gabrielle might be—but *her* story had convinced the young woman that poor, hapless Krista might actually be some kind of evil entity, a spy. . . .

Continue to think that, Gabrielle, she thought grimly. Twickenham had described the bard as such an innocent— babbled, actually. Her hair, her eyes, the legs, the little stick, her belief in the basic goodness of people. The kind of Goody Two-sandals Saroni knew you could make believe just about anything, if you went about it the right way.

She crossed the courtyard and entered the little hut, settled down on her narrow cot in the herbal room and tuned out the noises from the outer chamber with ease of practice. *Sleep,* she ordered herself. The next few days could be—interesting.

11

The deck under the warrior's back seemed almost as stable as dry land—and as hot as a desert, at the moment. Xena eased slowly and quietly from under the arm the sleeping Gabrielle had flung across her shoulders some time earlier, and quietly backed on all fours from the sheltering blanket. She sat back on her heels, ran a hand across her eyes, finally blinked up at the dark sky far overhead and the mast—and the crow's nest just barely visible as a darker blotch against that sky.

The ship was a quiet place at this hour. The first mate or, more likely in such a calm sea, his apprentice—manned the wheel; one of the ship's beardless boys would be lodged in the bow, watching for danger that might range from half-submerged rocks to approaching ships, while a youth kept watch from the circular platform above the mainsail. Yet another might be posted in the stern to watch the back path especially this near the Hittite shores, though that wasn't a given.

Everyone else—except possibly the cook and the navigator—would be asleep at this hour, and those who watched made sure they did nothing to waken the ship without very good cause.

Xena smiled. It felt good at the moment, being back aboard a ship and well out at sea. She drew a deep breath, savoring the mix of damp, salty air, the tar that coated the ship's hull, the faint but pervasive fishy odor that blended with an even fainter scent of some spice or herb down in the hold.

Dim stars were still visible to the north and west; the eastern sky showed a blood red, uneven line at the horizon. She rose quietly and gazed back along the rail. *Storm weather, when it's that red this early.* For Gabrielle's sake, she hoped it wouldn't be anything more than a passing late-day squall, but it didn't look that way to her.

The water was as flat as it ever got. Smooth, low waves slid past the hull, hissing faintly as the prow cut through them. Xena stood for some moments listening to the faint creaks of the ship and the whispery *ploosh* of water. The last stars faded and distant islands began to separate from the sea, hard black shapes scattered across a silvery-black surface. No other ships visible anywhere—and no sign of the long wakes she'd seen the previous evening, either.

Maybe they were gone. A corner of the warrior's mouth quirked. *Yeah, right,* she thought sourly. It was possible, of course. She didn't think it very likely.

There wasn't really anything else to do at the moment except stare out to sea, and visibility still wasn't all that good. She wasn't particularly hungry yet. *And you aren't up there sailing the ship or watching for ships to take, are you?* She yawned hugely, stretched, and slid back under the shelter next to Gabrielle.

The younger woman was deeply asleep, pale hair tangled across her shoulders except for one strand that lay across her face between lip and nose. Xena smiled faintly and moved it back behind her ear before settling into place.

She woke some time later to find the early sun hot on her legs and Gabrielle up and gone—though not far. She sat cross-legged with her back to the rail, running a brush through her hair and talking quietly to Briax, who sat with his arms wrapped around his knees; his face was very rosy. He wouldn't meet Gabrielle's eyes, though whenever Gabrielle looked away from *him*, he'd gaze at her with open longing.

Gabrielle, the warrior thought with amusement, was well aware of the young man's fascination, but doing her best not to let on. ". . . and that's why I think you should give this up, Briax, before you—" She paused; he nodded. Gabrielle sighed faintly and waved her free hand before his face. "Briax, are you even listening to me?"

He blinked. "I—of course I am, G-Gabrielle. I was just thinking, though; when I find the—the dish and return it to Sparta—"

"Briax," Gabrielle gritted his name out between her teeth. He cast a shy smile her way, then fell to studying his fingers.

"I know what you told me, Gabrielle—about there not being a quest and why the king's supposedly doing all this. But—but you know, Bellerophon explained it all to me, not long after we sailed from Phalamys, and he was there, after all. Like I was, except, of course—well, he knows more about things like this. Quests and the like. You know," he added thoughtfully, "it was so incredibly nice of him to let me travel along with him. I mean—well, I told you, I've never been far from Katerini, nothing like this. If it hadn't been for Bellerophon, I wouldn't have known what to do, which direction to go once I left Sparta. . . ."

"Yeah." Gabrielle gazed narrowly across the deck to where Bellerophon stood. Xena'd warned her about the young Corinthian's attitude, but it hadn't been necessary; she could see it in the distainful looks he gave her, and even the way he snubbed the warrior, though he was careful not to sneer when Xena was watching *him*. She could just bet Bellerophon had explained things. "It's a men's quest, Briax. Mere women can't be expected to understand this side of Apollo, it's not like inhaling steam and having visions, its . . ." *Yeah, you've heard it all before and all it does is make you mad. Give it up, you won't change him, and you won't convince Briax—even if he'd like to believe you just because it's you telling him.* Just now he was watching her sidelong and looking vaguely puzzled—probably at the grim expression on her face. "Yeah," she said finally. "He's a real prince, all right."

Briax gaped, then shook his head; he'd taken her literally again, Gabrielle realized. "I didn't know that he'd— oh, no, I'm sorry, I didn't understand what you meant. But I forget, he told me it's pretty much common knowledge. About—that. But, no one's sure about his father except maybe his mother, and she wouldn't ever say. So not even Bellerophon knows. I know that much, because he told me about it—all the rumors in Corinth, and of course, people were talking in Sparta.

"But it doesn't really matter to him whether he's a prince or—well, the other thing, you know. He says that so long as he can travel the world helping people and righting wrongs, that's all he wants."

At least, as long as everyone knows it's him that's do-

ing it, Gabrielle added silently. She kept the words in with an effort. *It won't do you any good to bad-mouth the snobby little monster,* she realized. *Because Briax already sees him as a good person—and for whatever reason he did it, at least Bellerophon is keeping an eye on the poor kid. Besides, if Briax is happy trailing around in Bellerophon's shadow, who am I to say that's wrong?* She laughed quietly. "Hey, the world could use a lot more people like that, Briax. And nice people like you, too." Oops, she thought. But the youth merely blushed and scrambled to his feet, the too-long, borrowed sword banging against the deck and tangling in his arms as he righted himself.

"I—better get back," he managed. "Ah—I'll, ah—" He was still mumbling as he turned away. Gabrielle watched him go and sighed faintly, then glanced at the shelter as Xena eased out into the open.

"You handled him just fine, Gabrielle."

"Yeah. Maybe. Except if I'd handled him just fine, he'd still be at home. Safe."

The warrior shook her head. "You know better than that. You're not responsible for his choices. By now, he could have come up with a dozen reasons to leave, besides a quest that might impress you if you ever heard about it." She got to her feet and held out a hand, drew Gabrielle up and turned to gaze out to sea. The water was rougher than it had been at daybreak but still fairly smooth, and the breeze steady and light. No clouds anywhere.

"It's gonna be hot," Gabrielle said as she glanced at the sky before settling her elbows on the rail. "I know; you're right. Menelaus's priest had already been there before I ever got to Katerini, and he was already excited about it. And his father—if there was ever a man who

177

seemed to be trying to drive his sons away, that's the one. It's just that—I meant what I said to him, you know. There aren't enough nice people in the world. Ordinary ones, who stay in their villages, live their lives, raise families and make things a little better—" She shrugged and fell silent. "I'd rather he didn't leave that behind and come all the way out here just to get himself killed." Xena laid a hand on her shoulder.

"I know what you mean. Still, if he was gonna leave home anyway, at least he did it for the right kind of reason."

"Yeah." Gabrielle laughed shortly. "I just—" She was silent for a moment, then turned to meet her close companion's eyes. "What if *he's* the one to find Helen? He's so naive and so full of good intentions . . ." She let the thought trail off.

"That's what's bothering you? That he'd just bundle her up and haul her back to Sparta? No matter what she said?"

Gabrielle shook her head, visibly frustrated. "I don't think he would—no, of course, he wouldn't do something like that. But Bellerophon? I can see him doing something like that. He'd never listen to her, and he probably wouldn't listen to Briax, either."

"But that would be true of just about any of them," Xena said. "They wouldn't have any reason to listen to Helen, and plenty of reasons to do what Menelaus wants."

"Yeah. It's just that—I don't know." The bard ran an impatient hand through her hair. "I—I just don't like any of this, everything that's going on lately, Xena. It's getting into my dreams and they're all bad. Last night—that priestess I told you about on Rhodes, the one with the wooden shoes?" Xena nodded. "I was back in that courtyard, but behind the risers where the audience sits, somehow I knew what it looked like, and I could hear that echoing *clonk, clonk, clonk,* like she was walking just ahead of me or just behind, far enough around the curve of the wall that I couldn't see her. Deliberately letting me know I was being stalked or something. And then, there was a pool—but when I looked in it, I couldn't see my face, just her hood." The warrior drew her close; Gabrielle leaned against her. "It wasn't really—that bad, or anything. Not scary, really. Just—"

Xena nodded as the other's thought trailed off once more. "Doesn't sound pleasant, though. Gabrielle, you *sure* you haven't been eating any of Joxer's stuff?"

Gabrielle laughed. "Nice," she said finally. "That reminds me, though, I could use some of that bread." She eyed the spray coursing back from the bow, then gazed out toward the horizon.

"With or without goo?" the warrior asked as she fished out the smaller loaf and felt in her pack for the wooden box.

"With," Gabrielle replied firmly.

The morning stayed calm and clear, the wind light. Gabrielle settled under the shade of the overhead blanket and worked on one of her scrolls for a while, then fell asleep. Xena watched the horizon for ships and saw three— all clearly merchant vessels and none of them on the same course as the *Yeloweh*. The air was clear enough she could still make out a smudge on the northeastern horizon that was Rhodes, and if she could still reckon things properly, the smudge more or less dead ahead should be one of the small outer islands to the east of Carpathos.

At their current speed, they wouldn't make land until

early the next morning—but that could all change if the weather turned as she expected it to, late in the afternoon. *If it does, Gabrielle's gonna be glad she ate that goo.* She glanced down at the sleeping young woman, then smiled as she went back to her study of the surrounding sea.

If a real storm blew up, the captain would head for deeper water, and well away from the islands. The harbor at Carpathos was nearly as tricky as the one at Phalamys and shallow water ringed the island for a goodly distance. Shallow water in a storm was no place for a ship, unless the captain was set on wrecking her.

At mid-morning bell, the captain came out to take over the wheel, snapping low orders at his men. Two swarmed up the main mast to take in sail while several others crossed the deck and dropped into the hold. Moments later three of them emerged with a roll of heavy canvas wrapped in ropes. The last man out was virtually wreathed in coils of rope, half of which he dropped on the deck so he could manage the steep stairs of the aft deck with what he still carried.

Tie-downs for whoever's on the wheel, and safety lines for those who'd need to cross the deck, she knew. She watched as crew unrolled the canvas and snugged it down over the hatch before moving off to other tasks. One of them paused to talk to Bellerophon and Briax; the village youth was pale when the shipman moved on and immediately fell to his knees so he could stuff things into his pack. Bellerophon squatted beside him, apparently soothing whatever fears the youth had, because Briax finally nodded, laid the full pack to one side and got back to his feet to gaze out to sea. Bellerophon turned to look up at the aft deck, beyond that to the eastern sky, then shrugged and began folding his one blanket around his sack of food and drink. He tied the leather thongs around the resulting neat bundle, attached a broad carry-strap to it and set it aside, then sat down cross-legged, set his blades out in a neat line in front of his knees, and began edging his sword. Briax's shoulders tightened as metal screeched against metal; he murmured something and moved away toward the bow.

She wouldn't get a better opportunity anytime soon, Xena decided, to talk to the young hero by himself. *Yeah, she thought, suddenly and grimly amused. Let's see how serious he was back in Sparta about taking on the traitor Xena.* She pushed away from the rail and crossed the deck.

Her shadow fell across the line of blades; Bellerophon tensed as his gaze fixed on her boots, but as he met her eyes, his hands were moving again, absently working on his sword. A faint smile turned the corner of his mouth in a wry smile, but his eyes were chill. "Xena," he said, and with a wave of his hand indicated the deck. She shrugged, and stayed where she was; he lay the sword aside and got to his feet. Silence. "I've heard of you since I was a boy, of course," he said finally. "Back in Corinth, you have—quite a reputation. Odd that we'd be on a ship together."

She raised an eyebrow. "Yeah, well. These things happen."

"Especially after Sparta." He studied her for a long moment. "I've already heard that you dislike the king and would do anything you could to thwart his quest to regain his treasures."

"Wrong," she put in evenly. "I despise the king, and I wouldn't trust anything he said as far as I could throw him, *and* his priest. You want to go find this trinket he puts so much value on, you do that. But Helen? Don't waste your time. Because even if you find her, you won't get her back to Sparta."

He brought his chin up. "Is that a challenge, Xena?"

"No," she replied softly. "That's a promise." The youth's dark eyes flashed, but whatever he would have said went unspoken as a sharp cry went up from the crow's nest; it was echoed from the stern, near the tiller. Xena pushed past Bellerophon to lean out across the rail.

Water spilled away from the ship, a spreading vee of whitecapped wavelets. This was broken by crisscrossing wakes. Something—two somethings—were coming up behind the *Yeloweh*, and fast. "Let me guess," Xena muttered to herself. She spun back to meet the youth's still angry gaze and leveled a finger at him. "We'll finish this later," she said, then turned and sprinted for the aft deck.

Bellerophon started to say something; it came out a startled squawk as a massive, blue-gray, snaky head rose from behind the ship, then dipped out of sight again. Water sprayed high.

She could hear Joxer's high-pitched voice behind her, and a startled cry from Gabrielle, who'd apparently been awakened by all the noise. Xena threw herself up the steps and onto the high deck to find a huddle of men against the rail above the main deck—as far as possible from the stern, she thought. The central upper deck was all but deserted: A towheaded lad clung to his perch on the tillerman's seat. His face was deadly pale as he gazed out and down.

The captain—a white-haired, vigorous, and sturdily built man—gripped the wheel hard; his mouth was set and grim. He glanced back as Xena reached the deck, then shouted, "Dyonis, get down from there!" The boy seemed not to hear him. He swore then, and scowled at Xena, who'd drawn sword and chakram.

"You aren't gonna fight anyone on my ship, woman!" he shouted. Water boomed, thunderlike, as a massive body slapped down across the waves and Dyonis cried out; the huddle of sailors crammed even more tightly together.

"Get those men off the deck and out of the way!" she shouted back. She vaulted forward in a tight flip, dropped the sword long enough to catch hold of the boy's shoulders and haul him back behind her, then shove him toward the terrified sailors. He staggered and fell into them and several other men went down.

"Down in the mess, the lot of you!" the captain bellowed.

Momentary silence. Their new traveling companions had apparently gone underwater once more. Xena could hear the creak of ropes and wood as the captain spun the wheel and the ship wallowed gently to a more southerly path. Gabrielle's light footsteps on the aft stairs, then, followed by Joxer's inevitable stumble and muted yelp of surprise. She glanced back as the two emerged onto the upper deck.

Bellerophon had the main deck to himself at the moment, a sword in each hand and half a dozen daggers jammed into the rail nearby. But she could see Briax now; he'd gone into the bow to pull the boy from his watch post and give him a shove toward the crew mess.

Water boomed again, and the ship lurched as a wave surged across the stern. The movement broke the frozen moment on the aft deck. Led by the boy Dyonis, the crew fled down the narrow steps, or over the rail, and out of sight. A door creaked and slammed. Silence once more.

Xena clipped the chakram onto her belt and, when Gabrielle would have come up beside her, she held out her free hand. "Wait there; watch my back. There's two . . ."

"Two what?" Gabrielle asked sharply. "Ahh—Xena?" This as the captain turned white as his hair and slowly slid down behind the wheel until he was folded up almost beneath it, one clawed hand clung to it, the other clapped across his mouth. Behind the women, Joxer began to laugh.

"That's right, you sailors, run!" he shouted giddily. "Seek the safety of your cabin, hide and cower! Joxer the *Mighty* is here, to turn danger aside with a—"

"Joxer," Gabrielle topped him—barely. "Will you *shut up*? Xena, just what is—ohmigods," she finished in a half-audible gulp as a large, snaky body rose from behind the ship to glare down at them through beady little eyes. The rest of the head seemed to be all spikes and points—and teeth.

"With a *glower, ha hah*!" Joxer finished triumphantly. He strode forward, teetering as he passed Xena and the ship lurched into a trough. The warrior grabbed his collar and set him back upright. He didn't even seem to notice; his attention was fixed on the massive creature hovering high above the aft deck—nearly as high as the mainmast itself.

"Joxer!" Gabrielle hissed urgently. *She* was pale, but she had the fighting staff at ready and had positioned herself at Xena's left shoulder. "Joxer, you're gonna get yourself eaten!"

"Eaten?" He swaggered, glanced back her way and gave her a knowing smile. "Relax, Gabrielle, it's just a big sea snake."

"Joxer, it's bigger than the ship!" she hissed.

He laughed and held out his sword. "Gabrielle, it doesn't matter how big a snake is, it's still just a snake, and there's only one . . ." A booming, explosive *clap* rang across the water directly behind them, silencing him. An incredibly deep grunt followed this. A long shadow fell across the aft deck.

Xena's gaze slid sideways to meet Gabrielle's, and both turned halfway. Joxer's eyes were white all the way around; he clung to the sword still but the tip dragged the deck as if he'd forgotten it entirely. He was gazing up, toward the aft mast, then along its thick length. Back beyond it, and farther back still. Gabrielle caught him when he would have overbalanced. She licked suddenly dry lips.

Joxer gazed straight up into the beady, pale gray, curious eyes of a second massive, snaky being. Water coursed from its scaled, sleek body, dripped from spikes, points, barbels and possible horns onto the rail just behind him, and splattered across the main deck. The would-be warrior's mouth fell open; the sea serpent's mouth went wide in what looked to Gabrielle like the worst travesty of a smile she'd ever seen.

Joxer screamed; the brute high above him drew back, then leaned low over the upper rail to stare at him, wide-eyed. Joxer staggered back, fell flat, and screamed again. The serpent cocked its head, for all the world, Gabrielle decided, as if studying a curiosity. *Or lunch.* Her grip tightened on the staff, but Xena laid a hand on her shoulder, and when the younger woman glanced at her, the warrior shook her head. "Wait," she murmured.

Back on the main deck, she heard Bellerophon shout a challenge and Briax's startled yell. No time to worry about them, she decided. They had their hands full right here.

"Poseidon's?" she asked Xena in a low voice.

"Poseidon's pets," Xena replied in like fashion. "He sicks 'em on people he doesn't care for."

"You, for instance?"

"Once before," the warrior admitted. "Fortunately, it wasn't *my* ship they turned into a collection of toothpicks. Actually, I'm not sure it was me he was after, anyway. This time, though . . ."

Gabrielle smiled tightly. "If they're supposed to be an improvement on that whirlpool Cecrops nearly got sucked into, or the tidal wave . . . Well, they're—different, anyway." Xena shrugged, then went into fighting stance, sword up and out as the serpent that was hovering over Joxer brought its head nearer the deck. Gabrielle caught her breath in a gasp and gazed up at the hovering serpent. "Hey! I don't think you want to eat him! I mean, neither of us can remember the last time he bathed—!"

"Gabri*elle,* do you *mind*?" Joxer hissed frantically. "I have everything under control here—and besides, are you trying to get this thing to drown me before it eats me, or something?"

"Why?" she shot back. "You got a preference or something?" She yelped and came halfway about at the strangled little sound near her feet, but it was only the captain, who was now curled in on himself so tightly she couldn't see his face at all—only the hand that still clung to the lowest point on the wheel. It was keeping the ship on a straight course, fortunately, but she didn't think it was on purpose.

Down on the main deck, Bellerophon shouted, "To me, my trusted companion! And beware, thou foul creature,

186

lest thou shouldst feel my wrath, and that of my blade! For know this is the sacred sword of. . . ." A loud splash silenced him. Gabrielle glanced that way to see the bombastic young hero pick himself sopping wet out of a pool of water. The second serpent hovered high over him.

Briax, who clung to the far side of the mainmast, leaned around it long enough to remark, "Um? I don't think I'd yell at him like that again, if I were you. I mean, he can spit an awful lot of water at a time, Bellerophon, and this isn't a very big ship."

Bellerophon swiped streaming wet hair out of his eyes. Gabrielle smothered laughter. The situation was not even remotely amusing—another minute or so might see them on their way to the bottom, or being picked off the water like . . . she fought the picture aside.

"Xena?" she urged in a hoarse whisper. Surely Xena could take out *one* of the pair! Maybe she, Joxer, and Bellerophon could distract the second until Xena could go after *it,* and . . . "Xena, we've got to do something!"

To her astonishment, the warrior sounded like she was fighting laughter. "Gabrielle, we've already done it."

"I mean, if we can keep this one—we have?"

"We have. Because—" An echoing *skronk* silenced her. Joxer gaped up at the creature far above him, and as the massive head slowly began to descend, he closed his eyes, swallowed hard, and licked his lips.

"Start with the head," he babbled under his breath. "That's all I ask, don't go for the feet first, just *chomp*! and that's it, I can *deal* with that."

Gabrielle changed stance and brought her staff up to the ready; the brute ignored her. Its eyes were all for Joxer; she shuddered as the tip of a very green, forked tongue slid briefly between snaky lips. To her surprise, the serpent stopped some distance away from and above the fallen Joxer. The corners of its long, mobile mouth curved upward, the eyes narrowed like those of a pleased cat, and it made a deep, rumbling noise not unlike a purr. Joxer slitted an eye open, gave out a muted yelp, and squinched both eyes tight, then folded in on himself much as the ship's captain had done; Xena kicked his sword aside before he could accidentally impale himself, then gripped Gabrielle's arm and drew her back two paces.

"Xena!" Gabrielle tried to shake the hand off. "What're you doing? You can't just—!" An echoing, deep voice filled her mind, bringing her around to stare at the hovering serpent. "It—spoke?" she asked wildly. "It—you spoke? You can speak?" The serpent ignored her and her question; its whole attention was fixed on Joxer.

"Awwww," it rumbled somewhere deep inside itself. *"Awww, it cute!"*

12

Dead silence. Gabrielle planted the end of her staff on the deck and took one wary step forward. "Excuse me? Did you just—*say* something?" The creature's gaze flicked her direction, then fastened on Joxer once again.

"Cute!"

Gabrielle shook her head as if to clear it, rubbed at her ear, and stared wildly at the deck. "Okay, fine. Either my mind's going or my ears are, because—"

Xena tapped her shoulder. "Gabrielle, it's in your mind."

"I was afraid of that. It was bound to happen, everything that's gone wrong since Thessalonika—no, it's that seasickness goo, whatever Ares did to it, I've finally flipped out. Terrific."

"Gabrielle, you haven't flipped out. The voice is in your mind. I can hear it, too." The two women gazed up at the sea serpent; their gaze slid as one down to Joxer, who lay motionless on the deck. They turned to look at each other; back at Joxer.

"Okay. I can deal with that," the younger woman said

189

finally. "But tell me I didn't actually hear it say—"

"Yeah, I know what it said," Xena murmured. She tilted her head sideways and eyed the swaying creature thoughtfully. "No one ever said they had good taste—"

"Let's not," Gabrielle broke in firmly, "talk about taste just now, if you don't mind!"

Xena grinned. "Not that kind of taste, Gabrielle."

"All the same—" Gabrielle caught her breath in a squeak as the sea serpent rumbled. It sounded ominous, or impatient. Either one couldn't be a good thing. She tightened her grip on the staff. *Yeah, this is gonna do a lot of good once that thing decides to attack.* Best she could hope for was to distract it while Xena went for the kill. . . .

"Not kill. Cute!" The words rang through her as if in response to her thought. She swallowed hard.

"Ah—Xena? They can't read my mind, can they?"

The warrior shrugged. "Don't think so—but I don't know. You can't tell everything *it's* thinking, though, can you?"

"How should I know? All I've heard so far is, 'cute.' And 'not kill.' Ah—you don't suppose that means what I hope it means?" She glanced at Xena, who considered this, then shrugged again.

"Kill?" Joxer gulped audibly and began slowly scrabbling backwards. He stopped as the massive head came around to block his progress. "Sorry, that was *not* kill, didn't mean to upset you or anything. Especially if you mean 'not kill' the way I hope you mean it? N-nice beastie, ahhh—n-nice beastie?" Silence. "Ah—if you don't mind, I'd like to get up, now," he babbled. But as he tried to ease up onto one knee, the serpent batted at him with one of its dangling barbels, and light as the touch seemed to be, Joxer went sprawling. Gabrielle reached for him; Xena caught hold of her elbow, and when the younger woman's gaze slid sideways to meet hers, the warrior shook her head and mouthed, "Wait. I think it's okay."

Gabrielle gave her a dubious look. "You *think* it's okay?"

"Look at it," the warrior murmured. "I think it's playing."

"Playing," the younger woman echoed. "Ah—you know, Xena, there's playing and *playing*, and right now that thing looks a lot like a barn cat going after a—"

"*Not* like that," Xena growled hastily. The creature gave Gabrielle what she would have sworn was a narrow—and unfriendly—look.

"Not kill!" it reiterated.

"Not kill, great!" Joxer rolled off his face and propped himself up on his elbows. "You know, I could learn to live with a philosophy like that." The serpent hovered so close he could probably have patted its massive snout if he'd wanted to.

Gabrielle's nose wrinkled as it blew a gust of fish-tainted breath all over the deck.

Joxer fell back flat and clapped both hands over his face. Enormous eyes stared up into narrowed ones that were nearly the size of his head. "Ahh—you know, you could really stand to chew some mint, or something," he said earnestly. "Not that I have anything against your diet or your hygiene or anything, but you'd probably have a lot more friends if you did something about the—well, that. You know?"

The smile—if it was a smile, Gabrielle amended her thought hastily—deepened, and two long, pointy fangs edged past blue-gray skin.

Joxer promptly rolled into a ball and squeaked, "Don't eat me! I wouldn't taste good, I'm stringy and tough and, besides that, I haven't even bathed in days, and—"

"No eat!"

Gabrielle let the staff fall and clutched her ears with both hands. Not that it helped; the sound seemed to ring through her head.

"Cute! Awwwwwwww," it repeated, even more loudly.

"Joxer," Xena drawled. "Relax, it's not gonna eat you." One dark, disbelieving eye peered up at her, eyed the hovering serpent with alarm, then vanished as the great head came even lower. "It said so, didn't it? And it thinks you're flirting with it."

The serpent turned its head to give the warrior a remote, chill look. *"She."*

The warrior flapped a hand its direction. "Sorry. *She* thinks you're flirting."

Joxer uncurled enough to gape at her. "I—flirt—I mean, it thinks—*she* thinks—?"

Xena nodded gravely.

His jaw dropped and he transferred the disbelieving stare to the sea serpent. "She thinks I'm flirting with her? What—that I have a—a crush on a—on a—?" Words failed him.

Gabrielle bit her lip. So far, the beast had ignored her; as far as she was concerned, that was just fine.

"Why not?" Xena drawled; her eyes were wicked. "We keep hearing about all these women who've got such a thing for you, Joxer. Like Meg?" He cast her a wild-eyed look at mention of the tavern woman who so closely resembled her. "Or all those women in that tavern back up in Bacchia? Bet they're *still* singing 'Joxer the Mighty'." His mouth curved into a self-satisfied smirk that vanished as the sea serpent's shadow fell across him. Xena nudged him with her foot. "Well, come on, Joxer, let's see that famous charm at work. She's fallen for you in a big way, you don't wanna let her down, do you?"

"She's—got a thing for me?" he asked, visibly stunned by the idea.

"I'd say she does. Can't you tell?"

He cautiously uncurled, just enough that he could look up. "I—no?" And, as the creature let out a low growl, "I mean, yes! Of course I can tell, it's written all over your face—I mean it's—! It's just that—I mean, I'm just not used to being—I mean—" He babbled himself out of words.

"Go for it, Joxer," Gabrielle murmured encouragingly. "She thinks you're cute. You don't want to disappoint her, do you?" He gave her a dirty look, glanced at the hovering creature and swallowed, then managed a wavery smile.

"Ahh—you know," he said at last, "it's really—ah—*nice* to have someone think you're cute, even if you're not even remotely alike or anything? And it's flattering; I—boy, am I ever flattered!" He tittered, swallowed hard, and floundered around for something else to say. "I—because, you know, it's not like anyone I've been around *lately* has called me cute. Not that I'm complaining, you understand!" he added quickly as Xena made a low noise in her throat. "People get used to other people being around them all the time, and they just don't bother with the—with the compliments, you probably know all about that? Well, or maybe you don't?" He sent his gaze sideways. "Xena," he muttered out of the corner of his mouth, "I do not seem to be *getting* anywhere here!"

"You're doing fine, keep it up," she replied.

"Yeah, right," he mumbled. "Ah—well, yeah! And—

you know, your eyes are probably really pretty, if you'd open them up instead of—of squinting at me like that?" Gabrielle backed up a pace as the creature's eyes suddenly went very wide indeed. They were blue-gray like the serpent's hide, speckly and bloodshot. Joxer managed a weak grin. "S-see? Really pretty." Another sidelong glance Xena's direction. "Xena," he hissed, "this isn't working!"

"Sure it is, she's all but eating out of your hand, Joxer."

He sighed heavily. "Xena, will you *not* use words like 'eat'?" He swallowed hard and went on. "Anyway, it's really nice of you to come all this far out of your way, just to tell me how cute I am. Because, I bet you've got a lot of stuff you should be getting done that's not getting done and I—ah—and well, stuff that you probably need to do, right?" Silence. The serpent continued to gaze at him, wide-eyed. Joxer swallowed again. "Well! Ah—you know, I just can't begin to tell you that—I mean—this has been—really neat. Nifty. And I'm glad we had this opportunity to meet, and believe me, I've got nothing against large, seagoing snakes or anything, but . . ." He squirmed around, gazed at his hands, muttered under his breath. Finally nodded. "Okay, fine. I just think you should know that—like I say, nothing personal here, but I've never been big on the whole idea of inter-species dating. Heck, I don't even swim so good, you know?"

The sea serpent immediately lowered her head to gaze deeply into his eyes; the corners of its mouth curled up once more, giving it the rather smug look of a camel. *Give or take all those teeth,* Gabrielle reminded herself. She swallowed past a dry throat. Maybe, just maybe—if Joxer didn't blow it—

He gulped audibly, turned aside to catch a breath of unfishy air, and went on. "I mean, it's good to get to know other people—and—and other—well, *things,* but the fact is," he was rallying rapidly, the way he always did when he started talking, "the fact is, this is just not gonna work out. I mean—well, eventually, I'm gonna have to get off this ship, and you don't look like a dry land kinda girl to me—"

"No get off. Stay here. Cute!"

Joxer gaped at the creature, then ran a hand through his hair and tried again. "Ahh—right. Well, sure, I suppose I could stay on this ship, that wouldn't be a problem for me. Long as you like, whatever. But, I gotta ask myself, what's in it for Joxer? Because, sooner or later, some big hunk of a guy serpent comes along. And all of a sudden, there I am with a broken heart, and you're off sharing squid with—" He considered this, finally spread his hands in a broad shrug. "I'm telling you, things like this just hardly ever work out the way you want them to."

"Pure. Sweet."

The inner voice had a different sound to it, this time. *Gods, there's two of them, remember?* Gabrielle tore her gaze from Joxer and his enormous suitor to look over the main deck. Briax was plastered against the mast, trembling so badly she wondered if he was able to keep to his feet at all. The second sea serpent was giving him the same besotted look. When Bellerophon shouted a wordless challenge and stepped between the two, sword raised, the creature used its snout to slap at the arm, sending the blade flying and the young hero scrambling on hands and knees after it. Briax would have moved then, too, but the beast's eyes hadn't left him. And frankly, Gabrielle thought, she doubted if the boy could so much as crawl at that point.

"Pure," Joxer's oversized "friend" agreed.

The inept warrior stiffened at that and began flailing about, trying to sit up. He finally managed it, using one hand to steady himself against the deck as he leveled a finger at the spiky snout. "Now, wait just a second here, you listen to me," he said rapidly. "We need to get something straight here. If you mean what I think you mean by that word, then—" His eyes flicked Gabrielle's direction; he managed a weak smile. "Um—do you think maybe we could go somewhere else, just the two of us, and—talk about this?"

"Joxer," Gabrielle began, "do you think that's a good idea? Because if she's not busting up the ship because she thinks you're a—"

"Gabrielle!" Joxer clapped a hand over his mouth; the name echoed across the deck. "Will you let me deal with this?" he hissed around his fingers. "You—whatever your name is, if you've got one? I don't quite know how to break this to you, but you've picked the wrong guy, because if there's one thing I'm not it's, ah—it's a—" His mouth hung slack as he searched for the right word. Gabrielle fought laughter—not very successfully—and Joxer cast her an injured glance.

"Hey, Joxer, c'mon, it's all right if you haven't—I mean, if you *have*—" She spluttered again as he blushed a deep red and began stammering. The sea serpent flicked its tongue and wrapped it in a strand of his hair. It was making the purrlike noise again; the sound vibrated the deck and made her feet itch.

"Gabrielle, for your—owww!—for your information, I have not only—owww, will you cut that *out*?—I have—" He clutched at his hair and pulled it free, fell back onto one elbow and eyed the serpent warily, then glared at her. "Well," he added loftily, "I *have*." He scowled up at the creature hovering over him. "So—I don't mean to disappoint you or anything like that, but you should probably just—I mean, if that's an important part of a relationship for you, then I guess you should just—just—" He sent his gaze the other direction. Briax had slid down with his back to the mast, eyes fixed on the massive head that hovered just above the deck and near enough his feet he could have shoved at it. Bellerophon had retrieved his sword, but seemed unable to decide what to do next. "See that guy down there?" Joxer indicated the youth with a nod of his head. "The big fancy hero in the shiny armor? Go talk to him, because if there was ever *any*one who had v-virgin written all over him, it's that guy."

The sea serpent turned its head obediently, but turned back at once. *"Too pure,"* it announced flatly.

Gabrielle stared. "Huh?"

"Joxer." Xena sounded as if she were fighting laughter. "I understand what you're trying to say, but I don't think that's what your big girlfriend has in mind. Not that kind of pure."

"Well, obviously she can't mean that," he mumbled; his eyes remained fixed on the serpent. "I mean, let's face it, a relationship between us could only go so far, and—" He made a face, drew a deep breath and expelled it in a gust. "Let's—not go there, okay? But—I guess what you're trying to tell me is, all those women don't mean anything to you, so long as—" He tugged at the strand of hair the serpent had caught hold of, made another face, and shook out his slobber-coated palm, then wiped it down his pants. "So long as I haven't dated another sea serpent?" he finished hopefully. "Um—well, I haven't, so I guess that's all right, and ah—" He ducked as the tongue flicked toward him. "You know, this just is *not* gonna work.

Wouldn't it be all right with you if we were just good friends?" The creature growled; Joxer squeaked and scooted backwards; a moment later, he crashed into the rail.

"Not kill, pure," the serpent insisted. Joxer sighed, but before he could say anything, Xena held up a hand for silence.

"Wait," she said and gazed up at the looming brute. "Are you trying to tell him that he's—ah—pure because he never killed anyone?"

"Pure," the beast agreed.

"And—the same for Briax down there?"

Gabrielle clutched her forehead. "Xena, can we speed this up? Because I am getting *such* a headache!"

The warrior chopped a hand for silence. "I'm doing the best I can, Gabrielle. Okay, I get it," she told the sea serpent. "I think," she mumbled. "But not Bellerophon? He's—never done anything. Hasn't killed anyone, hasn't had any women? So—too pure?" She glanced at Gabrielle. "So you and I wouldn't seem to qualify as pure, even if they'd fall for women."

"Thanks," Gabrielle said dryly. "I think."

"I don't get it," Joxer put in weakly.

"You don't have to," the warrior informed him dryly. "Just be grateful it works that way, or we'd probably all be good and wet by now."

The sea serpent was ignoring both women, and hadn't bothered to respond to the warrior's last question; its head was on a level with the rail now, peering over the wood or up the stairs at Joxer, who seemed to be adjusting to the idea of being courted by something at least ten times his size. Gabrielle stared at him as he grinned and wiggled his fingers; the massive head ducked back out of sight but a moment later came up directly behind him and the forky green tongue flicked lightly across the back of his neck.

"Hey, watch it!" Joxer protested and vigorously scrubbed at wet skin with his sleeve. "You know, if you're gonna flirt with a guy, you should learn what kind of flirting he likes. Now—the peekaboo thing is just fine, that's—it's cute. But the wet smooches are *definitely* not my kinda thing, okay?"

"Okay." The sea serpent batted its eyes at him. *"Cute."*

"And actually," he put in firmly, "that's Joxer. Joxer the Mighty . . ." He gave Gabrielle a sidelong look as the bard groaned feelingly. "Well, you *said* to go for it," he told her resentfully. "So I'm going for it. Or maybe you'd like a nice refreshing swim after all?"

"Joxer," Xena snarled, "I wouldn't push my luck, if I were . . ." She fell abruptly silent as the sea serpent scowled at her and bared its teeth. "Fine," she muttered. "Whatever." She backed away; the serpent turned away from her and let its head drop below the rail again. Xena kept moving until the port rail stopped her; she turned then and shouted, "All right, Poseidon! They're not gonna break up the ship for you, come and get them!"

Silence.

Gabrielle wrinkled her nose and turned her head aside to catch a fresh breath of air. Except, at the moment, there didn't seem to *be* any fresh air left on the aft deck. There wasn't any wind, either, she suddenly realized; the ship was rolling slightly, the sail hung limp and behind her, she could hear the terrified captain panting.

Suddenly both serpents straightened and turned to gaze back behind the ship. A gust of wind bellied the sail briefly and drove the vessel past them, but only for a moment. Silence again, this time broken by a loud gurgling noise. Gabrielle cast a disbelieving look at Xena, whose lips twisted. "Not *my* stomach, Gabrielle," she said dryly.

Joxer's sea serpent looked at Briax's. *"Hungry."* The inner voice sounded vaguely apologetic.

Gabrielle thought that was the second one—not that it mattered. Her own stomach tightened as the creature's gaze moved along the deck and past the ship. It hovered over Briax for a long moment, then simply turned and dove—straight for the ship, Gabrielle thought, but before she could even cry out a warning, the creature had surfaced on the far side of the vessel and was swimming rapidly south.

The other hesitated, then swung its massive head down close to Joxer. *"JoxertheMighty. Cute,"* it announced proudly, then arched its neck back and threw itself out of the water. It landed on its back with a resounding slap, rolled over, and slid beneath the surface as the resulting wave rocked the ship, and moments later was close on the tail of its companion.

Xena remained at the rail, sword still out, as the two vanished. *Waiting for Poseidon to answer her, maybe?* Gabrielle wondered. Or waiting for him to rise like a man-shaped column of water? Or just making sure his pets didn't come back? She leaned her staff against the rail and went over to kneel at the captain's side. "It's okay, you can get up now," she said. "They're gone."

He swallowed hard, opened one eye to look at her, let it close again, then shook his head firmly. "May be gone, but I saw how fast they move, they could be back—" He swallowed. "Never saw such things in all my days," he whispered finally.

"Yeah, I know what you mean. We were lucky."

"Lucky, hah." Predictably, that was Joxer, who'd pulled himself to his feet. He swaggered as Gabrielle glanced at him. "Lucky for all of you that I just happened to be aboard this ship, and lucky for *you* that I was here, that's what, Gabrielle. Because if it hadn't been for my charm and wit—"

"If it hadn't been for your 'purity,' you'd have been a quick snack," she replied sweetly and grinned as he turned a bright red; she turned her attention back to the captain. "Come on, it's okay now, they're gone."

Xena came back across the deck, sheathing her sword. "And we'd better get moving."

The captain eyed her with alarm. "They're not coming back are they?" he whispered.

"No—but remember why you battened down the hatch this morning?" He frowned, perplexed. "Storm sky, remember?" She bent down and hauled him to his feet; Gabrielle wrapped his hands around the wheel when he would have fallen, and gazed past him where Xena pointed. The entire sky north and west was filled with fat black clouds, and what little wind there was had begun to shift from the general direction of Rhodes. "Gabrielle, get down on the main deck and gather up our stuff; it's gonna get real wet here before much longer." The bard nodded and threw herself down the stairs as the captain hauled a metal bar from his belt and began banging on the bell next to the wheel.

The mess door slammed open, but Gabrielle noticed no one came out at first, despite the echoing clangor and the Captain's bellowed orders. Finally, one of the older men crept from the cabin and to the rail, where he stood peering about for some time before he turned to shout, "They're gone!" Sailors swarmed across the deck then, some stringing rope lines, others climbing into the rigging. Two middle-aged men carried rope up the main mast and vanished into the crow's nest, and moments later the two boys who'd been up there came shinnying down. Both were a ghastly white, and one looked as if he'd been ill.

Probably they'd had as close a view of sea serpent as *she*'d had. Gabrielle shaded her eyes and gazed up the mainmast—and up. "No," she told herself, "that would definitely *not* have been the place to be just now." Not at any time, as far as she was concerned. A gust of damp air soared across the deck and filled the sail; the ship began to come around slowly, until it was nearly on the same course as the sea serpents had been.

It took some moments to gather up her things and Xena's, and the rising wind nearly took the shade blanket as she tugged it free. She finally knelt on one corner and rolled it, then stuffed it away, and scooped up both packs. A quick look around for someplace to put them, now . . . one of the boys who'd been in the crow's nest came running over to her. "I can put those in the mess for you, if you want them to stay dry, miss."

"Great," she said, and handed them over. A glance at the aft deck: Joxer was gone—off gathering up his own stuff, she realized. Bellerophon was up in the prow, gazing out to sea. Watching the waves grow, she thought, and shuddered. The water was noticeably rougher than it had been moments earlier, whitecaps at times, and the wind was beginning to whistle through the ropes.

Briax sat where the sea serpent had left him, his back against the mainmast, his eyes huge and fixed on the distance. He was in the way, Gabrielle realized, but seemingly oblivious, even when two sailors began rigging a line from the prow to the mast. She shook her head and went over to get his attention.

13

Gabrielle ducked under a swaying length of rope and knelt next to the mainmast; Briax blinked and transferred his blank gaze from the distant horizon to her face. She flapped a hand in front of his nose. "Briax, are you all right?"

He swallowed; the corners of his mouth twitched. "That depends," he managed finally. "Did—I see what I think I saw?"

She nodded.

"Big, snaky thing, ugly eyes, lots and lots of teeth?"

She nodded again.

"My head aches," he said fretfully. "All that noise, except it wasn't really—noise, I guess," he finished lamely. He sent his gaze sideways. "Are they gone?"

"Gone," Gabrielle assured him firmly. "For good," she added.

"That's nice," he said faintly. "Because I—don't think I like being cooed over by something with that many sharp teeth."

"I understand," she said; she got to her feet and held

out both hands to help him up. "Come on, it's gonna rain."

He gave her a bemused look and staggered back against the mast. "They left because it's gonna rain?"

"They left because it was time to go. Hey, don't worry about it. Everything's fine." She swallowed hard as the ship rolled under her and sank into a trough, then wallowed out.

"Gabrielle?" Briax caught hold of her near arm. "If everything's fine, why do you look so—?"

"Pale?" she suggested as his voice trailed off, but he shook his head.

"Green, actually," he began.

"It's the light," she assured him firmly. "I always look green in the late afternoon when it's about to rain like crazy. Get your things off the deck, they'll let you toss them in the crew's mess. You can probably wait out the— the storm in there." Before he could say anything else, she staggered off toward the aft deck, where Xena was waiting.

The storm broke an hour later. Lightning flared across a black sky and the wind howled, driving the ship south across open sea. Gabrielle hid from driving rain and the roar of thunder in the captain's cabin, her face buried in Xena's shoulder, fists jammed against her ears. Wind shrieked through unseen holes, and the wooden cabin creaked alarmingly as the ship floundered its way through high seas.

"I think I'm gonna die," she mumbled as the wind briefly eased to the point where she could be heard. Xena stroked her hair.

"It's loud, that's all. It's not a very bad storm, just an

intense one," she assured the younger woman. "And it's not one of Poseidon's storms, either; those can be really nasty."

"I know," Gabrielle managed. "We were both on Cecrops's ship, remember?"

"This isn't anything like that. It'll pass pretty soon."

"Yeah, right," Gabrielle mumbled. "I *had* to pack everything up and let that boy take the packs, didn't I?" she added.

"You weren't thinking about the box of wafers right then, Gabrielle. You'll manage all right without them anyway. Take a nice deep breath, and let it out slow and easy."

"Yeah. Right."

"It works, trust me." Xena tugged gently at a narrow strand of hair, then eased it behind Gabrielle's ear. "You can always pinch your earlobe, you know. I won't let you eat anything."

"Great. Except, you *can't* let me eat anything," Gabrielle reminded her sourly. "Because the bread's packed away, too. And I haven't eaten anything since—" She jumped convulsively as blue white light seared across the cabin and thunder battered her half a breath later. "We're not gonna need those stupid serpents to sink the ship, lightning's gonna—"

"No, it's not, Gabrielle. C'mon, deep breath, let it out slow. Nothing's gonna happen, except the storm's gonna move on, and the sea'll go down. I'll get your bread for you as soon as you're ready to let go of me." She tugged another strand of hair. "You're doing a lot better at ships than you think you are, you know. Just thinking about food in a storm like this—"

Gabrielle fixed her with a dark eye. "*You* said it wasn't

that bad," she pointed out. "And I didn't say anything about eating, just that I was—"

"Hungry. I know. That's still an improvement." She smiled. "Trust me."

"Yeah. Right." Gabrielle subsided against her shoulder and drew a deep breath, let it out slowly.

"The sea'll be calm enough tonight, you'll sleep fine. And tomorrow early, we'll be putting in at Carpathos."

"Yeah," Gabrielle muttered darkly. "Dry land again. But we'll leave again tomorrow afternoon, or the morning after, and who knows *what* will be out here the next time? Besides another 'adventure'!" She was silent so long, Xena thought she might have fallen asleep, but just then she stirred again. "Xena, have I mentioned lately that I really, truly *hate* this kind of travel?"

"Gabrielle?"

"Yeah?"

"*No* one likes this part."

"Oh." Gabrielle leaned away from her to study her face. "You aren't making fun of me, are you?" she asked finally.

Xena smiled, shook her head and drew her close again. "Gabrielle, you know me better than that."

The younger woman's hands tightened on her arm. "Yeah," she said quietly. "I know you better than that."

The sky cleared just before sunset, but the wind was still strong—and chill—when night fell. Xena went out for a while and came back with the packs. "The captain says we might as well stay in here tonight, he's going to stay with the helm until daybreak." Gabrielle looked up anxiously. "It's usual," the warrior assured her. "When there's been a storm and it hasn't blown out by sundown, it's the

206

captain's job to make sure things are under control." She fished through her pack and held out a wafer. "Here, eat this, I'll dig out the bread."

"It's in my bag, under the scrolls," Gabrielle mumbled. "Next to the water bottle."

Wind still whistled through warped boards and small holes. Gabrielle draped the shade blanket around her shoulders as she ate; passing a water bottle back and forth with Xena. "Not much left in here," Gabrielle said.

"Finish it, if you're thirsty," Xena told her as she stretched out atop the captain's wide bunk. "The water barrels will be overflowing after all that rain."

Gabrielle pinched off more bread and tucked it in a corner of her mouth. "Everyone else all right?"

"Briax was asleep in a corner of the crew's mess when I went down to get our stuff and Bellerophon looked halfway there. Or maybe just bored. Joxer was—naw. You don't wanna know."

Gabrielle set the water bottle down. "Joxer was—what?" She shook her head and groaned faintly. "Don't tell me, I can guess."

"Five new verses," the warrior said.

"Too bad his new girlfriend didn't carry him off this morning," Gabrielle replied, mock-sweetly.

"Yeah, well, be grateful that 'serpent' doesn't rhyme with much," Xena told her. "Or there'd be a *whole* lot more than just five new verses."

"It doesn't?" Gabrielle considered this, began mumbling to herself and turning down fingers. She laughed suddenly. "You know, I'll bet Bellerophon just *loves* that! He gets ignored by two of Poseidon's pets—passed over for Briax and Joxer, yet!—and then Joxer takes over entertaining the crew—" She considered this, chuckled wickedly. "You know, he probably wouldn't be so bad if he didn't spend half his time giving me those superior looks—"

"—and the other half giving me the same looks when my back's turned. I know, Gabrielle. It's too bad about his education."

Gabrielle sighed faintly and drained the water bottle. "Yeah, I know he's not responsible for how he was raised, or what he learned to think about women. And maybe while he's out in the real world, he'll learn not to be so— arrogant."

"Maybe." Xena's voice was fading; Gabrielle recorked the water bottle and stuffed it into her pack, then eased over to lay down next to her friend. "But if he's got it fixed in his mind that heroes are like that, and that's what he wants to be, he may never change."

"Great," Gabrielle mumbled. "So long as I don't have to deal with it, once we're done with this stupid ship." She shifted her shoulders; the captain's bunk was lumpy and something was poking her. "Speaking of this stupid ship, how far is it going beyond—?"

"Gabrielle?"

"Yeah?"

"Go to sleep." The warrior's voice faded at the last word and her breathing slowed. Gabrielle eased up onto one elbow, partly to free whatever was sticking into her shoulder, partly so she could smile down at her close companion. Xena shifted slightly at the movement, then rolled onto her side, slid a hand under her face, and was still again.

Go to sleep. Something about the way Xena said it— growled it, most often—invariably warmed her. And left her feeling suddenly relaxed, ready to drift off. Even this night, with wind still shrilling through tiny cracks and the ship lurching through whitecapped water. *She's right, Gabrielle,* she told herself as she found a comfortable place for her head and shoulders. *Go to sleep.*

The last of the storm passed some time before dawn; by the time Gabrielle woke, the cabin was overly warm and muggy, and smelled like the indifferently-washed man who normally occupied it. She wrinkled her nose and clambered out of the bunk.

Xena was long gone, of course; she'd probably been up since first light. Gabrielle emerged onto the aft deck, both hands shielding her eyes in case the sun was full on the deck; the deck, wheel, and most of the rail were still shaded though, and the mast laid a long, skinny line of shadow straight up the main deck and onto the water beyond.

Gabrielle yawned and stretched, tugged her skirt straight, and ran a hand through her hair, freeing bits of straw and a few fluffs from the captain's ancient bedcover. The air was very still at the moment, and it was nearly as warm outside as it had been in.

To her surprise, the aft deck was completely deserted, though someone had tied the wheel off to keep the ship on a straight course. Not that there seemed to be a problem with that; as far as she could tell, the ship wasn't going much of anywhere at the moment. It rocked gently from side to side, and the mainsail hung limp.

Gabrielle frowned and held her breath as she listened intently. At the moment, it looked as if there was no one else on the ship—not a good thought, she hastily told herself. Not true, in any case. As she stepped farther onto the high deck, she could hear low, worried-sounding voices. She approached the rail and leaned out. The captain was down there, surrounded by what looked like most of the crew. Bellerophon and Briax were nowhere in sight, nor was Joxer, but Xena leaned against the bulkhead, next to the open doorway to the crew's mess.

"That's it, then." The captain raised his voice; what little mumbling there had been fell to nothing. "We've two smashed barrels that might hold half their normal water, with a little work and some pitch. There's the empty down in the hold. And there's a half-full barrel down with Cook. That's plenty, if we make Carpathos or another port by nightfall."

"And if we don't?" someone called out. "We made a fair passage of it last night, Capt'n, and beg pardon, but none of us have much notion where we might be, just now."

"Besides becalmed, that is," another put in.

Gabrielle licked her lips. The ship was still rocking side to side as small waves passed under it, but making no forward progress. And when she turned slowly in place to look all around the ship, she couldn't see anything that might be land, anywhere near. The faint purply line to the west—surely that was land, but mainland or more islands? *These guys should know which it is,* she told herself. They worked at this; they couldn't afford to get lost.

"So, what now?" yet another man demanded.

"We take stock," the captain told him. "You know that. No moves decided on until we have the best possible idea where we are. Wind should gather a little strength by mid-morning, but if it doesn't, we'll have to use oars."

"With half a barrel of water left? In this heat?"

"We'll manage," the captain said shortly. He clapped his hands once, ringingly, and Gabrielle jumped. "All of you! You have tasks, get to them!" There was some grumbling, but several of the men moved out to untangle rope safety lines from the night before, two others began working on the hatch cover, and the boys who'd come down from the crow's nest the previous afternoon swarmed back up into it; other men followed them partway up, to pull in a large portion of the sail.

Gabrielle retreated out of the way as heavy footsteps came up the aft stairs, and the captain strode onto the small deck, two men with him. One went to the wheel and released the tie-off, then settled down next to it; the other lay a worn-looking chart on the deck, and he and the captain squatted down to pore over it.

Xena came quietly up the stairs some moments later; she vanished into the captain's cabin briefly and returned with their packs, dropped them next to Gabrielle, and settled her shoulders against rough wood.

Gabrielle eased onto her feet. "How bad is it?" she whispered. Xena shrugged.

"It's not unusual for the weather to be like this after a rough night. It'll pass. What makes it bad is losing two full water barrels last night." She shrugged. "They've still got half a barrel, so nobody's gonna get too thirsty. And if we're still east of Crete and south of Carpathos, there's places to put in to fill what barrels they still have."

"We—don't know where we are?" Gabrielle managed.

"Not exactly." Xena gazed out across the bow, toward the distant line of purple.

The captain cleared his throat. "Ah—Xena? I—seem to remember you used to—ah—sail these waters. If—"

"I don't know where we are, either," she put in as he hesitated. "But I'll do what I can to help." She took a long look around, then bent over the chart. Gabrielle watched them for some time, then settled her shoulders against weather-worn wood. It looked to be a *very* long day.

To her surprise, the breeze did pick up within the hour— about the time she was beginning to worry in earnest. It wasn't much, just enough to keep the ship moving as fast as the oars would. Better yet, once they actually began to move, she could make out distant islands once more. Most of them seemed to be too small for people, let alone any fresh water. One or two of the more distant ones seemed vaguely familiar, until she remembered they all tended to look alike: high spiky peaks rising at sharp angles straight out of the sea, an occasional ledge overhanging deep water or jagged rock.

At some point not long after, Joxer wandered out onto the open deck. He teetered in place for some moments, then clutched his head and staggered toward the rail, where he flopped down in shade and stayed put. She bit back a grin. *One too many verses of Joxer the Mighty celebrated with one too many cups of sour wine.* Maybe some day, he'd figure that one out.

Briax came into the open shortly after, shielding his eyes against the glare to look all around. When his eyes caught sight of her, he smiled and waved, then vanished under the edge of the aft deck. Bellerophon stayed out of sight.

Halfway through the morning, the sun took over the aft deck. Gabrielle gathered up the two packs and went back down to set up the shade cloth over the piece of deck they'd previously claimed. Xena was still up by the wheel, conferring with the captain, studying the horizon and the chart. Gabrielle felt a little better about the whole thing with her up there, even though Xena was probably every bit as lost as they were. *She'll find a way, though. She always finds a way.*

Midday, the cook came out with a small bucket: one ration of water for everyone. Gabrielle's nose wrinkled as she drank hers down. The barrel had been used to ship something like fish before it had been turned into a water container—or the bucket had. It was fortunately faint. *Too bad we drained ours last night.* That particular bag tasted a little like leather, but she was used to that.

Late afternoon left her feeling damp and limp from the heat, but the wind had been gradually picking up and now there was enough of a breeze to cool her skin. The men had released more sail twice before, and now two of the younger fellows clambered out onto the crossbeam to loose more. A clear call came down from the crow's nest: "Land!"

Gabrielle scrambled to her feet and leaned over the rail, but there wasn't anything to see yet. The sun eased down behind a single, fat, white cloud, out again, and still she couldn't make out anything but water. Lots of it in all directions. She mumbled to herself, licked dry lips and sank back to the deck, under the thin shadow cast by the overhead blanket. *You should write some of this down,* she told herself. *In case you ever need to write about a lost ship, or you ever want to.* At the moment it didn't seem very likely, but, she decided, it would give her something to do while she waited. But when she finally pulled quill, ink, and a blank scroll from her pack, her mind went blank and stayed blank. She finally put things away and got back to her feet.

This time, there was a dark smudge on the horizon—a

little to her left and still well out there. Or so she thought at first. The island was much nearer than she'd initially thought because it was nearly flat. When Xena came down to point that out to her, she shook her head.

"And there's supposed to be water? Fresh water, I mean?"

The warrior shrugged; she looked tired, Gabrielle thought. "There's always a chance of water," she said finally. "If not—well, we should be able to figure out from that just where we are, and they can correct course."

"And—that will get us back on course for Carpathos?" Gabrielle asked. Xena smiled and patted her shoulder.

"And get us back to Carpathos. Gabrielle, it's all right. We got blown a little farther last night than the captain thought, and losing those barrels was bad luck. But if I'm right about where we are, we'll make Carpathos by tomorrow, mid-morning at the latest."

"Oh." She considered this. "And if you're—not right?"

The smile widened. "Well, we're not gonna sail off the side of the world or anything like that, okay? If I'm wrong, then we put in at Crete, or back at Rhodes—or if I'm really wrong, then you get to see the library at Alexandria a lot sooner than you'd planned on."

"Egypt? You really think—?" But Xena was already shaking her head.

"That's if the mate's right about what direction we went last night, and how hard the wind was blowing. I don't think he's even close." Xena settled down against the rail, cross-legged, and patted the deck next to her. "C'mon, relax, it's gonna be a while yet. They've gotta find a good place to either anchor out, or pull the ship onto the beach." She waited until Gabrielle was settled at her side. "Don't suppose you've got any of that cider left, do you?" Gabrielle shook her head. Xena sighed faintly, rubbed her shoulders into a more comfortable place, and closed her eyes.

The island looked like a jungle, Gabrielle decided; low, massively green, shrubs, trees, flowering things all growing in a wild tangle, right down onto the sand. It wasn't that large a place—the ship had circled it in no time at all—but the vegetation was so thick it was impossible to see much beyond the beaches. There did seem to be a few narrow paths leading back into the shade, though. And Xena pointed out the narrow, overhung swale that had been a running stream. What could be seen of it was dry. "That doesn't mean there isn't water if you follow it back in a ways," she said.

"And—what if you get lost in there?" Gabrielle wanted to know.

Xena laughed. "Gabrielle, you can see the size of it; you could walk from one side to the other in no time."

"Yeah. Unless you start walking in circles because you can't see where you're going, or where you've been."

"Well—then you'd better stick close to me."

Gabrielle leaned back to eye her companion warily. "What—you think I'm going in *there*?"

"You want a full water bottle or not?" the warrior asked reasonably.

"Is this a trick question?" Gabrielle retorted. Her eyes strayed to the lush island. "I don't know, though. . . ." Her voice trailed off.

"Gabrielle, c'mon. It's dry, solid land. Don't tell me you prefer the ship?"

"Land." The younger woman sighed faintly. "Dry, solid land. Yeah—I'll take some of that."

A short time later, a boat was brought up out of the hold and lowered over the side. Two barrels were lashed in and half a dozen men rowed the others who were saddled with water gourds, buckets, leather bags, and the like. The boat pulled onto the sand moments later, two men knee-deep in the waves holding it steady while the others freed the barrels and most of them went up onto dry ground. Four men rowed back out and picked up another load of crew, jugs, pots, and one barrel that ended just past the mid-stay. Briax and Bellerophon went with this load, Joxer with the one after. Gabrielle settled midships with the final load, the two water bottles and her cider bottle draped over one shoulder.

She peered forward as the island drew near. The sun was low in the afternoon sky behind the island; this side seemed dark and rather ominous. "Xena? Why can't we see anyone?" she asked. Xena gazed at the vacant strip of sand and shrugged.

"Because they've all moved back where it's shady, filling the barrels probably," she said.

"All of them?" Gabrielle asked. The warrior shrugged again. The boat creaked its way into shallow water, then plowed a furrow up the sand. Gabrielle jumped out and moved up toward the wall of green, barely aware when the boat shoved off.

It was quiet. Unnervingly quiet, she suddenly thought. *There should be birds—insects, even.* Of course, this many people might scare birds and the like into stillness— but at the very least, they should be able to hear men moving through the undergrowth, twigs snapping. People talking to each other. "Xena?"

"Yeah?"

"How come it's so quiet?"

Xena raised an eyebrow. "Because no one's yelling? Gabrielle, how should I know?"

"Fine," the bard said. "But we've been here"—she turned slowly in place—"long enough for that boat to make it back out to the ship. And in all that time, we haven't heard a single thing out of Joxer? No trip, no stumble, no yelp when he falls in a hole or falls facedown in the mud?"

Xena considered this as the men who'd come ashore with them moved up the nearest narrow trail. She tugged at her sword, changed her mind, and unclipped the chakram, then stole quietly along the sand toward the dry waterway.

"You may have a point, Gabrielle," she said quietly. "Stay here, and I'll—"

"Stay here?" Gabrielle echoed as she shook her head. "Not a chance, Xena! You go in there, I'm staying right with you."

"Fine. Then stay close," the warrior ordered. The overhanging branches seemed to reach for her, Gabrielle thought nervously. But Xena didn't seem to have any such concerns; she turned from side to side as she moved stealthily up the shaded waterway, eyes constantly moving. Gabrielle cast up her eyes, got a two-handed grip on her staff, and followed.

14

It was cooler than she would have expected under the matted overhanging branches. Gabrielle kept her eyes fixed on Xena's back and followed her friend off of the sand and onto a bed of rough, tumbled stones. Her ankle turned, and she flailed for balance, caught herself on a thick treetrunk, and leaned against it to catch her breath. When she looked up, there was no one in sight. Including—She opened her mouth to call out, then hesitated, frowning. "I better call her before she gets much farther ahead of me," she told herself. The words seemed to hang in the air. "Call—wait a minute." She scowled at the seemingly solid wall of green, then at her hands. "What's her name?" She considered this as she slowly turned in place. Green everywhere, and the only path was this dry waterway. "Umm, it's—wait a minute, I know it, it's. . . ." Nothing came. She finally shrugged, stepped cautiously onto a flat stone. "Maybe I'd better go back in case she's waiting?" She eyed the course in both directions—nothing to be seen but green, and more green. She considered the options, shook her head in bafflement. "If I came from there—no, if *we* came from there, then that's the way I gotta go to get out of here." Another long pause. "Wherever *here* is."

She tugged at her hair, thought some more. "But if I go *that* way, and it's the wrong way . . ." She shook her head, raised her voice. "Hello? Anyone there? It's me, ahhhhh—" She swore under her breath. "Okay," she demanded of the vining thing that swung low just short of her head. "So, who am *I*?"

No answer. Except—she held her breath and listened. There seemed to be someone talking—that way? She turned away from the stream bed, but as the staff trailed behind her and clonked loudly on the dry bank, she turned back, shaking her head. "Oh, no," she murmured to herself. "That's an old trick, and I'm not falling for it, nosir! They're trying to get me away from this nice clear path, so they can . . ." She clapped the free hand over her mouth, listened some more. Now all she could hear was a faint breeze rustling the leaves far overhead; it was too dense down here for any of the moving air to make it through to where she stood.

"They?" she asked herself finally in a whisper. "All right—there was one somebody else just now. I think," she amended more honestly. "And a bunch of others, and water . . . ?" *A ship,* the thought offered itself. She considered this, shrugged it aside. Maybe a ship. Meantime, she needed to get out of this jungle so she could *see*. "That way," she told herself, and started off, plunging more deeply into the island.

She walked one direction, then another, finally stumbled onto what seemed to be a path beaten down in the grass. This went up a small incline, down a few steep ledges, and eventually came out in a small clearing. Another one—maybe the same one—she was vaguely aware she'd completely lost her sense of direction and was ambling aimlessly, but felt no urge to stop.

There was a different clearing eventually; a clear pool of water that felt cold on her hands and forehead and tasted of nothing at all. Now she could hear other voices—well, one other voice, she decided. *Singing? You could* call *it that, maybe,* she thought judiciously. It didn't sound particularly dangerous, but she kept a tight grip on the staff as she skirted the pool and eased her way under a low-hanging fern.

A man lay on his back, hands tucked behind his head, brown hair standing on end, eyes fixed on the green canopy overhead. He yelped in surprise as a twig cracked under her foot, and he rolled away from her, gasping. "Who're you?" he demanded. "Do I know you?"

She spread her arms in a wide shrug. "I don't think so. Do I look familiar to you?"

His brows drew together as he studied her, but he finally shook his head.

"Is there anyone else here?" she asked. He shrugged and settled down cross-legged.

"Have you *seen* anyone else?"

He shrugged again.

She sighed faintly, walked past him, and plunged into the forest on the other side.

"Hey!" he yelled. "You—whoever you are—wait a minute!" She could hear him scrambling to his feet and thrashing around. She sighed again, but waited for him to catch up. He tripped over a low vine, barely caught himself before he could fall flat, and practically ran her down. Dark brown eyes stared bemusedly into hers. "Are you *sure* you don't know me?" he demanded finally. "I mean, everyone knows me, I'm . . ." He boggled at that point.

"Everyone knows you?" she inquired dryly. "Fine—then what's your name?" He simply stared. She nodded. "Thought as much," she said, and was pleased with the logic of her comments as she strode off. Behind her, she heard a flurry of movement as if he'd tried to follow, a crash and a thump.

"Owwww. I hate it when that happens," a reedy voice complained. Silence. "I *think* I do," it added.

She half turned, puzzled. *Why does that sound familiar?* she wondered.

But at that moment, he began to sing again, a low, bumbling sound. Half or more of the words were missing, and finally he stopped altogether. "Homer the Mighty? Ahhh—wait, *Aphrodite* the Mighty? No, can't be that, it's too long. . . ." The voice trailed off. She shook her head, rolled her eyes, and walked on.

The path hadn't been much more than a game trail to begin with, and now it petered out. Fortunately, Gabrielle thought, so did the woods. She gazed down into a small, rocky bowl, a few tufts of dry grass clinging to the edge, two or three low, thorny bushes near the bottom.

Nothing there. But as she gazed across to the far side and another solid wall of greenery, dark blue eyes met hers. She caught her breath in a gasp and started to cough rackingly. Tears filled her eyes; she went onto one knee and thumped her chest, trying to clear the air passage. She was vaguely aware of the leather-clad woman who stepped briefly from the trees to stare at her, aware of the round weapon she held, ready to throw. The woman uttered a terrifyingly shrill, eldritch screech, turned, and sped back into the trees. Gabrielle whooped for air, backed away from the stony hollow and into shelter of the trees again.

"Who or *what*ever that was," she wheezed, "I don't wanna see it again! I coulda been killed!"

The day was fading, she suddenly realized. Shadows were longer than they had been, and the sky was a very deep blue, what little of it she could see from her current vantage. "I gotta find my way out of here," she told herself. "There was—yeah, I'm *sure* there was sand, and salt water, and a ship. . . ."

People, too. Especially the one person she'd been with—She clutched at her hair with both hands. "Auugh! This is crazy! I all right. It wasn't that weird guy, the one who was trying to sing; Aphrodite, or whatever he called himself And it wasn't—" It simply wasn't any good. The harder she tried to remember a face—or worse yet, a name—the more blank her mind went. "Logic," she told herself finally. "Forget the name stuff, all the rest of it. Find a place where you can see the sky, so the sun's in front of you or at your back, and *keep* it there until you get out of all these trees!" It felt like there was a flaw in her reasoning somewhere, but she wasn't going to try to find it just now.

Somehow, she found herself back at the edge of the trees and the rock bowl. It took time for her to convince herself that the odd and dangerous woman was gone, that she was alone here, that it was all right to move out into the open. She drew a deep breath and took two steps forward.

"Okay," she told herself quietly. "The sun's—over there. So that must be—west?" It sounded right. It didn't matter, so long as she kept moving in the same direction. Now—which way to go. If she returned the way she'd come, the sun would be at her back. "I can't remember any real obstacle between here and—well, wherever *there* is," she murmured aloud.

One last look around, she decided. Just to make sure there wasn't a real path anywhere on this side of the bowl at least. *Remember which way that madwoman went,* she reminded herself as she slowly turned in place.

She yelped in surprise as her eyes crossed the bottom of the stony dell. A tall, black-haired man stood there, watching her, and she was ready to swear there hadn't been anyone around a moment before. She clutched at her throat and stumbled back a pace, fetching up against a tree trunk hard enough to set her ears ringing. "Who are you, and how'd you get down there?" she demanded. He smiled lazily and started up the slope. She brought the stick up, a last possible barrier between them. "Don't you—you stay away from me!" she yelled.

"Don't you remember me?" he asked softly; his voice was deep and resonant, and should have been soothing. For some reason, it made her even more wary, but before she could move, he was between her and the bowl, one hand casually holding her shoulder, pressing her back into the tree.

"Why?" she panted. "Should I?"

He chuckled. "What—I'm not memorable looking?"

He was definitely *that,* she decided as she eyed dark, deep-set eyes, neat beard, and a moustache surrounding a wry-looking mouth. An incredibly well-muscled body was barely concealed under a black, leather, sleeveless shirt. "Maybe," she said finally. "So, if you know me, how about helping me get *out* of here?"

Silence. He studied her face for a long moment. "You

"know," he said finally, "you're never gonna believe this, but that's why I'm here."

"I'm not?" She eyed him warily. "Why wouldn't I? I mean, we *do* know each other, right?"

"We know each other, right," he agreed. His free hand toyed with her hair. "Been through a lot together," he added softly and leaned toward her. She ducked just as his lips would have touched hers, and only an agile twist kept him from falling face first into the tree. "Hey, you had your chance," he murmured, and snapped his fingers as he stepped back from her.

A deluge of seawater slammed down onto her, soaking her clothes, plastering the hair to her face, and sloshing into her boots. Gabrielle gasped, choked, and scrubbed water out of her eyes, spat saltwater, and sneezed violently. When she looked up again, her eyes were very aware, and narrowed in anger. "Ares!" she snarled as she spun the fighting staff. "This time you've got a good one coming, and *this* time, I don't have Xena here to tell me not to—"

"Back off," he snarled back. "You remember who you are now, right?"

"I'm Gabrielle, what's the point?" she demanded, and suddenly leaped at him. He sighed heavily and shoved her back into the tree.

"Shut up and listen a minute, will you? You're on Lethe."

"Shut up? Why should I—? Wait a minute." She gazed around warily, then looked at him, a faint line between her brows. "Lethe? *That* Lethe? The forget-everything place?"

He smiled faintly.

"I thought it was a river—"

"It's an island," Ares broke in. "Look, can you save all that for later? You want to get off this island before it gets dark, all right?"

"Why?"

"Because if you don't, you stay here. For good," he added. "That's like, forever, if you catch my drift."

"Got it," she said, but the frown remained.

"What?"

"I'm just curious," she said warily. "I mean, what's in it for you? Rescuing me?"

"Oh, it's not just you," he said. "Xena's been a good ally in the past, and she's one of the few decent adversaries I've got. It would be a waste of good talent to let her rot on Lethe. You with me on that?"

She nodded.

"Good. Now—the reason you got wet is, the only way to keep your head once you're off the sand is to have seawater on your feet. So, if it's in your boots, you're okay, that making any sense to you?"

She considered this briefly, nodded again.

"Good. Now, what you're gonna have to do is get back to the water, make sure your feet stay wet, find Xena—"

"You're kidding?" Gabrielle broke in. "I mean—Xena, sure. But you know how many of the crew of that ship came ashore? I'll never find all of them before it gets dark!"

"Yeah, you will," the god of war said flatly. "You got no choice, okay?" But he spoke to her back; Gabrielle was already running toward the shore, her boots squelching wildly. Ares watched her go and shook his head. "Xena," he murmured, "you are gonna owe me big time for this one." He vanished in a blare of light.

• • •

It was exhausting, but not as bad as she'd feared, Gabrielle realized. Because she found Joxer and half a dozen of the sailors on her way back down the dry streambed and persuaded them to follow her. *Remembering a couple of verses to that stupid song sure helped me there,* she thought. Coupled with her promise to let Joxer know what the name was he so urgently sought so he could properly bellow out the words. By now, the crewmen he'd been regaling with his half-recalled adventures were almost as curious as he was. And once she'd led them far enough out into the breakers to get thoroughly wet from the waist down, it was fairly easy to explain what they needed to do, and why it was so urgent.

One woman searching the island at this late hour of the day would've been a sad joke. One woman joined by a dozen sailors, who in turn restored others of their kind. . . .

The sun was hovering near the horizon when a third boat-load of men rowed back to the ship. Bellerophon had been easy to find, but Briax had been hiding under some low bushes and she'd nearly missed him. Several of the sailors—including the captain—had run deeper into the woods when she and Joxer had gone after them, but they'd been near the narrow end of the island at the time, and they'd run straight across a pebbly beach and into the sea.

Another boatload, and another. The water barrels had been filled and were being hauled aboard. "And still no sign of Xena," Gabrielle murmured to herself.

Xena—she recalled the wary look on the warrior's face when they'd almost run into each other in that stone bowl. Xena didn't know who she was, but she had enough memories to work with that she'd been hiding, stalking those trying to find her and get her safely off the island. Gabrielle tugged at her hair, suddenly wild with frustration. "I'll lose her if I can't get her out of there!" She tipped back her head and shouted, "Ares! You owe me this one!"

Joxer tapped her arm. "Gabrielle, are you *sure* you're okay? I mean, it's not like you to call on Ares—is it?" he added in a worried voice. He backed into the waves to get his feet wet again, scooped up a leather bag of saltwater, and ran dripping hands through his hair. "I hope you realize it's gonna take me forever to get all this salt out of my boots," he added with a grimace of distaste as he shook water down around his feet.

"I know." She sighed faintly. "We've got everyone but Xena, haven't we?" she added.

He nodded.

"And—the sun's down," she said bleakly. "Another hour at best, and . . ."

"Gabrielle, how do you know he isn't lying to you?" Joxer urged quietly. "I mean, wouldn't he do that just to give you grief? Sure he would," he answered himself before she could. "If you can't find her right away here— well, I'll go back to the ship, get some torches, we can keep looking—"

"Go on back to the ship, Joxer," Gabrielle broke in wearily. "It's okay, you go ahead when the boat comes out. Send them back for me when it gets dark, will you?"

"You're sure?" he asked; she nodded. "Because I can—"

"I'm fine, Joxer. Go on. I'll—yeah, I'll manage." He cast her an unhappy glance, but when she started back toward the dry streambed, he made no move to follow her.

• • •

She detoured out into the water one last time, squelched ashore with the dripping water bag dangling from one hand, and started inland once again. It was extremely gloomy away from the water, and what breeze there had been had died away. Gabrielle took two steps forward, feeling her way with her feet, then paused to hold her breath and listen.

There could—just maybe—have been a faint noise ahead. Somewhere between her and the stream, *maybe*, she thought. She almost called out Xena's name, but kept quiet. The woman wouldn't recognize the name or Gabrielle's voice; most likely she'd run away, but if she didn't, it would be because she was stalking. . . .

"Don't think that," Gabrielle told herself in a faint whisper. As close and dark as these woods were getting, she could scare herself half silly with such a thought.

It was utterly silent as she stepped away from the loose stones of the streambed and onto the narrow path the sailors had tromped down through the grasses, bringing out water. The woods opened out all at once, and she could hear the faint bubble of water over rocks. It was nearly dark, even here, but she could just make out the huddled shape sitting next to the water. Xena, she realized, and swallowed a lump.

The warrior was aware of her at the same moment; she half turned, coming onto one knee, chakram in her hand. Gabrielle dropped the water bottle and held out both hands. "It's all right," she said quietly, soothingly. "Xena, it's me. Gabrielle. I won't hurt you, I'd never hurt you."

"I—do I know you?" Xena's voice was husky—she sounded *afraid*, Gabrielle realized with a pang.

"You know me, Xena," she said. "It's all right. Everything's going to be all right, but we have to get you out of these woods right away. This—this isn't a good place for you, Xena. It's not safe."

"Safe. . . ." The warrior rose awkwardly to her feet and turned in place, her eyes wide and wild-looking as she gazed into the woods and high overhead. "There are things out there," she whispered. "Ugly, nasty things." Her lip quivered. "I was afraid."

"I know." Gabrielle held out both arms, and as Xena hesitated, she took a small step forward. "It's all right. I'll keep you safe." A thought occurred to her. "I have something here, magic, it'll protect you."

"Magic." The dark blue eyes went wide. "Are you a witch?"

"No, not a witch. I'm a friend, Xena. Your friend. And you can trust me, I swear it."

Xena hesitated again, then took one step toward her. Gabrielle held her ground, resisted the urge to run forward, catch the woman close, knowing Xena would likely turn and sprint into the woods and be lost to her forever. It was getting hard to make out her face. *Getting dark,* she thought, and her heart sank. But Xena took another step, wavered, and reached for her; eyes brimming with tears, the warrior staggered forward and fell into Gabrielle's arms.

"It's all right, you're safe now, everything's all right," the younger woman soothed. "But we need to get out of here, before it gets completely dark."

"It's dark, it's already so dark," Xena sobbed. "Get me out of here, please?" she whispered, her hands clinging painfully. Gabrielle eased the grip on her shoulders the least bit, caught up the bottle of seawater and turned to lead the way back to the shore.

230

A glance overhead assured her it wasn't full dark yet. *Get her out to the sand and walk her into the water,* she decided. If she tried to pour the jug of water into Xena's boots, snugly as they fit around the warrior's knees—if she missed, she might never get another chance.

To her surprise, Joxer sat waiting for her, two torches dug into the sand behind him and a small, lit, oil lamp at his feet. Xena started and would have pulled back, but Gabrielle had an arm around her waist, and the fingers of her other hand twined in the warrior's belt. "It's ok, he's a friend," she said soothingly. "Come on, just a few more steps."

Xena eyed Joxer warily but edged past him, only to hesitate at water's edge. "I don't wanna get wet," she murmured fretfully.

"Sure you do," Gabrielle replied. "It's part of the magic, didn't I tell you?"

The warrior gave her a confused look. "I don't understand, how does getting wet have anything to do with magic?"

Gabrielle stepped into the low waves and tugged, hard. "Trust me," she said firmly. "In a moment, I promise, it'll all make sense to you."

The sickle moon was just rising behind the ship when the captain gave orders to cast off. Gabrielle leaned back against the rail, her head on Xena's shoulder as the vessel creaked and rocked and finally began to move north, a cool evening breeze puffing into the sails. "I don't think I will move for the next three days," she murmured. "My feet hurt."

Xena wrapped an arm around her shoulders. "I don't doubt it." She stared off across the open deck. "That

231

was—the strangest thing. I remember walking into the woods ahead of you and then—nothing. Except eyes, everywhere. Following me. Like I was being stalked by a bear or something." She considered this. "I haven't been scared like that since I was a little kid, and one of my brothers pretended he was a bear, followed me through the trees, growling . . ." She laughed quietly. Gabrielle's head slipped against her arm to fall heavily against her shoulder. "Gabrielle?" the warrior murmured.

Silence.

She smiled down at the exhausted young woman, leaned back against the rail and let her own eyes close.

15

The voyage back to Carpathos took two days, but fortu
nately was otherwise uneventful. Gabrielle slept most of
the time, and Xena stayed close by, ready to offer bread,
a drink of cool water, a damp cloth for her forehead. The
younger woman was so exhausted, she didn't even seem
to notice she hadn't had her dose of goo since before the
storm that had driven them nearly to Lethe.

At one point, Gabrielle smiled up at her and shook her
head. Xena spread her arms in a wide shrug. "What?" she
asked.

"You're spoiling me," Gabrielle accused.

"Well, maybe you've earned it," Xena replied softly.

Gabrielle shook her head. "I didn't do anything special.
Nothing you wouldn't have done for me."

"Maybe. But I didn't go looking for a heavily armed
crazy woman in deep woods like you did." She hesitated.
"I could've hurt you, Gabrielle. Killed you, even, and I'd
never have known it."

"Well, I didn't feel like I was in any danger," Gabrielle
began, but Xena laid a hand across her mouth.

"Don't," she said quietly. "I know better." She shifted and scooped up the loaf of dark bread, now so hard she needed to saw at it with one of her daggers. "You want any of this?"

"Pass," Gabrielle said. "If that's the best we've got around here, I think I'll go back to sleep."

"It's better than ship's biscuit," Xena said around a dry mouthful of bread.

"Pass on those, too." Gabrielle yawned and settled back down on her side.

Xena adjusted the overhead blanket so she'd be in shade, finished the crackerlike bit of bread, and wrapped the remainder of the loaf. With luck, she thought, they'd reach Carpathos late in the afternoon.

It was nearer sunset than not when the *Yeloweh* maneuvered up next to the stone pilings mid-harbor—there were no berths in the small bay at this hour, and the ship would probably not be able to unload any cargo until midday. The boat was hauled out of the hold and dropped down into the harbor. Xena and Gabrielle sat near the bow, Joxer just behind them, and Briax at the far end of the same bench. Bellerophon hadn't decided whether he wanted to come ashore yet. Sulking, Gabrielle privately thought, but she didn't say as much. Briax openly admired the fellow and would be uncomfortable hearing such remarks.

All the same, the young Corinthian had barely managed to be civil to her when he'd found out what had happened on Lethe—*as if it was my fault Ares picked me to find everyone, instead of him,* she thought sourly. Frankly, the way her feet still felt, she'd much rather have given him finding rights and left her to find Xena before it had gotten so frighteningly close to the deadline.

Xena touched Gabrielle's shoulder to get her attention; they'd come bumping up against the pier, and she hadn't even noticed. Gabrielle got to her feet, staggered as the boat lurched and caught at the pier, two-handed. Xena stepped ashore and tugged her onto solid ground, then caught Joxer, who stubbed his toe on a warped board. He staggered off, grumbling under his breath. Gabrielle got her balance and stepped back out of the way as one of the crew tied the boat off and held it against the pier while it emptied out. "You all right?" the warrior asked.

"Fine," Gabrielle said. She drew a deep breath and let it out on a happy sigh. "Something smells *really* good," she said. "I just hope that whatever it is, there's a *lot* of it."

Xena tugged at her hair. "Well? Let's go find out, shall we?"

Briax seemed suddenly shy around her—something to do with being found by her, hiding under a bush, she was afraid. He followed Joxer into the tavern portion of the waterfront inn as the two women settled onto a bench near the kitchen, and a boy came hurrying over with cups and a pitcher.

What she'd smelled was stew. Rich, dark broth brimming with chunks of meat and vegetables—very plain, barely spiced, incredibly filling; particularly since it came with a heavy loaf of seed bread. Gabrielle finally pushed aside the empty bowl and settled her elbows on the smoothed wooden table, watching absently as Xena swiped the last drops of gravy from her bowl with a final wedge of bread. The warrior drained her mug of ale and set the cup down with a thump.

"Gonna live now?" she asked.

Gabrielle sighed happily and nodded.

"You get enough of that?"

Gabrielle propped her chin up on one arm and blinked. "Why—is there more?" Xena's eyes widened in mock alarm; Gabrielle laughed. "I'm fine." She glanced toward the open doorway, where the last rays of the setting sun lay across the harbor. "What now?"

"Fresh supplies, at least for tomorrow morning," Xena replied. "And maybe a look over the market."

"I don't know," Gabrielle said. Her eyes strayed toward the next room, where sailors and local men were drinking and shouting over one another's voices. So far, she hadn't heard anything out of Joxer, though she'd caught a glimpse of him now and again. "I mean, we grab Joxer, and Briax will—" She shrugged. "I suppose it doesn't matter, except if Briax learns we're interested in pottery, then Bellerophon will find out, and . . ."

"Even if he learns that much, it won't do him any good because he won't know why." Xena tipped her cup back, remembered she'd already emptied it, and shoved it aside. "But I don't see why we need to haul Joxer along with us. There's nowhere he can go tonight, and I don't think he's gonna try anyway."

"I—" Gabrielle considered this, finally shrugged again. "Yeah. Even if he wanted to get away from us, there won't be any ships going out of here tonight. But I don't think the idea of going off on his own has even occured to him lately." She glanced toward the other room. Briax was walking toward the bar; no sign of Joxer. She cast her close companion a grim little smile. "He'd better not start thinking about it, either," she said. "Because if I have to chase him down again, after everything else that's hap-pened lately—" She got to her feet. "You hold him, I thump, right?"

"I hold him, you thump," Xena replied gravely.

• • •

The market was one of the smallest Gabrielle had seen so far. A handful of meager stalls and blankets in the town square were grouped around the central fountain and pool. There was no logic to any of it. The baker sold bread and a few dull-looking chipped daggers, a woman who kept a pair of fat milking goats in a pen sold kerchiefs and used boots, while the cloth merchant had a rack of dried, seasoned, meat strips hanging between the roped lengths of dyed yarn and fabric. At first there seemed to be no one selling pottery, new *or* used, but Xena talked to several people and finally ran down a rickety bench behind the goat pen, where a frail old woman had piled everything from cracked, clay cups to a massive glazed tray that was one of the ugliest pieces she'd ever seen. Gabrielle smiled pleasantly, letting the old woman size her up, before she began picking up individual pieces and asking about them. Gabrielle cheerfully answered the usual questions—including, "why isn't a nice young woman like you married?"—and traded a couple of harrowing stories about life on the road for the old woman's shaky memory of a ship's journey from Naxos to Athens, back when she was younger and ship travel (according to her) much more perilous.

Gabrielle listened closely, laughed at the right moments, applauded the old woman's courage, and finally brought out the little clay figure. "I was hoping you might have something like this," she said. The woman's fingers trembled as she took the little piece, and Gabrielle held her breath until the figure was safely back in her own hands. "Because I only have the one, but I'd like . . ."

"Nothing like it," the old woman said firmly. "Never saw anything like that." Watery old eyes blinked and her gaze slid away from Gabrielle's. "Never at all," she said, and forced her lips tightly together.

Gabrielle glanced at Xena, who minutely shook her head. "I—see. All right." She shoved the clay figure carefully away; the old woman seemed relieved with it out of sight. "Maybe—you wouldn't mind if I took another look at what you *do* have?" She glanced beyond the woman's shoulder as Xena beckoned with her eyes. "Ah—excuse me a minute, I think my friend needs to borrow some dinars or something." The old woman watched her closely, but as Xena led Gabrielle over to the baker's stall and knelt to pick up one of the daggers, she seemed to lose interest, and got up to rearrange some of her cheaper looking pieces.

Xena's lips twisted as she gazed at the warped blade. "Keep your eyes on it, like it matters," she said softly.

"Got it," Gabrielle replied, as quietly. "What's wrong with her?"

"She recognized that piece, I'm sure of it."

"Yeah, that's what I thought."

"Either that, or she knows who made it, and maybe even where she is. And she knows it's important that no one find out from her."

"You think so?" Gabrielle glanced up as the baker came over, a broad smile on his face. "Ah—we're just looking, all right?" He nodded and stepped back. "Well—that makes sense, I guess. Do you—do you mean she might be *here*?"

"Maybe, Gabrielle. But I doubt it. Carpathos is a little off the regular shipping routes, but not that far. And it's small enough that she'd stand out, even if she was careful."

Gabrielle looked around the little market and finally

238

nodded. "Yeah, you're right. A stranger would stand out in a place this size, and it's all so close to the harbor—unless there's another town?"

"Just the one. And the only land good enough for farming or herding goats is right around the town."

"Okay." Gabrielle gazed down at the dagger, took it from Xena and dropped it back on the blanket. "I can't believe someone would actually buy something like that," she said.

Xena's mouth quirked. "Wanna bet *he'd* been even more surprised than you, if someone did?" She got to her feet.

Gabrielle shrugged, cast the merchant an apologetic smile and let Xena haul her up. "So—now what?" she asked.

"Two choices," Xena said finally. "We can try to talk to her now—or we can wait until she closes up shop for the night, and find out where she lives."

"You think she might tell us something if we follow her home?" Gabrielle asked.

The warrior raised a shoulder. "I think our chances of persuading her to listen are better than they are out here in the open market," Xena said. "It's worth a try, don't you think?"

Fortunately, they didn't have long to wait. As torches began to flutter along the harbor, the woman with the goats dropped a thick cloth over the pile of boots, pulled the gate aside, and flapped her apron at the goats, who obediently pranced up the street ahead of her. The baker followed some moments later, a heavy basket of loaves and rolls strapped across his shoulders. When the old woman drew a corner of the trailing scarf over her wares and fastened it down with a lumpy little statue that reminded Gabrielle of Salmoneous, the two women held back long enough to make certain the woman wasn't aware of them and that no one else in the market paid them any attention.

The woman moved slowly, with the tottery caution of those who didn't dare chance a fall, and she stopped frequently to catch her breath. In the encroaching gloom, they would have lost her, but Xena's keen ears picked up the sound of harsh breathing, and her eyes picked out the narrow doorway between two low, stone houses.

The doorway led into an alley that emerged behind the houses. Half a dozen small huts clustered against a dusty wall; most of them looked uninhabited. Xena held up a hand, indicating Gabrielle should wait where she was, then stole softly up to the farthest of the little hovels. Nose wrinkling, she shook her head and moved on. At the next to last of them she froze for a long moment, then nodded and vanished inside. Gabrielle moved, stopped short of the cloth-covered doorway. It smelled like goats, she thought, and felt sudden pity for an old woman who hadn't any place better to live than this. Xena's low voice reached her.

"Gabrielle? She says it's all right; come on in."

The old woman was a frail huddle in the faint light cast by a tiny oil lamp that smelled fishy. *Cheap oil,* Gabrielle knew. All she could afford, and probably she considered herself lucky to have that much.

"I had a feeling, you know," the woman said abruptly. "When you asked me, earlier. About her little figure. I knew somehow, knew you'd come here, that you'd find me."

"I'm sorry," Xena said softly.

"We wouldn't have bothered you if it weren't so important," Gabrielle added.

"Important—yes." The woman nodded emphatically. "She knew she could trust old Arana right from the first. I was—no one important, you know. A servant—not one of *hers,* of course, they took young ladies for that, and I was—a herder's daughter. A woman who'd had a man, and children, not good for much but building fires, and sweeping out the ashes after. But—but when she went to Sparta as—as queen—I was one of those who went with her." The woman smiled faintly, her eyes fixed on the door curtain. "I remember when she first noticed me, it was..." She sighed. "Well, that's not important. She knew, though; knew I understood what kind of a man her husband was. Knew how—what a tyrant he was to her." She glanced up at Xena. "You'll probably not believe it, but I knew because mine was the same, right until the day he died. Cold-blooded brute, with never a kind word for me."

"I believe you," Xena said quietly.

"When she—went from Sparta, *he* kept the household servants, but the rest of us were dismissed. I was too old to earn my keep, even if the laws had let me. Probably I'd have starved, but my eldest daughter learned where I was and how bad off. She'd just married a fisherman, down in Phalamys, and he let her bring me in; kind man, he was." She sighed. "Drowned four years ago, off Naxos, he was, and after that, she and I went to his mother's people, here. When the fever took her—well, there's none of them left now, just me." She shifted uncomfortably. "Lass, would you fetch me water? There's a cup and a jug from the well on the sill yonder." She fought a dry cough, took the cup Gabrielle held out for her and sipped at it. The two women exchanged a look over the tossled white hair, but when Gabrielle would have spoken, Xena laid a finger against her lips, held it there until the younger woman nodded. Arana finally set the cup aside.

"I hadn't much of anything after my daughter died," she said. "Just a few extra bits of pottery. But, all I need for myself is a cup and a jug, and maybe a bowl or a small plate. Anything else—well, there's always someone who'll give you a copper or two for something that's new to them. I started like that, and found that while the sailors didn't much care what I had, a few of the other people who came through Carpathos did, and often, they were willing to trade." Her mouth trembled. "When that man— I can still see his face—when he came to me with a piece of *her* blackware, I didn't know what to think. She'd been gone so many years, you see, and everyone knew the war'd ended badly for Troy. No one hereabouts knew, though, whether she'd died with the city, or if he'd found her and taken her away. But that little pot . . . her mark on it and everything."

"How'd you know that?" Gabrielle asked. The old woman gave her a watery smile.

"Why—who do you think built the fires for her kiln, and raked the pieces out when it cooled? Old Arana, that's who. I was the only one she trusted, because I was the only one in all that time who never broke so much as a cup."

Silence. Gabrielle glanced at Xena, then gazed at the old woman, who gazed levelly back at her. The warrior finally cleared her throat. "Do you know where she is?"

"If I did," Arana replied cautiously, "would I be fool enough to say so?"

"As much as you've already told us," Gabrielle began, but the old woman shook her head.

"Told you nothing that isn't common knowledge. If I did know more, no one's learned it in all my years on Carpathos, and there's no reason I'd have to tell it." She looked up at Xena, visibly unafraid. "At my age, there's nothing I want, and nothing—including death—that I fear."

"I understand," Xena replied. "But we've got reasons of our own for needing to know anything you can tell us." Another silence, a stubborn one, which Xena finally broke. "Gabrielle," she said wearily. "Tell her."

Gabrielle made a fairly succinct story of things, but even leaving out Joxer, the long maddening journey to Sparta and much of what had happened since, it took time. "The important thing is," she said finally, "the king hasn't given up. Normally, I would never want to know where H—where she is. Xena absolutely would not want to know. And if there's some way for you to warn her without letting us know where she is—that's fine, we can deal with it. She may be doing a good job of being careful, but with Menelaus launching this new quest for her, careful may not be enough to keep her safe."

Silence.

"If you can reach her yourself, send her a message somehow, tell her that it's Xena who's looking for her."

"If I could do that . . . but how would she know you're *really* Xena?" Arana demanded.

"She'll know. Ask her to remember the question I asked her—the one no one else ever bothered to ask her."

Another silence. This one stretched. Off in the distance, Gabrielle could hear men laughing as they strode up the street, out beyond the narrow little alley, and farther up the hillside, a dog barked.

Arana stared down at her hands. She finally shook her

head. "If I could—I'd send that message. I don't know where she is, and that's the truth." She looked at Xena. "Oh—that she's alive, yes. Or, she was. Because she came through Carpathos not two years ago."

"You—saw her?" Gabrielle said.

"She got off one of the ships down there—came up into the town square, just another robed and hooded woman, I thought at first, walking around town to get the stiffness out of her body while she had the chance. That little piece of blackware—I had it displayed right in the middle of my wares, even though I knew no one around hereabouts would ever pay what I was asking. I nearly fell over when *her* voice asked what I'd take for it. And when I looked up—" She smiled. "She hasn't changed, not a bit, all those years. I nearly spoke her name, but something in her eyes warned me, so I named my price—ten dinars, I told her, and no bargaining for such a fine piece, either. Imagine my surprise when she handed over the coins without a murmur, then scooped up the little thing and shoved it deep in her sleeve." She sighed faintly. "That evening, she did just what you did tonight—followed me, though it was to a cleaner place than this. She was still—it upset her, not because it was me, I don't think. Just to see anyone living like that.

"She warned me then that I must never tell anyone I'd seen her. That she'd been making the blackware again, enough to pay her way, but that she'd seen someone she'd known, one of Menelaus' captains, and she'd had to move on. Naxos, I think that was. She had one of those little people with her, something new—for children to play with, I think. Something Menelaus wouldn't recognize, she said, though he never paid much heed to her pot work." She picked up the cup with trembling hands and

244

took another sip of water. "When she left that night, it was the last I saw of her. Now and again, one of those little people will come through, but they could be traded from anywhere." Xena stirred; Gabrielle got to her feet. Arana watched as they moved toward the doorway. "I don't expect to hear from her, or to learn where she is. But if I do, I'll pass her your message."

"That's all we can ask," Xena said quietly. Gabrielle moved over to refill the woman's cup, and quietly slipped a dinar onto the blanket next to the jug, where Arana would find it later. She quietly followed Xena out into the drab little courtyard, and back down the alley.

They moved steadily back to the harbor, stopping at the tavern long enough to see Joxer was no longer there. Briax was; he was talking to Bellerophon, who sat at the table where the women had eaten earlier, long legs splayed out before him. Dark eyes stared down at the cup he was turning in long-fingered hands, and Briax finally seemed to realize the man wasn't paying any attention to him. He sighed, and turned toward the door. Xena gave Gabrielle a shove past the open doorway and down toward the harbor.

"Let's get moving, before he catches up with us," she said in a low voice. "We gotta talk."

Fortunately, the boat was tied up to the pier, the young seaman in charge of it half asleep over his oars. He came awake with a start as Gabrielle clambered down into the stern, waited only long enough for Xena to cast off the bow, and rowed them out to the *Yeloweh*, yawned as the women climbed aboard and turned to row back over to shore.

Joxer was curled up on his blankets, pack under his ear and helmet balanced over his face; muffled snores issued from beneath the metal brim. Gabrielle gave him a side-long look and snorted. "How does he *do* that without it waking him up?"

Xena shrugged, led the way over to the opposite rail and dropped down onto their blanket.

"Poor old woman," Gabrielle added as she got comfortable. "Living like that—all her family gone, and then . . ." She shook her head.

"It's hard," Xena agreed. "Fortunately for her, she's learned how to deal with it."

"You'd have to," Gabrielle agreed. "Helen, though. She was actually here, two years ago—I know, if Arana isn't lying to us."

"Or changing her story enough to make sure we don't look in the right places," Xena added. She shook her head. "I was pretty worried when you first showed her that little statue of yours—a woman that old, that—well, it would've been clear to anyone that she knew something about your piece. I thought she'd spill everything she knew."

"Well, she didn't. Which is good, except it means we're no closer to finding Helen than we were." She considered this. "Unless you think she *knows* where Helen is, and she'll pass on your message?"

"Gabrielle—right now, I haven't got the faintest idea what to think," the warrior admitted. "Except it's late." She drew the sword belt over her head and set it against the rail, eased under the shade-cloth and settled her shoulders against the deck.

"You sleep," Gabrielle said absently. "I'll think."

"You do that," Xena replied sleepily, and closed her eyes.

16

Xena woke early to find the ship quiet and Gabrielle slumped sideways, as if she'd fallen asleep where she sat the night before. The warrior eased her carefully down and draped the end of the blanket over the younger woman's shoulders—it was cool at the moment, though it probably wouldn't stay that way once late morning sun finally worked its way down to the water. She settled back down next to Gabrielle, who murmured something in her sleep and closed her eyes.

Sleep evaded the warrior, however. Too many things to wonder about—or worry over.

That old woman could have been telling the truth last night, only omitting that Helen had remained behind, on the island. It didn't strike Xena as very likely, and that besides the arguments she'd given Gabrielle the night before. It wouldn't be like Helen to allow Arana to live in such squalid conditions if she were around to keep that from happening.

You don't think she would, another thought intruded. She didn't really know Helen. And it had been a long time now, since she'd last seen the woman. Years of living like a commoner, of traveling by foot, maybe living by her wits and whatever little coin she could scrape together by selling bits of pottery—a life like that could harden people. Getting older, maybe losing some of her fabled looks—they might have meant more to the woman than even Helen herself realized, until they began to slip away from her.

She finally forced all that aside. If and when she came face to face with Helen, she might get answers to some of those questions. For now, she could only guess, and that wasn't at all useful.

She did feel fairly safe in assuming Helen was nowhere on Carpathos, however. People in small towns talked—whether about mysterious veiled strangers or incredibly beauteous newcomers, the result would be the same. The woman wouldn't dare chance such a thing.

All right, she told herself. *If you were in her sandals, where would you feel safe? And anonymous?* Two possible answers: in a big city, or in someone's court.

Mainland cities: She still felt safe in assuming that Menelaus had had his spies' search Athens, Tirins, and places like that. This current quest, she was willing to bet, hadn't come about until the man was reasonably certain the woman was nowhere on the mainland.

Which left plenty of places to consider. Egypt was a possibility—Cleopatra was said to have a strong lock on the loyalty of her court and her servants. Anyone trying to spy for the Spartan king wouldn't stay hidden there for long. The Hittites tolerated Greeks but wanted nothing to do with Menelaus and his, mostly because of Troy. Aside from that—she had one or two other ideas, and at least

248

one of those would probably be eliminated in the next few days.

Next item: To stay with the *Yeloweh*, or leave her here? *Might as well stick with it,* she thought, and stifled a yawn as Gabrielle stirred and rolled toward her. She opened an eye briefly, but the young woman was already breathing deeply once more. After that storm, and Lethe, *Yeloweh*'d given up on Alexandria this trip, the captain hoping to recoup losses in the Cyclades. The ship would make two more ports on local islands before it docked on Crete and then worked its way north across two days' worth of open sea to Melos. There'd be good opportunities to find something in Crete heading south or back east. Meantime, it was almost pleasant, the way the captain and his crew simply accepted her presence. Far cry from that red faced buffoon out of Phalamys—the one who'd dumped them the first chance he'd got.

Next thing, she thought, and yawned again as she rubbed an itching shoulder against the deck: What to do with Bellerophon and his young companion? Because even if she hadn't overheard the young Corinthian hero when Avicus and Menelaus had tapped him for the quest, she'd have been wary of him. The way he looked at her and Gabrielle, his attitudes—he wouldn't be able to do a thing to or with Helen if Xena didn't want him to, of course, but she didn't want to be in the position of having to silence him.

That might handle itself, however. After Lethe, she wouldn't be terribly surprised to find the two young men switch to another ship. *Since before Lethe,* she thought drowsily. Bellerophon wasn't the type to follow anyone, particularly a woman. *Particularly me,* she thought with a faint grin, remembering all the things he'd said to

Avicus back in Sparta. Traitorous woman, was it? She noticed he hadn't confronted her about Helen's whereabouts, despite Avicus's earlier assurances that Helen might be with her.

Joxer—she wasn't sure what he believed about the whole thing these days. It was probably as much habit as anything that kept him tagging along with her and Gabrielle. Fine with her; it was better than having to haul him around by his collar. Even if she *did* wind up hearing a *lot* more of "Joxer the Mighty" than anyone in her right mind would want to hear.

She smiled, rolled onto her side and prepared to doze off; one last thought flitted through her mind as she did so. *I wonder where Draco's got himself to.*

Draco, at the moment, was standing on the *Wode*'s aft deck, scowling into early morning sunlight, trying to pick out what Habbish was pointing out. He finally managed as a thin veil of cloud got between him and the glare, and he shrugged. "It's a ship. So?"

"It's a ship," Habbish agreed waspishly; the man tended to be ill-tempered so early in the day, the warlord knew. "And t'is the same ship as was out there yesterday *and* the day before."

Draco eyed him sidelong and with clear disbelief in the set of his mouth. "What—you're being followed? You don't think Xena—?"

"It is no merchant ship," the Gael broke in flatly. "And for why would the woman follow my ship?"

"Because she thinks I know where Helen is? How should I know?"

Habbish shook his head. "If she thought that, she wouldna tossed you overboard."

"Oh—I don't know about that. She can be just as straightforward as you'd like to think, Habbish—but she can be just as devious as they come, too."

"Whatever," the pirate mumbled. "That, though, that's a raiding ship. I've seen it about, mostly nearer Rome than here."

Draco turned to stare at him. "Rome? You don't think—?"

"Rome interests itself in Greek waters," Habbish replied as the warlord's voice trailed off. "But I doubt it's one of theirs, either. I just wonder," he added softly, as if to himself, "why it follows the *Wode*?"

Draco stretched massively. "Well, I'm no sailor," he said finally. "But if I wanted to know the answer to that, I'd wait around for them to catch up, and ask."

Habbish cast him a sidelong glance, then turned to scowl toward the eastern horizon, and the distant ship. He grinned suddenly. "Ask 'em, the man says," he chuckled. "D'you know, warlord, I b'lieve we'll do just that!" He turned and strode for his cabin, motioning the dark man to follow. Inside, he lit two lamps from the little oil lamp that was kept burning at all times, set them at opposite corners of the heavy wooden table, and partly unrolled two charts before finding the one he wanted. He flattened this out, set the lamps on it to hold it down, and bent down to peer at the maze of water and islands set there.

Draco gave it a passing glance, then settled down to wait. Charts were enough different from maps that they confused his eye, and he didn't figure on being at sea any longer than he had to, to accomplish his current goal. After that, as far as he was concerned, he'd never set foot on another ship.

Habbish mumbled to himself, moved the two-pointed

little measuring instrument back and forth, eased a stubby finger along a thickly inked line, mumbled some more, and finally nodded as he shifted the lamps to let the chart roll back up. He dropped it next to the other two, blew out one lamp, then fished two cups and a jug from the litter at the table's far end. He poured a dollop into each cup, handed one to Draco, set the jug aside and blew out the other lamp, leaving them in semi-darkness. "To Crete," he said finally, and raised the cup in a toast. "To Crete with her long-fingered eastern tip, and all the lovely little bays where a ship like the *Wode* might hide."

Draco grinned and tapped his cup against the other man's. "To Crete," he agreed. One of the bigger ones, he thought. Bigger than Rhodes, even. Maybe. There was a great palace somewhere on Crete, he seemed to remember. Maybe a fancy enough place to house Helen.

Remember what you promised Xena, he reminded himself—though he really didn't need to. He'd let the woman talk if he found her. Ask her if she was afraid of Menelaus, like Xena said. Either way— He swallowed, and his face felt warm. *I'd like to tell Gabrielle. Either way, however it worked out.* Remembering the stammering, gibbering, blushing mess she'd reduced him to on Melos, though. . . .

Well, there was a time for such things. Maybe, when all the fighting was behind him, and Helen was safely wherever she wanted to be—maybe then he'd find a way to talk to Gabrielle.

When the *Yeloweh* sailed from Carpathos two days later, it carried a bale of tin that had been left for forwarding to Melos, a crate of aromatic tea for the king's kitchens in Knossos, and three passengers: Xena, Gabrielle, and

Joxer. Briax had been unhappy over the separation from Gabrielle, but unwilling to let Bellerophon go off by himself.

"He's—been really nice to me, Gabrielle," he explained awkwardly. "I mean—you've been nice, too, but, I just feel like—well, you know. And—really, he doesn't feel as if he'll have any chance of—of doing the right thing, if he's with you and Xena."

"As long as you feel you're doing the right thing," Gabrielle replied. She was personally of two minds about the whole thing. Glad to be rid of Bellerophon, but still worried about where he'd go and what he'd do if he got to Helen first. And unsure what to say to Briax that might make a difference in how things worked out, if that was the case.

Probably it wouldn't do any good to say anything to Briax; it would just make him unhappy, regardless of whether he actually wound up doubting the supposed half god or not. And she sincerely doubted he'd ever dare thwart the man. He just wasn't the type for that kind of conflict, particularly against someone he so openly admired.

There wouldn't be any point in saying anything directly to Bellerophon, of course, she thought sourly. He hadn't spoken to her at all since Lethe, and little enough before that. He wasn't likely to believe a word she said, especially about Helen. *I'm a woman, after all. Anything I say is suspect, because I'm a walking bundle of emotions, and no brain to speak of. Ahh—let it go,* she ordered herself in disgust.

And Briax—*Xena's right,* she told herself firmly. *He looks young, he acts young, he's incredibly naive—but he's as old as you are, Gabrielle, and he's gotta learn sometime. You did.* Bellerophon was no Xena, but maybe Briax wouldn't need that much guidance. She could only *hope* he wouldn't need that.

At the very least, he didn't seem to share her early enthusiasm for eateries with "atmosphere."

She'd come up with half a dozen different threats to use on Joxer if he decided to go his own way, but fortunately the would-be warrior didn't seem to have even considered it—not even after Bellerophon's announced decision to find his own ship out of Carpathos.

The water outside the harbor was rough, and the wind sharp—a little cooler than she normally liked. After the warmth of the harbor, which had made her sleep more than anything else, she rather welcomed the edge to the weather. She still spread the goo on her bread first thing in the morning, but only about half as much as Xena was willing to allow her. Xena might be right about her adjusting to the sea, she thought gloomily, as *Yeloweh* wallowed through white caps, but travel by water was about as boring as it got.

She rested her chin on the rail and stared out to sea. Water was water, and the changes it went through weren't all that different. At the moment, she could see a few scudding clouds, a few islands. *Same as the last time, and the time before that* . . . Water sparkled under the sun or looked like dull metal when it was cloudy; white-capped waves shone at night, or now and again reflected starlight off smooth ripples. It was still simply water.

Walking, now. She sighed faintly. The trip from Thessalonika to Sparta hadn't been any picnic, but it was a *lot* more interesting than *this*. And the journey up to Thessalonika from Athens—she'd enjoyed that. A good path to follow, good company (if you ignored Joxer's occasional case of the sulks, that was), and either a good fire and her own cooking to look forward to come nightfall, or an inn with good food or good cider—sometimes both. Forest led down to farmlands or up to alpine meadows, and you could encounter just about anything in between. The higher you went, the trees changed from elm and oak to sharp-needled fir and the like. Water in the mountains was often a pale, milky green that meant bone-chilling cold. . . .

Her thought shifted suddenly. *I wonder where Argo is— how she's doing?* Xena had left the mare behind at other times, of course, but this seemed like a particularly long stretch for the two to be apart. *Xena's got to really be missing her. Heck, even I miss her!*

She considered this, finally shook her head. She and Argo had long since grown used to each other, and these days, she found it hard to imagine life without Xena's beloved mare. "I wonder how much longer we've got to go," she murmured. No real answer there. Even if they found Helen tomorrow, it might not be reasonable for them to simply warn her and leave. Xena might decide the woman needed their protection—or their help to get to a new place of hiding. The way things had gone so far, she wouldn't be the least surprised if it was snowing in Thessalonika before they got off ship.

She turned and settled against the rail, her gaze distant. Helen might very well need all the help they could offer her. She might have found protection from one of the island lords, of course—but there weren't many of them, and probably most of them would think twice before siding with Helen if it meant siding against the jealous Menelaus. *And Helen doesn't have the protection she had when she first left Troy.* Gabrielle shook her head sharply.

She didn't want to let herself think about poor dead Perdicas just now—not even the gallant young figure he'd been when he set out with Helen for the next city beyond Troy.

Something suddenly occurred to her, and she rummaged in her pack to find the little clay figurine that so reminded her of the boy he'd been.

Helen had known him, too. She'd forgotten that. She smiled down at the familiar face. That nose. The mouth. Her fingers closed around it and her heart briefly lifted. Maybe the resemblance wasn't a coincidence after all.

Yeloweh put in that night just offshore from a small island fishing village most of the way to Crete. Gabrielle looked around her most of the late afternoon and early evening, fascinated by the constant stream of little boats that came out, offering fresh fish, some jerky that smelled so bad even Joxer wouldn't buy any of it, dried fish, salted fish— and an assortment of other goods like plain-woven rugs and mats of undyed wool, a few ratty-looking rings and bracelets missing half their stones, pots of some kind of mead that Xena tried and proclaimed much too sweet, plain clay jugs and stoppered drinking vessels—practical stuff and nothing marked with a swan on its base. Trading was heavy, with many of the sailors buying for their own personal use, or to take home to Paros or Icaria.

Eventually the sun dropped below the horizon and the procession of little boats went away. Gabrielle gazed out across the darkened sea later to see the winking of torch-light here and there. Night fishing, Xena had told her. It seemed like a particularly dangerous way, to her, to get food on the table. Unnerving at best—a torch would illuminate the water immediately around the boat, not anything in its depths or beyond the circle of light. Anything could be lurking. . . . She shuddered and forced the thought aside.

But when she told Xena later, the warrior laughed. "There are a lot more dangerous things around the sea than things waiting in it to eat you," she said.

"Never mind," Gabrielle put in hastily. "You can tell me all about them once we're back on solid ground for good."

The Spartan palace was dark and quiet, the priest's private quarters deserted for the moment. Avicus sat cross-legged on the low bench in the god's private chamber behind the reception throne, eyes closed, waiting.

Not that he expected anything from Apollo at this hour, In fact, he rather hoped not. The last two times the god had bespoken him at an hour past midnight, he'd been increasingly tearful and inclined to be snappish at whatever his priest needed to know. *Yes, I do understand the god has his own view of the matter—but he fails to realize that Menelaus also has such a view, and my king is at least as arrogant—and as snappish—as the god.* The priest's stomach hurt at the moment; it often did, anymore. That came of walking the fine line between two such imperious masters.

Menelaus had finally learned that several of his heroes were missing the badges they'd been sent out wearing—and though Avicus had chosen his words with care, he didn't doubt the king knew Xena was responsible. First Draco, then Joxer. Those two on Rhodes would have been perfect for keeping watch over the woman and her chattering little companion, but she'd dealt with them not long after that tubby little boat sailed out of the harbor.

Unfortunately, the device his assistant had attached to Joxer's gear wasn't as much use as it might have been. *A man with any wit at all would have attached it to the* outside *of the arrow case!* Where it was—well down the inside lining of the case—it was far less likely to be found, of course. But unless the case was tipped on its side, it couldn't see anything but an occasional glimpse of distant rigging and the sky beyond it.

He rubbed a hand across tired eyes. Fortunately, Saroni had been successful in getting to Gabrielle. *Silly young woman, calls herself a bard! Anyone with a measure of wit would be suspicious of a strange person just walking up and nattering at her, never mind embracing her on such short acquaintance!* Fortunately, Gabrielle was still naive, and so, marked. The only place Saroni had been able to attach the device was something of a problem, however, because the view from the back of that tiny little green top gave him a headache if he concentrated on it too long. The bard moved too sharply, leaving him feeling as if the wind were whistling through his ears, and it was decidedly odd seeing things in reverse.

And there were things he still didn't fully understand. What had she been up to, wandering around that gloomy little jungle of an island? And what by the name of all that was holy had the god of war been doing there?

Ares has a soft spot for Xena—or did, he reminded himself. It had looked to him as though the god had a roving eye, though, the way he'd been all over Gabrielle. Somehow, he didn't think Xena would be one for sharing his affections, even if she was as fond of her young companion as they said. *Particularly if*—but he let that slide. Gossip, or a closely guarded relationship, whatever; either way, it wasn't his business, and it didn't interest him, either. Besides, the warrior had dropped Ares when she'd decided to turn good, everyone knew that.

It was unfortunate the patch devices were much better at vision than hearing; he'd caught only a word or two of the conversation on Carpathos to be intrigued, but not enough to sort out who that ancient woman was, or her connection—if any—with Helen. But Helen would not be hiding out on a grubby little spot of dirt like Carpathos, and he sincerely doubted anyone who did live there had the faintest idea where she might be. *She's clever enough to have avoided Menelaus all these years,* he reminded himself grimly. *She's not foolish enough to make a mistake like that.*

He let his thoughts move on: Draco. He still had some hopes for the warlord, if only because the man seemed to be sincere about impressing Gabrielle with his good deeds. The priest's mouth twitched. *What is it with that woman, anyway?* He couldn't begin to see the appeal—certainly not to the point where a perfectly deadly warlord would give up control of an army and all the power and wealth such an army guaranteed. For what—love? He snorted. Not just love, but for *that woman?* Well, he might not be able to understand it, but plenty of people obviously did.

He dismissed that; it was something he'd never understand.

Draco's badge was long since gone, of course, but he knew where the warlord was. At least two of Habbish's men carried their own badges, and there was a small device in that ever-burning oil lamp the old Gael kept in his cabin. The smallest *rhodforch* yet, he thought with pride.

Avicus grinned suddenly. All that planning the two men had done, and he'd caught every last bit of it. Enough to pass on to the *Hammer*, which had been following *Wode* ever since it had skirted Rhodes. Menelaus' own personal raiding ship, manned by a picked crew made up of men who'd supposedly deserted Sparta right after Troy. *His* idea, actually, Avicus thought—well, a suggestion of the god's, but he'd been the one to put it to Menelaus in a fashion the king couldn't turn down. Not just a ship to keep an eye on things for Sparta, but whatever raiding was done, the king took first cut off the top.

Unfortunately, it hadn't located Helen for him as he'd hoped, but Avicus had never thought that likely.

He drew a deep breath, let it out slowly, and considered what message to send to *Hammer*. There wasn't any good reason for *Hammer* to attack *Wode*—except that wily old Habbish might start wondering what the Romen-based raiding ship was really up to if it didn't at least feint in his direction. Besides, the priest thought, it had been some time since *Wode* had sent any decent percentages to Sparta. Habbish knew better than to withhold the king's share of any ill-gathered spoils, but the man was just stubborn enough, jealous over his rights as a freebooting captain, and stingy like all his northern kind—well, the man'd never know where the goods went, after they left *Hammer*, would he?

The faint rattle of water drops against hard stone caught his attention, all at once. Avicus sat up straight and smoothed yellow silk robes. A moment later, Saroni's face hung in the air above his small gazing-bowl, and the priestess began to speak.

Midday, and the long, bony shape of Crete now blocked all view of the southern sea. Gabrielle dismissed it as one more island—larger than most but no more picturesque—

but Joxer stared avidly at the high ridges capped in stubby trees, and despite her clear lack of interest, he continued to point out various landmarks. She finally sighed. "Joxer? I mean, really, why should I care about Crete?"

He considered this, shrugged. "No reason, except it's— Did you know the palace in Knossos is five times as big as the one in Athens? That makes it almost *ten* times as big as the Spartan one, and that's just the building, not the grounds." He stared beyond her. "And then there's the maze . . . I mean, that all by itself would just be. . . ." He sighed happily. "Imagine getting to walk through the maze. You'd—"

"Be lost before you got through the first three turns," Gabrielle interposed neatly. "I know all about the maze, some guy named Daedalus designed it, and it was so twisty and turny that even *he* couldn't find his way around it without a ball of twine."

"Oh yeah?" Joxer gazed down his nose at her. "Says who?"

"Says bardic tradition, that's who," she replied. As usual, Joxer had no ready response to this; as usual, it visibly frustrated him. "C'mon, Joxer. I can think of a lot better places to get lost in than a great big, old, walled, underground place that probably still smells like minotaur."

"Oh yeah?" he repeated. "Like, where?"

Gabrielle sighed faintly, settled her elbows on the rail, and leaned out to gaze at the water. There were dolphins in these waters, she'd already seen three today, just none close by. It could happen, though, she thought. "Where?" she murmured. "Woods, or maybe a wide open field just covered in wildflowers. Or a road . . . a road that goes from someplace like Athens to someplace far away, a village so small it's not on any map . . ."

Joxer snorted, breaking the thread of thought, and she scowled at him.

"Gabrielle, you're landsick," he informed her, and strode away.

"*I'm* landsick?" she shouted after him. "Joxer, *I'm* not the one staring at that big old island as if I'd like to *eat* it!" Someone farther up the deck laughed jarringly; Gabrielle clapped a hand over her mouth and turned away with what dignity she could manage to resume her study of the water between the ship and the island. *Dolphins,* she reminded herself.

Xena came over to join her some time later; when Gabrielle explained her preoccupation, the warrior laughed easily. "You'll stand a much better chance first thing in the morning, and last thing in the evening," she said. "What was all the shouting about?"

Gabrielle slewed around to face the deck, rubbing her stiff neck. "What else?" she asked and shrugged. "Owww. Joxer, of course. He decided I need a full lesson on the geography of Crete, and—owww." Xena batted the hand aside, turned her companion back to face the sea, and dug her hands into either side of the younger woman's neck. Gabrielle gasped, then suddenly relaxed, her head hanging loose over crossed arms, hair swaying with the ship's motion. Xena worked at her for some moments, then clapped a hand on her shoulder.

"Better?"

"Mmmm—a lot better. You know, I think that—" Whatever she thought went unsaid as a loud warning yell came down from the crow's nest.

Xena tensed, then vaulted onto the rail, one hand caught in the rigging as she stared intently forward.

Gabrielle eyed her with alarm, rose onto tiptoes to stare ahead. "What?" she asked finally. "I don't see a thing from here!"

The voice from high above answered her before Xena could. "Sea raiders dead ahead! Two ships fighting it out, and one of them's afire!"

Epilogue

Xena swung onto the ladderlike rigging; Gabrielle cleared her throat nervously, and the warrior looked down at her. "What?" she asked blandly.

"Look, I know you used to crawl around on that stuff, and you're probably still pretty good at it—"

"Whadya mean, *pretty* good?" Xena demanded. "Who got up into the crow's nest on that floating disaster of Cecrops's, *in* a full storm and right on the edge of the whirlpool?" Gabrielle muttered something under her breath, and threw up her hands. The warrior flashed her an urchinlike grin and clambered a little higher, one hand shielding her eyes from glare off the water. "They're right," she said finally. "One of them's a raider—long, lean, and fast-looking." She stared into the distance. "I got a bad feeling the other one's Habbish's; that looks like his sail."

"Habbish? Who's Habbish?" Gabrielle wanted to know.

"He's the old Gaelic pirate I borrowed to catch up with you, Gabrielle. The one Draco was traveling with, last I saw of him."

"Draco?" Gabrielle caught hold of the rigging and drew herself up off the deck. "You don't—?" She shook her head and fell back onto the spray-dampened boards. "What are you gonna do about it?"

Xena shook her head. "I don't think there's anything I can do, Gabrielle. *Yeloweh*'s no match for anything like *Wode*, and that other ship looks like it could sail circles around Habbish. Besides, the captain won't go anywhere near those two; he'd be a fool to even think about it." She swung out over the water as the ship came jerkily around to starboard and began working its way north, away from the island. Gabrielle caught her breath in a squeak and closed her eyes. "Will you cut that out? I'm *okay* up here," the warrior said; she sounded mildly exasperated. "I—it's hard to tell what's going on right now, there's smoke everywhere."

Gabrielle held her breath and listened hard; it seemed to her she could make out the distant shouts of men and the clang of heavy swords, but that might have been her imagination, or something rattling around in the merchant ship's hold.

She started as someone came clomping up behind her. Joxer, of course, she realized as he cleared his throat. "What's going on out there, Xena, and why are you playing around on those ropes?"

"Couple of pirates taking on each other, instead of coming after a nice easy target like we're riding," she informed him. "And this?" She switched hands and vaulted off the rigging in a tight flip, coming up almost under his chin. He yelped and stumbled back. "Because I can," she said evenly, and walked off. Joxer watched her go, a frown knitting his brows together.

"You know, Gabrielle," he said thoughtfully, "I think she's getting as landsick as you are."

"I'm delighted to hear what you think, Joxer," Gabrielle retorted. "Go away now, okay?" He gave her a long, expressionless look, and walked away. Gabrielle cast her eyes heavenward. "Why do I even bother?" she asked herself. "Yeah; I know. Because he's so easy—and because I can." She caught hold of the rigging and stared toward the thick cloud of smoke. Impossible to tell what was going on in there, or who, if anyone, was winning.

Things happened, battles like that, she knew; Xena'd told her about enough of them back when she'd never imagined spending so much time aboard ship herself. Sometimes the two ships left a few holes in each other's sails, or set a few minor fires. Now and again it happened that one ship got off a lucky shot with its catapult as it was going down, or managed to come around and ram the ship that had holed it fatally, and both sank.

Her fingers were wrapped so tightly in the ropes that she couldn't feel them, she suddenly realized, and forced herself to ease her grip. "It's two ships full of pirates," she told herself. "Cold-blooded men who hunt down ships like this, and kill men who're just trying to do a job and feed their families." It didn't make her feel much better, and she wasn't sure she liked the reason niggling at the back of her mind.

Draco. Whatever he wanted, he was no more her type than—well, than Joxer. Or even sweet young Briax. But the man was making an honest effort to change his ways. As he'd said back in that temple, to "do . . . good." It made her smile, remembering how he'd gagged over the word, how he'd so cheerfully announced he'd only let his army kill the old men when he raided a village. *He really*

didn't get it at all, she thought. But back on Melos—
maybe some of what he'd said, the way he'd acted, had
been a put-on to get her attention. She didn't think so,
though. *He wasn't like that before, he was cold-blooded,
ruthless and downright scary—but he was straight about
it.* On Melos, he'd come across as less sure of himself,
maybe even abashed by her company—but still straight.

He deserved the chance to see what he could do with
himself, she thought angrily. "It would be—stupid and
pointless for him to die like that," she whispered.

The ship changed course slightly once more, to parallel
the island. Once it was well past the still-raging battle,
the captain corrected once again, this time heading back
toward the island.

Gabrielle leaned out to look back. So far as she could
tell, the two ships were moving apart, and the sleeker of
the two seemed to be riding low in the water. Smoke
poured from the stern of the other ship, and she thought
it was being rowed back out of reach of its adversary.
Smoke covered both then and hid them from view. She
shook her head and settled down out of everyone's way,
her back against the rail, the shade blanket flapping faintly
in the rising breeze.

They reached the mid-island port late in the afternoon, to
find the docks crowded and everyone talking about the
sea battle, or wanting to know what had happened. Xena
waved off those who came at her, indicating the ship and
its busy crew. "The boys who were in the crow's nest can
tell you more than I can, they saw it all." When a stubborn
old man tried to plant himself in her path, she growled at
him; startled, he fell back, and she brushed past him,
heading for the road beyond the piers with her usual

ground-eating stride. Gabrielle dug her staff in as she half ran to keep up; Joxer trailed well behind them, grumbling and muttering to himself. Xena slowed once they reached the main road and turned to call back, "Joxer! Get yourself up here right now, or you'll walk all the way up to Knossos!"

"Knossos?" Gabrielle asked rather breathlessly. "That's where we're going?" The warrior nodded, her eyes moving along the road that lay mostly in shadow at this hour.

"There used to be carts," she muttered to herself, "but things have changed a lot since Minos died."

"You—you knew Minos?" Gabrielle asked. Joxer came up to peer uncertainly down the road.

"Yeah," Xena replied shortly. "We met, once, anyway. He kept this place pretty well organized, but. . . . Wait, here comes one," she said. Joxer stared where she pointed.

"There is? Because I don't see any—oh," he broke off as a slat-sided affair drew up, two mismatched donkeys pulling it. "That's a cart?" he asked, his voice heavy with disbelief. Gabrielle eyed the thing with visible misgivings.

"Are you sure this is a good idea?" she asked. Xena shrugged and pointed high overhead, where weathered cliffs blended with the sky.

"You wanna walk it instead?" she asked, but before Gabrielle could answer, she bundled the younger woman into the cart, tossed in her bag, waited for Joxer to clamber in and get settled, then vaulted lightly over the side and dropped down cross-legged next to Gabrielle. "Get a grip," she said; Gabrielle gave her a wide-eyed look and Xena laughed shortly. "I'm serious," she said. "Get a grip, something to hang on to. The road's pretty steep, and these things aren't made for comfort."

"Great," Gabrielle muttered. "Anymore words of encouragement, while you're at it?"

"Yeah," Joxer put in from the other side, "like, don't fall out?"

"Don't fall out," Xena told him, her face expressionless; she turned to Gabrielle as the cart lurched forward. "It's easier than walking, trust me. And better than the way Minos used to get to the top."

"You're kidding me?" Gabrielle clenched her teeth together; she'd nearly bitten her lip when the donkeys had started off. The warrior grinned at her.

"Yeah. He had a sedan chair and eight guys to carry it."

Joxer fussed around most of the way up, especially once they cleared the lower turns of the road between the king's city and port, and he could make out the trail of smoke that marked the earlier battle. "You know what?" he said finally. "I think the skinny one's sinking."

Xena rose onto one knee to peer out to sea, but dropped back down when Gabrielle uttered a wordless little cry of dismay and shut her eyes tight; her fingers digging into the rough handholds that had been attached to the floor of the cart at various odd spots.

"We should be able to see better a little further up," she said at last. "Or from the top, of course."

Gabrielle swallowed dread. "Of course," she echoed. Xena patted her arm.

"Nice deep breath, Gabrielle," she urged quietly. "These things look and feel like a collection of junk parts, but they don't fall off the edge."

The younger woman licked her lips. "Ah—how sure are you about that?"

"That's what the donkeys are for," Xena replied cheerfully. "Now, something like a heavy sedan chair on poles, with two guys to a pole, working their way up a slope like this—something like *that* could fall. Except," she shrugged, "as far as I know, none of them ever did." Gabrielle grimaced and cautiously shifted her grip on the floor cleats as the cart creaked its way around a bend and started back across the slope. "Enlighten me," she said finally. "*Why* are we even going up here?"

Xena considered this, finally shrugged. "Call it a hunch," she said finally. "Besides, I used to know a few people up here. Seemed to me I'd be more likely to get answers if I came to see them in person, instead of sending word from the harbor."

"After this," Gabrielle panted, "you had *better*." She glanced back the way they'd come and abruptly lost color. "Oh no," she moaned. Xena reached out to touch her face.

"You're not gonna be sick are you?"

"No—not just yet," the bard replied unhappily. "I'll save that for when we start the trip back down."

Fortunately for her, the road leveled out after the next switchback and moved back off the slope and into a deep, dusty stretch of woods. When she could next see any distance at all, the awful drop wasn't visible. Another bend, and another climb up what looked like—and felt like—an abandoned streambed, and the cart heaved up onto level ground. Gabrielle opened her eyes as the thing creaked to a halt.

There weren't many trees up here, just a lot of open, dry-looking ground surrounding a monstrosity of a palace. Whitewashed walls seemed to go on forever, and fat, stubby-looking columns of every possible color held up tiled roofs. Off to one side, she could make out an amphitheater easily four times the size of the one on Rhodes, and beyond the palace, she caught a glimpse of the massive, stylized gilt horns that were the symbol of Knossos—sign of the bull.

The bull was gone, and so was Minos, but his heir kept the old ways, meeting the guests at the entry himself, and seeing to it they were properly housed before ordering servants to prepare cool baths and fetch food and drink.

He was an odd little man to be king, Gabrielle thought. Short and chubby, and while he wore the signet ring with the bull's horns on it, he seemed otherwise unadorned and definitely not one to stand on ceremony. When the warrior addressed him by title, he brushed that aside. "I was Nossis when my father ruled, and I am still Nossis," he told her. If he recognized Xena, he gave no sign that Gabrielle could see, and he was just as cordial to Joxer as he was to her. The two women were given adjoining apartments, Joxer another as sumptuous, a few doors away. "My queen is no longer among us," Nossis said as he readied to leave, "but the woman who tutors my children will come in a little while, to guide you to the banquet hall." He inclined his head, then, and left.

Some time later, clean, dry, and wrapped in silk the color of the sea at sunrise, Gabrielle wandered into Xena's bedroom to find the warrior swathed in red and gold silk, stretched at full length on an expanse of canopied bed, eating grapes. "Mmm, I love these things," she said.

"Half as much as I like being clean again?" Gabrielle asked as she settled on the edge of the bed. There were cherries, too. She scooped up a handful of them and popped one in her mouth. "I don't suppose this," she waved a hand, "had anything to do with your decision to ask questions up here?"

Xena raised an eyebrow. "It crossed my mind," she admitted; her teeth crunched into another crisp grape. "But it also occurred to me a while back, when I was thinking about alliances—you know, who had one with Menelaus before and after Troy, and who didn't? Well, Knossos wouldn't have a thing to do with him, especially after Paris died."

"Nice thought," Gabrielle said as the warrior ate another grape. "Of course, that would have occurred to Menelaus, too . . . ?"

"I'm sure it did. In fact, I wouldn't be surprised to learn he had a spy here at some point. But with no Helen—"

Gabrielle considered this, finally shook her head and dropped the cherries back on the pedestaled dish. "Xena, I swear it gets more confusing by the day! If Menelaus *had* a spy here, then he probably *still* has a spy here—right?"

"Wrong," Xena replied. "Knossos has its own protection, something I don't fully understand—but then, no one does except maybe another Cretan." She wiped her fingers on the mat under the tray and sat up as someone tapped lightly at the door. "Anyway, we should be able to learn more tonight—*come in*!—if there's anything to learn . . . that . . . is . . ."

Gabrielle stared at Xena, who was gazing glassily beyond her; the younger woman swallowed dread and turned to see what had caught the warrior so off guard.

Two servants had just come in, one carrying a silver box, the other a whiteware clay ewer, its only decoration a spray of black branches. They stepped aside, heads bent as a lithe woman came into the room. She stopped short, smoothed the cloud of dark hair back from her face and gazed into Xena's face. The warrior slid off the bed and smoothed her skirts. "Hello, Helen," she murmured. "Tutor to the king's children?"

Helen of Troy gazed up into dark blue eyes, her face expressionless. "Xena," she said finally. "I—somehow I knew, if anyone found me, it would be you."